Between the Star and the Cross: The Choice

Book 1

Fourth Edition

Laura L. Valenti

Between the Star and the Cross: The Choice – Book 1

Cover Art & Photography by Bailey Reid
Publishing Coordinator – Sharon Kizziah-Holmes

INDIE PUB PRESS
Springfield, Missouri

ISBN -13: 978-1-960499-86-8

Come to me, all of you

Who are weary and heavy laden,

And I will give you rest.

Matthew 11:28

ACKNOWLEDGMENTS

First and foremost, my heartfelt thanks to God, because truly the stories here are His, about His people. They are stories that are simply given to me to pass on. Without His love, there would be no point at all. Each and every day of my life is filled with gratitude for His incredible, amazing grace and the many ways it is manifested in my life.

Someone recently asked if the hardest part of writing a book was getting started, and I assured her it was not. The hardest part is finishing and that would never happen without the love, support and assistance of many others. They include, but are not limited to the following, and my deepest appreciation goes out to one and all.

To Sheriff Bob Dotson, who gave me a job when I needed it and taught me so much over the years about honor, hard work and not quitting until the job is done.

To colleagues Sgt. Bill Monroe, the late Lt. Joseph Huffman, Deputy John Young and many others for their respect and their friendship. They say you don't really know someone until you live with them, and the folks in law enforcement come pretty close to just that, working endless hours together, side by side. I never expected to last ten minutes in a world I knew very little about; instead, I stayed ten years and learned a lifetime's worth of lessons.

To fellow writer Ellen Gray Massey, for so generously sharing her time, her editing and writing skills and encouraging me and so many others along the way to always continue writing.

To my dear ones who proofread and edit, Francesca Rich, Tiffany Valenti, Judy Dotson and Debbie Blades, as they shared their individual perspectives with me. They keep me grounded, keep me going and keep me inspired at every step of the journey.

To Susan Kirkpatrick and Linda Leicht, professional editors who were kind enough to lend their skills and expertise to this work. It means so much more than I can say!

To my Camino sister, Mary Lambert and novelist D.B. Barratt for sharing their knowledge and the spirit in which this book was written.

To Carmen McCulloch and Philip DeMoss for their specialized assistance with parts of this manuscript.

To Eric Adams and Bailey Reid for their excellent work on the cover of this book.

To Sharon Kizziah-Home, Publishing Coordinator of Paperback Press of Springfield, MO., for her assistance in this Third Edition

To Sheriff Richard Wrinkle, for giving me a chance, despite the politics and controversy involved.

To countless nameless hundreds who passed through my office, and later through my jail cells, and shared their stories, literally, their lives, with me for a time.

To Francesca and Jón, Lisa and Clayton, Ricardo and Tiffany, Emmanuel, Dante, Dominic and Jessica, Austin, Cooper and Tyson, for teaching me what's really important in life.

And last, but never least, to my husband, Warren for more than 40 years of love, patience and most of all, believing in my dreams, all of them.

To each of you, I extend my never-ending appreciation. As Milagro would say, *Díos les bendiga*—God bless you all!

Chapter 1

Her golden hair sparkled in the shaft of morning sunlight coming through the living room window. The melody of her gentle laughter echoed down the hall as she glanced back over her shoulder at him.

“Where are you going?” he asked. He stood with a towel wrapped around his waist, one foot in the bathroom, the other in the hall, watching her dance away from him. She wore only one of his old shirts, the long tail and scooped sides emphasizing her slender legs.

“That storm door is banging again. Didn’t you hear it? Thought you were going to fix that. I’m just going to close it.” She was looking back at him with a fetching smile and a wink as she turned the knob.

An alarm went off in his head. How many times had he told her not to open the door without checking first? He started to say it again, but what he saw was the dull gleam of the shotgun barrel, then the shaggy blond mane of the man behind it as he leveled the gun upon them.

“Bonnie!”

She turned back and he leapt toward her, but it was a reach

too far and his world exploded.

He awoke with a start as he had dozens of times, a hundred times since that day. He longed for the moment of innocence that came on mornings like this, just before he opened his eyes, when he could still feel her beside him. He lingered a few moments more in the sultry warmth of the sheets before rolling out of bed.

The last streaks of crimson were fading at the eastern window. He took a hard look in the mirror, washing, reaching for the razor. He was always surprised by the fact that he did not look as old as he felt. There was no gray in his chestnut hair, although life had done its best or worst to put it there. He wasn't forty yet but more than the beginning of some serious wrinkles could now be seen around his eyes. Laugh lines, his mother used to call them. Maybe. Once.

The radio crackled in the next room, bringing him back to the world that waited. He climbed into his gold pickup truck, still listening to the radio, and decided to get coffee at work rather than on the way. The telephone was ringing as he came through the door and he reached over the front counter and snatched it off the hook.

"Crossland County Sheriff's Department." He listened a moment before speaking again. "Yes, this is Sheriff Harper, Mrs. Davis. I appreciate that those boys are a headache to you. I'm sure I can convince them to put up a new mailbox for you. Yes ma'am, to replace the one they tore down. Yes ma'am, living in the country is hard sometimes, I know. Take care now." He hung up the phone as a tall, rawboned redhead in tight blue jeans and a fitted checkered shirt rounded the corner from the back room.

"Morning to you, too," she shot at him while chewing a

large wad of pink bubble gum. "I guess you've heard the radio this morning. Big wreck out on the highway. Weldon Johnson is in the drunk tank again. Came in about four this morning and Freddy Ganst got mad and stopped up the toilet in cell three and flooded everything, so they put him downstairs with Weldon and moved the boys out of cell three into two other cells. Now everyone's crowded and complaining. And Commissioner Ravens called and---." She stopped in mid-sentence.

"Uh-huh," he murmured as he looked over the jail roster in one hand and the radio log in the other. His eyes never left the clipboards that held each as he nodded slightly in rhythm to what she was saying.

"It's been all I could do to get some coffee made this morning. You want some or not? Have you been listening to a word I've said?"

"Yes, Wanda. You said the sergeant is already out on the highway, helping with traffic. And they wanted Jimmy out there, too, but you told them he's on vacation out to Arizona."

"I never! Well, yeah, I did. But that was twenty minutes ago on the radio!" Her tone rose with her level of exasperation.

"You asked if I was listening. People who don't speak English out there, I gather?"

"Best I could tell a trucker fell asleep and turned over his rig. The car he run off the road had a woman and her son in it who were headed south. The trucker and the boy both left the scene by ambulance but they was having a hard time explaining it all to the mother. I don't think she's hurt, just shook up. The sergeant is bringing her here."

"Hmm. And are you going to talk to her? Has Jimmy been giving you lessons or something?"

"Don't you think I'm smart enough to learn that lingo?" She deliberately batted her eyelashes at him in time to the gum chewing.

He laughed unexpectedly. "Wanda, I think you and I do good to speak English and we'd best leave the other languages to folks that can, like Jimmy."

A county cruiser pulled into the carport outside the front door. A short, dark-haired woman was escorted inside by Sgt. Roy Baker. The officer lifted the breakaway portion of the front counter up and to the left, and whisked the woman to a seat in the back. Wanda handed her coffee in a Styrofoam cup, which she accepted with a weak smile. She took a sip and then began to cry softly, obviously not for the first time that morning.

"¿Dónde está mi hijo? ¿Cómo está? Quiero ir con él. Por favor."

"I tried to explain things to her, but without Jimmy to speak Spanish to her..." Sgt. Roy Baker shook his head in exasperation. "The ambulance guys wouldn't let her ride in the back. I'm not sure but I don't think the kid is in very good shape. Tommy was working on hauling off what was left of their car with his wrecker. I'm a-telling you, to see it, they were both lucky to get out alive."

"And the truck driver?"

Sergeant Baker shrugged. "Still breathing, but can't say much more than that. Out of Oregon, I think. State Patrol has his name and particulars. I just wasn't sure what to do about her."

"You know," Wanda drew the sheriff off to the side, "Jimmy was telling me there's a new Spanish girl running the Main Street Mission. Maybe she could help."

"Sounds good to me. Roy, you want to take her down there?"

"I would, but I got to do this report for the state patrol and there's that Federal drug guy coming in this morning to talk about the latest and greatest in drug control they want to start here." He stopped. "You said to get with him, right?"

"Yeah, you meet with him. What's this mission girl's name, Wanda?" He turned to the woman who had been watching their faces over her coffee cup, apparently discerning little of their conversation.

"Lady, come with me. We'll go for help."

She followed meekly.
"Good luck," Wanda patted her hand when she walked past. The silent woman smiled her thanks as Wanda turned back to the ringing phone. "Crossland County Sheriff's Department. No, I'm sorry, Sheriff Harper is not in the office right now. Can I take a message for him?"

* * * * *

The Main Street Mission was a cobbled together group of buildings at the west end of the commercial district of the small city of Serenity. What had once been separate businesses, including a roller rink, an outdated motel, and a few tiny shops, had been remodeled together to serve a more pressing purpose on the humble side of town. Beyond them, the railroad tracks stretched across the rolling fields to the northwest while a thin ribbon of asphalt forked off to the southwest. The mission provided food and clothing for those in need, a daily hot lunch for all who came through its doors, and shelter for those who had no other home to call their own.

From time to time, sheriff's deputies delivered the occasional abuse victim to these doors, but recent developments at the center had threatened its very existence.

A plump grandmother of a woman bustled into the front vestibule at the bell that sounded when the sheriff opened the door and escorted his charge inside. The smell of stale disinfectant he had long associated with this place had been replaced with the aroma of a robust breakfast. The sheriff could identify fried sausage and freshly baked biscuits, and it made his stomach growl with envy.

"Hello, Aunt Martha. I‘m glad to see you’re still here. Last time we talked you weren’t too sure if you were staying or going."

"Well, Dale," she drawled his name out longer that its single syllable. "Our former director may have got caught with his hand in the cookie jar, so to speak, but the work goes on. There's still lots to be done, people who need help, so I guess I'll stay as long as they'll have me. Whatcha got here?"

"Yes, well, I'm glad you're here, just the same. This lady and her son were caught up in a wreck on the highway this morning. Her son is in the hospital and we need to get her over there, but the problem is she doesn't speak English and Jimmy, my deputy who could talk to her, is gone. Wanda tells me you've got someone here who might be able to help."

"Our new director. She got here last month. You haven't

met her yet, have you? Let me see, she was checking on things in the kitchen."

A slim woman with long, dark curly hair and matching ebony eyes stepped from an inner hallway while Martha was still speaking. "Here she is."

The newest arrival moved immediately to the shaken woman who was still following the sheriff's every move.

"Buenos días. Pase adelante. Sientese, por favor. ¿Qué le ha pasado? ¿Quiere algo de tomar?"

"Sí, aguita, por favor."

"Martha, can you bring a cup of water?" The younger woman showed the visitor to a small sofa as she continued to speak. It was several more moments before she seemed to notice the man still standing at her side. "Good morning. I did not mean to ignore you. It is only that she…"

He shook his head. "That's what I came here for, someone to talk to her. You're doing just fine."

"And what is your name?" she asked.

"Harper. Dale Harper."

"*Sheriff* Dale Harper," Martha corrected as she came back into the room with the requested cup of water. "Dale, why don't you ever wear your uniform?"

"'Cause nobody likes talking to uniforms. Haven't you ever noticed that?" He shrugged in defense, tugging at the sleeve of his light blue denim jacket.

She made a face at him on her way back to the front

counter as the sheriff turned his attention back to the two women seated on the couch.

“Would you like to sit down?” The new director asked him as she indicated a chair across the room.

“No, ma’am. I’m just fine standing.”

"Sheriff Harper,” she continued, “this is Guadalupe Alvarez, and she is very concerned about her son. She tells me they were driving back to California when their car was hit by a truck. He was hurt and her car is destroyed. She is now without a car and without money and…" As she approached the end of the story, Guadalupe began to cry again. "Can you tell me where her son is?"

"Yes, he was taken to the hospital on the other side of town. I can take her but I didn't figure she'd find anybody over there to talk to her either. I was told that her son speaks English, but he's not in very good shape at the moment and I wasn't sure…”

"Not sure? About what? I shall go with her to serve as an interpreter and I am certain we can provide a place for her here, yes, Martha?"

Martha nodded.

She hardly seemed to take a breath as she hurried on. "So we shall begin there. I shall be only one minute." When she returned, she had a small purse dangling from one shoulder and a sweater over her arm. The sheriff noticed the long earrings of gold beads and tiny pearls that sparkled against her dark thick curls.

"Vamanos donde su hijo." She reached an arm around Guadalupe's shoulders. "We shall go to your son.” She

turned back to the sheriff as they headed towards the front door. “I had you on my list.”

"Your list?" He raised an eyebrow.

"A list of people I want to speak to about our center. My name is Milagro Palacios. I hope you will come back and I can show you what we have here and what we want to do."

"Sure, I guess I can do that." The sheriff stood by the counter rolling the brim of his gray felt cowboy hat in his hands.

"Tomorrow." She called back over her shoulder before the door closed. "Come for lunch."

He turned back to Martha. "Mil-, Mil-, what did she say?"

"We just call her Miss Millie around here." Martha’s smile was wide. "I can't get my tongue to roll around words the way she can."

"I can appreciate that. See ya around, Aunt Martha."

* * * * *

Back in his pickup truck, Wanda was calling on the radio. "You're needed at the Walton place immediately, on North Highway 57." Her voice was steady despite a sense of urgency. "Shots fired. Number 356 is on scene, but subject with a gun says he will only talk to you. His son says he's not been right since his wife died." A long pause followed. "Oh, I'm sorry, Dale."

"It's all right, Dispatch," he cut in. "Go ahead."

"He says he'll only talk to you if you bring him a bottle. He said you'd know what kind."

"10-4, en route."

The highway out of town past the Main Street Mission offered the shortest route, with a couple of quick cuts across well-worn dirt roads. He drove along the ridges through the woods, the sunlight playing a rapid staccato through the bare trees of early spring as he flew along the gravel roads. These were the times that he was actually thankful for having grown up in this county, learning to run the back roads as a kid, trying to avoid cops as often as not.

Certainly he drove a better class of pickup truck now than he did back then. He almost grinned as he looked around at the gleaming black leather interior. The sparkling gold exterior, trimmed in chrome accessories, carried a Crossland County Sheriff's Department decal on each door. Under each decal were the words, written in white *This vehicle confiscated from a convicted drug dealer.* He remembered the day Judge Billy Joe Randolph had given him the keys to this truck after the out-of-state dealer's conviction. The oversized motor lent this vehicle speed like he had never experienced as a kid or even in a county cruiser. The only things he had added, other than the lettering, was a siren, the radio and a set of lights across the top. Still, it was a hollow victory since the one he most wanted to share it with was gone.

Harper thought about the man he was going to see. He and Earl had spent some long nights together, especially those first weeks after Bonnie had been killed and he had been released from the hospital. He'd fought hard to get his desire for the bottle under control and he had told himself, *Never again!* but now here he was on his way to Earl's place once more. His thoughts wandered back to Wanda's comment on the radio, "…he's not been right since his wife died."

He pulled back onto the black top a few miles on the north side of town. Looking across the open fields, he took an unconscious pleasure in the many shades of spring, spread before him like a great green Ozark quilt. From the golden green that outlined the oak trees laden with strings of pollen, to the rolling jade velvet of the fields, to the emerald ravines along the edges, it all spoke in eloquence of new life. Raggedy wild cedars and dark green pines of all sizes dotted the canvas, completing the picture of spring in the Ozark home country. He pulled into Smokey's Short Stop, a couple miles further up the highway.

He was grateful not to recognize the old man behind the counter as he entered the tiny store.

"Give me a pint of R & R," was all he said.

The clerk plucked the small bottle from the couple dozen varieties of liquor bottles that lined the wall directly behind him. He slipped it into a paper sack and handed it to the sheriff who paid cash.

Back in his pickup, he flipped on the lights for the first time, with no siren, and breezed the last few miles up the highway to the waiting Car #356.

"Now what?" the sheriff asked as he walked up beside the sergeant who was standing casually behind his car talking with a state highway patrolman.

Sgt. Roy Baker shook his head. "Earl Walton is in there and he's really tied one on. His daughter-in-law said she found him this morning, threatening to shoot hisself. When we got here, Doreen said Jack had put up all the guns because he was afraid of something like this, but I guess Earl found a pistol his son didn't know about." Sergeant Baker jerked his head in the direction of the couple standing to the far side of the drive near a new pickup truck. "Earl fired a shot out the front door at us and said the only one he would talk to was you. Did you bring him a bottle?"

"Yeah, I picked up something on the way."

Baker snickered. "Wanda'll have your hide for that one. Let's see, how does that play with the politics? Sheriff stops in official county vehicle to buy a bottle of--"

The corners of Harper's mouth twitched slightly. "Yeah, well, sometimes you just got to do…" He left the thought unfinished.

The sergeant continued. "Earl says he wants to see you unarmed. I'm not sure this is a good idea, Dale. We can hold out awhile."

The sheriff shifted his weight from one cowboy boot to the other as he looked at the powerfully built officer before him. They had been through too many tough situations together to even begin to count and he knew fear was a reason that Roy Baker rarely allowed to dictate any decision. Today was no exception.

"Maybe you want to spend all day out here with that drunk old man," he answered, "but I don't. Let me go over and say a word to Jack and Doreen and then I'll be ready."

He walked the short distance to their truck, trying to look calmer than he felt.

"Hey, Jack." Harper greeted his old friend with a hearty handshake and tipped his hat to Doreen. "This ain't where I like to see you two, you know."

"Morning, Sheriff." She spoke first and attempted a smile. "To be honest, I'd rather be serving you coffee at the Four Leaf Clover, too." Her words caught in her throat, and she stopped to dab at her eyes with a tissue.

Jack looked down in embarrassment as he spoke. "Sorry, Dale. I thought I'd taken care of things better than this. Thanks for coming. You know, I love my father, but that old man's gonna be the death of me and I'm fresh out of ideas. I've tried more than once to get him out of that shack and off this postage stamp piece of ground, but it's like he's nailed to it." He sighed heavily. "There ain't much in the way of retirement benefits for old cowboys and old deputies."

Harper grinned. "Don't I know it. Hey, don't worry. We'll get him out of there in one piece. You know he doesn't really want to do this or he'd have had it done already."

"I hope you're right, Sheriff," Doreen answered with a sniffle.

A half dozen shots interrupted their conversation. Twigs showered down over the two officers still standing by the patrol car. The younger officer flattened himself on the ground instantly while Sgt. Baker casually squatted down behind the vehicle.

"Where's that sheriff? I thought you said he was on his way! He's the one I want to talk to!" The terse voice from the house followed the gunfire.

"Earl, you got no call to be shooting at us!" Baker yelled back.

The sheriff quickly instructed his friends to get into their vehicle and move it a short distance down the drive.

“Earl, this is Harper,” he called out. “You need to put that gun down and come on out now! You're upsetting a lot of folks and there’s no need. Let's quit before somebody gets hurt!"

"You can come in and get this gun, Harper, if you want it so bad. Don't you bring no weapon in here neither. Come on. I won't hurt you. You know that."

The sheriff walked back over to his car and retrieved the whiskey. "He won't hurt me." He tried to reassure a doubtful Baker as he walked past.

"Maybe not on purpose,” the sergeant growled, “but he's a drunk with a gun!”

Harper tossed the bottle back and forth between his hands and then pulled his .38 pistol from its holster on his left hip and tucked it securely in his belt behind his back. He tugged the brim of his hat a bit lower over his eyes and started up the driveway to the house.

"Earl, I'm comin’ in. I've got your bottle here." He held it slightly above his head in his right hand. The silence was broken only by the hollow thud of his boots on a hard-packed dirt road that had not seen gravel in the sheriff's lifetime.

"Earl?" He hesitated at the darkened door of the tattered shack where the screen door lay twisted to the side, pulled awkwardly from its hinges.

"I'm here, Harper." A heavy-set man with white hair lurched from the shadows. "At least you brought the Rich and Rare. Wasn't sure you'd remember."

"Yeah, I remember." The sigh that escaped him was heavier than he intended.

"Not too smart coming in without your gun. I got mine." The old man brandished an ancient revolver.

"Earl, what are you doing anyway? You must have had a lot more than usual if I need a gun to come and see you. Shoot, your nose is blue. Your nose always turns red, then blue when you've had too much to drink. Put that thing down, will ya?"

"No, Dale. I'm gonna do it this time. I'da had the job done today but I wasn't drunk enough. Ran out of booze and then Doreen come in here, seen the gun and started screaming." He swayed as he spoke and reached for the side of the house to steady himself.

"It's gonna be all right, Earl, now just put the gun down and..."

"No!" Newfound resolve strengthened his voice as he swung the antiquated revolver unsteadily in front of the younger man. "I tell you I'm gonna do it! Just give me my R & R and get out, if that's what you're about."

"Hey, calm down." The sheriff was conciliatory. "This is what you want, right?" He offered the pint tentatively, still held high and to the right, but he pulled back immediately as Earl reached for it. The old man moved faster than the sheriff had anticipated. He got his fingertips onto the bottle top as Harper jerked it away. A quick swing brought the .38 from behind his back on the left in one fluid motion as it caught Earl on the side of the head. Glass and whiskey spewed across both of them as the bottle smashed against the house and Earl Walton fell heavily to the ground.

"Earl, this ain't the way." The sheriff jerked a pair of handcuffs off his belt and had the old man's hands cuffed behind him as the others ran up the driveway.

"Geez, Sheriff." The young trooper spoke without thinking. "You smell awful!" He helped Sergeant Baker haul the older man to his feet and support him.

"You shoulda kilt me, Harper. It woulda been easier." Earl Walton's anger dissolved as his eyes filled. "Dale, I just don't want to live no more, don't you know?"

The sheriff did not answer but simply clapped his old friend clumsily on the shoulder as he moved away.

The two uniformed men escorted their prisoner up the drive towards the waiting vehicles. The sheriff returned quietly to his and pulled off his jacket before climbing inside. Under the surrounding trees, he sat in the shadows and breathed deeply of the overpowering aroma that emanated from the jacket he still clutched in his arms.

"Yeah, Earl," Dale Harper whispered unsteadily to Sergeant Baker's departing car. "I know.

Chapter 2

The mission director stood outside the building, watching a crane bring down a city landmark.

"You're taking down the neon cross?" The sheriff walked up quietly behind her.

She seemed completely engrossed in the work before her. "Yes, it has not worked properly in years they tell me. We have a new one." She pointed to a large cross lying on a nearby flatbed truck.

The sheriff moved in for a closer look. "That ain't exactly like the old one, is it?"

"No, it is different. It is still lighted but with many colors, because after all, we serve many different people here, yes? It goes with the new name, Foot of the Cross Mission. *Pie de la Cruz.* You see, it works in both languages."

"A new name, too? All kinds of things going on."

She took her eyes from the old cross long enough to peer at him from beneath her hand which was guarding her eyes from the sun.

"It was decided, after the problems that were here before I came that some changes were needed on the outside and on the inside. It is to let people know that things truly are different now." Her voice was as steady as her gaze.

"I never said it wasn't a good idea," the sheriff stated in a half-apologetic tone. He joined her, watching the progress of the work. “I remember this cross, shining white, when I was a teenager. It’s true the lights in it haven’t worked for a very long time.”

"And now they will. Come see what else we have."

He followed her inside and down the hallway from which she had first appeared the day before.

"Look, here." She guided him into a large room that was covered with raw sheet rock, lumber scraps and plaster dust. “We are making a day care center. We have children who live here already and some who only stay a short while. Still, there are others in the town who need a place to go while their parents work."

The sheriff picked his way through the project under construction, watching the slender samba of her walk before him as much as any of that which she was intent on showing him.

"And whose children will come to this center?"

"Who we always serve," she answered with a smile. "We will not serve the children of the doctors or the bank presidents. We will serve the children who have nowhere else to go."

"And is that all right with you?" He stepped around a ladder, heavy laden with a trough of drywall mud and the accompanying tools.

It was a question that seemed to catch her unawares. "What do you mean?"

"Is that who you want to come?"

"Of course. Who else would we serve in a mission like this? The least of these, as Jesus called them, is who we are always about," she added, with a little smile.

"Just wondering." He returned to her side, ready to proceed with the tour.

"You know, of course, about our rooms on the other side." She led him out to a courtyard in the center of the buildings. A cluster of wooden picnic tables, numerous wash lines and children's patio toys claimed much of the area. She pointed to the little obsolete motel rooms on the far side of the patio area.

"That reminds me. How is, what was her name, the lady I brought here yesterday?"

"Guadalupe. We shall see her. She is doing very well, I think."

They crossed the courtyard to a doorway where, once inside, he stopped to take a long look around.

"You know, this was the old skating rink when I was a boy," he told her as he looked at the rows of tables before him that made up the local soup kitchen. A half smile creased his face. "It takes me a minute sometimes, when I come through here."

"I understand," she replied, viewing him with solemn regard.

"It must seem a foolish thing to you," he continued, as they moved towards the kitchen that loomed at the far end of the room. The yellow hardwood floor, left over from the building's previous life, echoed their footsteps despite the noise of those crowded around the tables in front of them.

"No." She hesitated. "I was thinking it must be both a good and a bad thing to remain in the place where you grew up. Good, if your memories are kind ones from the past, but also sad because nothing stays as it was when we were children."

"That pretty well describes it. Do you get to go back to the place you grew up? South Texas?"

"No." Her smile was tinged with sadness. "I was in San Antonio as a teenager before I came here, but my days as a child were much further to the south."

"And do you go back?"

She shook her head and turned away, her face hidden by her long, shimmering black curls and the sparkling earrings as she ushered him past the tables.

"We serve lunch every day. I hope you do not mind if we eat here." She handed him a soup bowl on a tray with the accompanying flatware. "We have some very good cooks." They stepped to the rear of the line where those already standing encouraged them to go ahead.

"Miz Millie, please." The elderly lady immediately in front of her stepped aside. "You must go ahead. You, too, Sheriff."

"No, it is not necessary." She tried to assure them, but it was apparent she could win no ground.

"Come." She turned to her companion. "It is the only way to make certain they wait no longer."

The young blond woman dishing up the steamy chicken, vegetables and noodles, gave the sheriff a shy grin.

"Hello, Jenny," he greeted her.

"Hey, Sheriff," she responded. "Long time since I seen you."

"That's probably good. Looks like you're staying busy."

She giggled. "I help with the cooking here. Helps keep me out of your place."

He nodded as he followed along the line. Two thick pieces of home-baked buttered bread were added to his tray before they made their way to a table by the far wall.

He watched as she said a silent prayer over her food and they ate without speaking for the first few minutes, time he used to cast a look around the room. A few faces were familiar but most were strangers, a fact that brought both relief and disquiet.

"If I'd known Jenny could cook like this, I'd have put her in the kitchen rather than let her waste time in jail." He spoke as much to himself as to the woman across from him.

"She told me she was in jail before she came here. There are several here, yes?"

"I recognize some of the faces," the sheriff nodded.

"Well, not everyone who comes here has been in jail. The mayor ate here last week and also one of the judges. Judge

Randolph, a very tall man. He was very nice."

"Yes, he is. You guide each of them around, too? I guess I shouldn't feel too special that I got a personal tour from Director…what do they call you? Millie? That's not the name you told me yesterday."

"My name is Milagro. It is Spanish for miracle but it is difficult for people to say, so they like Millie better. That is fine with me if it is easier for them. I know what it is to learn to pronounce difficult words."

"I bet you do." He leaned back in his chair and took a long look at the caramel-skinned, dark-eyed beauty before him. "How long have you been in the U.S.?"

"Half my life."

"So you came when you were what? Twelve? And no English?"

"Just a little," she smiled in spite of herself. "And I was fifteen. My father lives in San Antonio and friends insisted that I come to live with him when I was not quite grown. Now, I can say it was a good decision." She shrugged.

"And your mother? She still lives in--"

"She is dead." Her voice went flat and the business manners returned. "I invited some people like you and the mayor and the judge to come. Others, like Commissioner Ravens, he invited himself."

"He came here?"

She nodded. "He came to complain."

"Complain? About you or the mission?" The sheriff raised an eyebrow in surprise.

“He did not like it that I let people sleep on the front porch," she explained while stirring her soup.

"Why? He is the county commissioner and you are located in the city. What does he care?"

She frowned and pulled the heavy crust from a piece of bread. "I asked him about that and he said it was because we were close to the city limits. He thought he needed to check us out. And also that we serve some county residents. That part is true. But another truth is that some of the people we serve are not comfortable staying inside. They will sleep outside no matter the weather so I said they could sleep on the front porch. They are happier and we cannot let them inside if they have been drinking. That is not safe for the others. They do not hurt anyone there so I thought it was a good plan, but the commissioner did not like it. It is never more than two or three and they come late and leave early." She shrugged with her hands lifted in the air.

"Great heavenly days! Oh, pardon me, sister, but that sounds like him. Why does he care anyway? At least on your porch they have a roof over their head and they’re not wandering down the side of the highway causing an accident." He shook his head in disgust. "So Dickie Ravens came to complain."

"He told me his name was Richard."

"I'm sure he did." The sheriff laughed in spite of his irritation. "Sorry. We went to school together and it's hard to forget who he was. He hasn't changed much. He just likes to pretend that he has."

"He is, I think, a man who likes to pretend many things."

"Yeah, that's him. How long did you talk to him anyway?"

"In the country where I grew up, there is something called *malicia.* The word means bad or wicked, really, but the country people use it differently. It is that nervous feeling you have when someone or something is not as it should be or when a person is not telling you the truth. There are men in my country, some who are quite dangerous. They pretend to be one thing but really act in a completely different way. The people who understand *malicia,* who feel it, who know it before something bad happens…" she hesitated before continuing. "Often they are the ones who stay alive. Commissioner Ravens is a man who reminds me that I was always pretty good at *malicia."*

"And what country is that?"

Her gaze was leveled full upon him as she answered. "I am from El Salvador."

He winced. "Then our problems must seem pretty tame to you by comparison."

The smile that came his way lit her entire face, making her even more beautiful, he thought. "That is not the answer I usually hear."

"Still, you've seen more than your share of misery, haven't you?" He leaned back in his chair as he asked.

"Hunger and cold and misery do not know nationalities. Even though much of what has gone on in my country involves civil war and death, sometimes I think it is just a different kind of dying. Death by drugs or alcohol or hopelessness or even poverty is still death. Here, it seems like it starts many times with death of the spirit."

He nodded. "I can't say I ever thought of it that way but you may be right." He finished the chicken-vegetable soup and had pushed the bowl aside when it was quickly replaced by a serving of chocolate cake. Sheriff Harper looked up to see Guadalupe, appearing much improved from the day before. “Why, thank you. How are you? And your son? Oh, gosh, I'm sorry, how dumb--" He turned in embarrassment to Milagro. "Will you ask her for me?"

Guadalupe giggled at his frustration. She touched his arm as she bent down to bring her face closer to his. "Bet-ter," she pronounced the word slowly.

He looked at Milagro and she agreed. "As you can see, Guadalupe is feeling much better and insisted that she wanted to help in the kitchen today. She baked the cake she brought to you now."

“Well, thank you again." The sheriff reached out and shook her hand.

"No.” She shook her head. "Thank you." She scooped up their empty soup bowls and headed back to the kitchen.

"So she's staying here?" The sheriff watched her walk away.

"Her son has a broken arm and a broken--how do you call this bone across here?" She motioned across her upper chest, just below her shoulder.

"His collar bone."

"That is the one. And some cracked ribs but his lungs are fine now and the doctor says he needs to rest to get better.

She and I, we are going back to the hospital this afternoon. Guadalupe talked to her family in California and they are sending money for bus tickets as soon as he is well enough."

"Wow, that may be awhile, don't you think? Is she going to stay here all that time?"

She shrugged as she continued with a warm smile. "That is what we do, yes? It will be fine. She is a very good person. Already she is worrying about sending money to us when she returns home. I do not know if she will because really, I do not know that she has anything to send but I like that she is thinking of it. In the same way, she is already thinking of others here. We will be fine with her, no matter how long she stays."

She started to say something else and then stopped. "What is wrong with your hand?" The concern in her voice caught him by surprise. "You are left-handed, yes? But I've been watching and..." She hesitated, then blurted out, "your hand is purple!"

"Yeah, it is. Just bruised, is all."

"What did you do?"

"Yesterday, after I left here, I hit a man."

"A bad man?" She looked startled. "Do you do that often? Does it hurt?"

He frowned as he concentrated on picking at the chocolate cake with his fork. "I had to separate an old man from his bottle, his gun and his plans to do something his family would regret. He's just old and sad and when he drinks too much, well, it's not a good thing for anybody."

"You know this man? He is a friend?"

"Once. It's a long story. He worked for my father. He had an old pistol so I hit him to make sure he didn't get a chance to hurt anyone, including himself." A sad little smile crossed his face. "I had my gun in my hand when I did it and I caught my thumb funny. My hand is pretty sore today."

"And what will happen to your old friend?"

"He's been sent off for a mental exam. That's what we do nowadays with people who threaten to kill themselves."

"And will that help him?" she asked as she popped the last bite of chocolate cake into her mouth.

“If he's lucky, I suppose, and if he gets some good help. Maybe it will. Maybe not."

"What do you think?" She watched him closely as she asked.

"I think he has a lot of problems that probably no doctor can fix."

“Then I shall pray for him,” she said as she sat back from the table.

“But you don’t even know him.” The sheriff surprised himself at how defensive he sounded.

“That makes no difference,” she stated in the same matter-of-fact tone. “What is his name?”

“What?”

“What is the name of your friend? I can pray for him by name or just as your friend. God knows who he is already but it is sometimes helpful when making the prayer to know the first name. You do not have to tell me if you do not want to.”

“Well, I suppose under the circumstances, it sure couldn’t hurt,” he sighed. “His name is Earl.”

She gave him a smile for an answer. “It never hurts to pray,” she added gently.

He pushed the now empty cake plate away as he stood up. "I'd best be getting back to the office. I thank you for the lunch but there is always work waiting."

"We have that in common, no?" She followed his lead out of the skating-rink-turned-dining-hall. They walked side by side, without speaking, to the front of the building.

He reached to his waist to hitch up his pants as he walked, and he winced as he thought of Earl again. It had never crossed his mind before that it took two hands to button a pair of blue jeans until he woke up this morning with a seriously bruised hand. He would have a regular reminder of Earl and his predicament for several more days, he realized. In spite of his doubts, he hoped Milagro’s prayers would be of some help.

They arrived in time to see the new cross being settled into its final resting place.

"The sides are different colors and it is a little bigger than the old one, but most important, it will have light, and that will be better, yes?"

"Better than one that does not work, I suppose," he

commented dryly.

"No, really better, do you not think so?"

It struck him that it was important to her to receive more of an answer than that.

“Yes, it will be better. Now tell me, why did you need to hear that from me?”

She seemed to recoil ever so slightly from the question, and then with a deep breath, she began. "In this world, every person must make the choice if they will make some contribution, no matter how great or small, that is a gift to others. Between the star at his birth and the cross at his death, Christ made the choice to follow and do and say what his Father promised, what the prophets had foretold. The result is that He became the greatest gift the world has ever known. Each of us has to make that choice at some point, between our star and our cross. This cross is our reminder, a sign for those who are lost, to come back to the greatest gift and the greatest giver. This should be a place where people can do that. And for that, we need a cross that can be seen, a cross that reflects the many different colors in our world, a *De Colores* cross, one that shows the true light of life."

He nodded solemnly as he contemplated her anew. “I can appreciate that.” They watched a few moments more and then he turned towards his truck.

"Thank you for coming,” she told him. “I wanted you to see that we have a place for the ones like Guadalupe who have no place to go, for the beaten ones, for whoever you think needs to be here."

"Who I think? Why me?" He turned back to look directly at

her.

She looked up at the cross before them. "Because you are a sincere person who will send only the ones who really need to be here."

His frown only deepened.

"I know an insincere man from a good man when I am fortunate to meet one." She took a quick breath and then added, "That is a part of *malicia,* too, and you are nothing like your Commissioner Ravens."

“Hold on there! Dickie Ravens is not MY anything!"

"I know.” He heard her giggle for the first time. “I could not help it. I just wanted to hear what you would say."

Despite his protests, Sheriff Harper drove away with a smile on his face.

* * * * *

“It is my turn to ask for a little help,” Milagro Palacios told Wanda a few days later upon her arrival at the sheriff's department. “I would like to ask him about something that happened a long time ago, if he is not too busy.”

“Let me check for you.” Wanda gave her a big smile and picked up the telephone. A few seconds later, Wanda ushered her to a small private office in the back.

Milagro cast an eye around the room, taking it all in as she found Sheriff Dale Harper seated behind a heavy oak desk. The walls held little in the way of decorations, only a couple of long guns and a few awards that looked as if they had been hung up as an afterthought. A photograph of a lovely blond woman stood out, low on the wall and close to the desk, away from the other frames. The most impressive item, however, was a large wooden carving that seemed to take command of the entire room from its place high on the back wall. It was surprisingly ornate and carried the state seal in the center as well as the words, *Crossland County Sheriff's Department, Sheriff D. Harper*.

Dale Harper's eyes followed her gaze. "It was my father's," he explained, without the question being formed into words. "Darrel Harper. He was sheriff here twenty years ago."

"I see." Milagro nodded solemnly.

"See what?"

"Oh, many things," she smiled. "The wood, it looks old, older than the rest of the room."

He shrugged. "That, the desk and this barrel chair were all his when he was sheriff, so I had them brought back in here after I was elected. I wasn't sure about that." He waved a hand towards the wooden plaque. "But my wife liked it and said I should hang it up, so I thought, why not?"

"Your wife? Is that her?" Milagro turned toward the picture by the desk.

"It was." His voice was quiet in a misty sort of way.

"Was. I am sorry. Martha said she was killed almost a year ago."

"Ten months, twenty-two days." The voice was lower yet.

"What was her name?"

"Bonnie." He changed the subject. "But you said, many things. What else do you see?"

"Oh, we spoke the other day of staying in the same place you grew up but I did not know your father was also sheriff. I am thinking, does that make your job harder or easier?"

"Hmm…I'd say that depends on what day you ask." He chuckled slightly as he turned the conversation again. "So, did you get lost on your way uptown?"

"Oh, no. I came to find some help for a lady who arrived at our door late yesterday. She is looking for someone she knew a long time ago, but she has only little pieces of information. And she does not know the name of the woman."

Dale Harper grinned. "She wants to find someone but she doesn't know her name? That could make things kinda hard, don't you think?"

"Yes, but this is what she told me. Maybe you can put it together."

The sheriff's barrel chair creaked in protest as he leaned back.

"She arrived last night. She is not young anymore and she was very tired. She is also, I think, without much money. She said when she saw our *De Colores* cross, she knew that meant we would be a good place to find help. Her name is Anna Mae, and many years ago she was traveling with her daughter who was trying to make a career, singing country music. They met another young girl, and the two girls became a pair for a short time. Her daughter used the name Bobby Sue and the other girl was Linda Lou. Those were their names for their act…fake names, how do you call them?"

"Stage names," he added.

"Yes, stage names," she continued. "Anna Mae remembers that Linda Lou was from Serenity and she remembered that because her brother was killed while they were on the road together. She said the brother was not quite right, mentally. He could work and help with farm chores but he was only thirteen and did not go to school anymore. He was working at an older lady's house out in the country. Then one day, something went terribly wrong because the boy shot the older lady and himself. That is really all Anna Mae knows, but she remembers how upset Linda Lou was to get the news when she called home. Anna Mae and her daughter took care of her for a little while, but not very long after that she decided to leave and go home to be with her family. So that is the story, and now she wants to find the woman she knew called Linda Lou."

The sheriff continued to sit without moving, as a chill ran up his spine. Milagro waited quietly and was about to ask him something more when he broke the silence.

"The old lady's name was Dunstan, Eunice Dunstan. She had a farm about ten miles out of town. The boy was just like you said, not quite all there but a harmless sort, not a mean bone in him. His name was Rupe Jensen, short for Rupert. I remember him in school when we were younger. And like you said, he couldn't keep up. The work was part of the problem but some of the other kids was the rest of it. That means the woman she's looking for is one of the Jensens. There were ten kids in Rupe's family, as I recall, and he was the youngest. I'm not sure which one of his sisters it is but it shouldn't take long to find out."

"You remembered so quickly." Milagro was impressed. "I thought it would be much more difficult to find this information for Anna Mae."

Dale Harper looked down at his boots. "Well, we don't get those kinds of shootings around here too often and I'm thankful for that."

His mind was reeling, remembering the details of the twenty year old case. He could still hear his father's voice, ranting and raving downstairs after he believed Dale had gone to bed.

"My father was sheriff then." He chose his words carefully.

"He was?" He could hear the surprise in her voice. She leaned forward. "And what did he do about this shooting?"

"Not much really. He worked on it what he could but this county had even less money then for a sheriff's department than it does now. He died just a month or so after that."

"While he was still the sheriff?"

The sheriff sighed. "Yeah, he was still in office. He had a heart attack and died on his way to the hospital." He stood up and walked around the desk. "So where is this lady now?"

"Oh, she is at the mission. I wanted to talk to you to see what I might find out before I said any more to her. She was so tired last night. Can you talk to her and explain how she might find her friend?"

"Sure, but let's check one thing first. Wanda!" He yelled rather than reaching for the phone.

“I’m a-coming.” Her footsteps could be heard tapping along the linoleum. “Can’t you just use the phone like a civilized person?” She came around the corner, slightly flustered, chewing her bubble gum even faster than usual.

“This way we can say we’re a modern sheriff’s department,” he said with a serious expression on his face. “We got voice mail and that was it.”

“Oh for pity’s sake.” Wanda was not amused.

“Hey, which one of the Jensen girls is it that you are such good friends with?”

“Jensen? Good grief, Sheriff. Her name has been Mrs. Lou Ann Fleming for nearly eighteen years now. She was Lou Ann Jensen. We were in school together, and we’ve been friends ever since. Why?”

“Ever hear of one of the Jensens referred to as Linda Lou?”

“Oh my stars!” Wanda exclaimed. “I haven’t heard that name in years!”

CHAPTER 3

Within a couple of hours, the former Lou Ann Jensen was standing outside the Foot of the Cross Mission. "Thank you so much for bringing me to town, Sheriff," she said as she turned towards the man who had just delivered her. "When I heard Anna Mae's voice on the phone, I just couldn't wait to see her. Hank won't be back from hauling milk for hours yet. And with my car broke down, I didn't have a way to get here. I really do appreciate this."

"It's not a problem, Lou Ann," he replied. "Just a favor for you and a little old lady. Glad to help."

They went inside to find a tiny woman seated on the front room sofa where the sheriff had first met Milagro and Guadalupe a few days before.

The two women reunited with squeals of delight and an embrace that lasted for a long moment. "It is so good to see you! I can't believe you came all this way! How are you? How is Bobby or I should say, Roberta? That is her real name, isn't it? You were the only one who ever called her that!"

A cloud crossed the older woman's countenance. "We lost

Roberta right after Christmas." She choked on the words. She took Lou Ann's hand in both of hers as she sat back down and pulled the younger woman in close beside her. "Cancer." She shook her head as the tears rolled down her cheeks. "It was a long time coming, a lot of suffering. When it was over, I was just glad for her sake that it was done. I suppose that's part of why I had to find you. I remember how you two were together on the road all those years ago. You were the closest thing she ever had to a sister. I just wanted to be sure you were all right." She patted the hand she still held.

"I'm so sorry. I had no idea. I wish she would have written or called."

"We wanted to, but you can't imagine." She laid her hand along the side of the younger woman's face. "We lost the address you gave us to write to you here in Serenity. And then I couldn't remember your real name. Linda Lou was such a pretty name but I knew it wasn't quite right. Roberta couldn't remember either, so I didn't know how we'd ever find you." She leaned back with a tired heartfelt smile. "Why, if it wasn't for this kind sheriff here, I might never have found you at all!"

Sheriff Harper touched the brim of his hat in their direction as he stood a respectful distance away at the counter talking with Martha.

"The other day when you were here, I considered that official business." Martha sounded surprisingly brusque. "But today, I don't think so. I think your mother, my sister, raised you better than that." She frowned at Dale and he laughed, looking down at the floor.

"You're right, Aunt Martha." He leaned over the counter and gave her a peck on the cheek.

"Aunt Martha?" Milagro joined the conversation as she entered the room. "You are his aunt?"

"Yes, I am." The woman behind the counter answered with more than a touch of pride. "My sister, Penelope, Penny we call her, is his mother, even if she is all the way off in Florida these days." She shook her head in a disapproving manner.

"I am surprised no one said anything the other day," Milagro continued.

"Miss Millie, you know what they say about folks in small towns, or at least, about this one. Everybody's related somehow!" Martha laughed at the look of consternation on Milagro's face.

"It's true," Dale Harper nodded. "You are one of the few people in town who is not related to anybody, but you never know. If you look hard enough, you might find…" He hesitated with a twinkle in his eye.

"Oh, I do not think you have to worry about that." Milagro corrected him quickly.

They were interrupted by more laughter from the reunited pair. "Well, the truth is," Lou Ann Fleming slapped her ample thigh, "Linda Lou is in here somewhere, but she's buried under a lot of cornbread, apple pie, and years of home-cooking. My husband, Hank, likes to eat, and I'm afraid I'm not too good at pushing away from the table when I should, either. We got five kids, too, so what can I say? That's only half as many as my folks had. Seems like a pretty small family to me, but it's a houseful. Anna Mae, why don't you come and stay with us? It's a busy place but we'd love to have you there."

"Oh, sweetheart, I appreciate it but I'm just going to be a few days here and then I'll be on my way. You don't need another one under foot at your house, surely! Miss Millie and Miss Martha have been so good to me and they said I could just stay here, if you don't mind. It's pretty quiet here and that's good for me, too." She began to pat Lou Ann's hand again.

"Well, of course that's fine, if you are comfortable here."

"Oh yes, don't you remember how many terrible motel rooms we survived in the old days? It is very nice here, really."

"Yeah, some of them were pretty rough as I recall. 'Course I was a kid and so excited about the idea of being a singer on the road." She laughed out loud at the memory as a distant glow lit her face.

"You had such a beautiful voice. Tell me, you do still sing, don't you?"

Lou Ann smiled in response to her friend's praise. "Yes, ma'am. Plenty of Sundays at the Catholic Church and I do the occasional solo at weddings and funerals, too."

The sheriff tipped his hat once again to the two women immediately before him. "I trust I can depend on you ladies to get Lou Ann back home a little later today. After talking to her, I just had to offer her a ride into town to see this lady but for now, I've got to get back to work."

* * * * *

It was late afternoon when Dale Harper heard raised voices coming from the direction of the front counter. He stopped digging through the boxes of old paperwork that surrounded him in the back storeroom and listened for a moment, hoping the crisis, whatever it was, would pass. With a sigh, he wrangled the box he'd been searching for, free from the others and made his way down the hallway.

"Commissioner, I cannot let somebody out of jail on your say so!" Wanda's face was as red as her hair tied up in a tight bun on top of her head. She addressed the two men on the other side of the counter.

"So what's the problem here?" The sheriff dropped the box of records with a loud thud.

Commissioner Richard Ravens flashed a politician's perfect, yet heartless, smile. "Dale, all we need here is a little in-county cooperation. Oh, you remember my cousin Carlton?"

"Carlton Dunstan." The commissioner's companion offered an unusually formal handshake which the sheriff chose to ignore.

"I remember Carley Dunstan." His voice was flat as he looked at the rail-thin man standing next to the commissioner.

"Now, Dale, all I was trying to do was explain that when we need some extra work done at the courthouse, the easiest thing for everyone involved is for me to simply come over here to the jail and get an extra hand or two to help paint and do a little construction repair. I just told Wanda who I'd like to have come over and work at the courthouse for the afternoon and she took it all wrong. I wasn't trying to—"

"Dickie, did you read the sign on the front door when you came in? Last time I checked, it says Sheriff's Department, not Ravens' Employment Agency."

"You should call me Commissioner, Dale. After all, I'm here in an official capacity."

The sheriff gave him a skeptical look. "Yeah, just like you call me Sheriff. I don't care for you to take out one of the drunks who's sobered up if he wants to do a little work as a trusty. But last time you picked out the biggest feller we had back there, and he was in for aggravated rape and attempted murder! You can't take a guy like that out to prance around the judge's chambers with a paintbrush in his hand! Why don't you go hire someone to do what you need in your *official* capacity? I appreciate tight budgets as much as the next guy, Dickie, but you give new meaning to the term tight-fisted when it comes to money!"

Commissioner Ravens dropped the polite pretext. "Dale, there you go with that unreasonable attitude you get every time I ask for a little cooperation between county offices. Then you wonder why there's a problem between us? If I have to go to the judge to get an order allowing me to get a little help from this department, then that's what I'll do but it sure don't look good for you, especially come budget time, next year when I have to—"

"Geez, Dickie, take a breath!" The sheriff cut him off. "I'll look into it. I can probably have one of the drunks ready for you by tomorrow. But you remember they ain't always the best workers. Some will, some won't. Work, that is. You best keep an eye on whoever it is and if they do run off, I'm telling Judge Billy Joe you were the responsible party. Got it?" The sheriff picked up the box of records at his feet and turned back towards his office.

"Fine Dale, fine. We'll wait until tomorrow." Ravens' political mask was back in place. "What is that you got there anyway? Does that box say ‘Dunstan’ on it?”

Both men on the front side of the counter peered carefully at the box in the sheriff's hands.

Dale Harper swung back halfway around.

“As a matter of fact, it does, but it’s just some old records, Dickie. Nothing for you to worry about.”

“But it’s about my aunt’s old murder case, right?” Commissioner Ravens tried once more.

“It’s an old case, that’s for sure,” the sheriff answered as he turned towards his own office. “Just files that need to be stored away and I’m taking care of that right now.”

The two men went out the front door, grumbling to each other as the sheriff put the box down in his office. He waited a few seconds, making certain the visitors were gone, before walking back to the front desk.

“You okay?” he asked, addressing Wanda’s back.

She swiveled in her office chair to face him. “Yeah, I’ll be all right.” She chewed her gum more slowly than usual. “Why is it always like that with him? Does he not have a brain in his head?”

“Oh, he’s got one. But like anything else that’s a little complicated, he doesn’t have a clue as to how to use it. Dickie’s one of those fools that once he has the least bit of power, he’s got to make certain everybody knows he’s got it.”

“And Cousin Carlton?” she asked. “Does he look the worse for wear or what?”

"Who knows? That's Carley Dunstan. He was born up the road and lived there his whole life until he ran off when he was a teenager. He went to California, they say, but then he came back a few years later, not too long before his mama was killed. I don't know what all that was about just now. He hasn't lived around here for years but I'd heard he'd come back this last year. Still, Carlton Dunstan, like we don't even know who he is. You're right, though. He doesn't look very good."

The smile was back on Wanda's face as he made his way back towards his office.

She looked in on him as she was preparing to leave for the day. "What are you doing?" she asked, as she found his desk covered with the various files and papers he had pulled from the box he had retrieved earlier.

"Just looking over the details of an old case, that's all." He looked up from the papers he had been reading. "Can't say there's a lot here, really. Don't even know what I was looking for. Just curious, I guess." He dropped his boots to the floor from where they'd been resting on the corner of his desk and followed her back to the front of the office.

At the front counter, jail roster in hand, there remained one last thing he needed to attend to before calling it a day. Thirty-seven souls sitting in the jail, he thought as he looked over the list of inmates he held in his hand. Thirty-five men, two women. Half were here because they really didn't have what it takes to live in regular society, go to work, pay their bills, get along with their neighbors and stay out of serious trouble. He wasn't sure what you called that certain quality it took to live like a normal person in America today, but a lot of these boys just didn't have it.

Freddy Ganst was a good example. He was one of the most

regular drunks they had. Dale Harper had worked for the local police department for ten years before becoming sheriff, and he dealt with Freddy and his brothers several times each year. Every one of them had some sort of problem with drinking or worse. Freddy wasn't a bad sort when he was sober and in a mood to talk, and any time he sat in the jail for awhile, he was both. Dale had used him as a trusty before, someone to help cook, do laundry, pass out meals, and wash dishes, but this time, Freddy was in real trouble. Sheriff Harper decided to have a little chat with him anyway.

"Freddy," the sheriff called through the bars as he approached one of the larger upstairs cells that held eight men.

"Yes sir, Sheriff." Freddy hopped off his bunk and over another inmate, sprawled on the floor reading a comic book.

"Come talk to me for a minute." The sheriff turned the heavy key in the lock and opened the door far enough to let the husky-built Freddy, clad in an orange jump suit, slip out of the cell. The sheriff closed the door with a clang that seemed louder than it actually was in the quiet cell block. Several other inmates looked up and a couple scurried to the front of their cells.

"Sheriff, Sheriff, I need to ask you something."

"Sheriff, do you have a minute?"

"When I come back, fellers," Sheriff Harper answered as he escorted Freddy to the end of the hall and down the steps. He took him into the large glassed-in booth at the end of the front counter. The sheriff showed Freddy to a chair but the lawman stayed on his feet, leaning against the far wall.

“You’ve got yourself in a pickle this time, don’t you?” The sheriff opened the conversation. “This ain’t like before when we had you in here for public drunkenness, and then Driving Under the Influence. This time they picked you up with drugs on you, Freddy. Methamphetamine. What’s that about?”

“Oh, now, Sheriff.” Freddy began to shuffle his orange rubber flip-flops while seated. “You know how it is. I mean, a feller’s got to have a little fun once in awhile. It don’t mean nothing really.”

“Freddy, they didn’t find no tiny little personal use packet on you. You had a sizeable amount of the stuff. Enough to sell. The question is where did you get it? Because it means that, with your record, this time they could send you to state prison. Now if that don’t mean nothing to you, well all right then, but I didn’t think—”

“Sheriff, I don’t want to go to prison,” Freddy began to whine. “You know me better than that. I ain’t a bad guy. You tell ‘em. I’ve always worked for you when I was in here before, didn’t I? I was a good trusty. I worked and didn’t give you no sass, no trouble. We got along good. You know me. I ain’t no criminal. I’m just a drunk. You can get them to give me another chance. Sure as the world I’ll make it work this time, Sheriff.”

“Freddy, I ain’t the deal maker. You’ll need to talk to your lawyer for that and then he’ll lay it out in front of the judge.”

“I don’t wanna talk to no public pretender.” Freddy’s face drew up in a childlike pout. “I don’t trust them lawyers. You can talk to the judge for me, Sheriff. You’re the only one I know, I can talk to you. There's things you should know and sure as the world, I can help."

"The lawyer is the public defender, Freddy." The sheriff stood with his arms folded across his chest, working to suppress a grin. "I'll see what I can do but no promises. If I can get you a deal, you better have something good."

"Oh, it's good, Sheriff. I won't make you sorry."

"Well, while you're at it, keep your mouth shut upstairs, ya hear? If anybody asks, I'm just looking for a new trusty. I can't do anything about that right now, with this drug charge hanging over your head, but we'll see about it later."

"Thank you, Sheriff." Freddy Ganst jumped to his feet, re-energized. "Thank you so much. You won't be sorry you took a chance on ol' Freddy, I promise."

The sheriff escorted him back to the cell and pulled out another familiar drunk, Weldon Johnson. "Weldon, you want to do some painting around on the courthouse tomorrow?" the sheriff asked, after fielding a few of the other questions that came his way as he walked down the hallway between the rows of cells. "The commissioner is needing a little help over there. You'll have to look sharp and mind your manners, but you got at least thirty days in here and it's a chance to get out and stretch your legs if you're interested."

Weldon Johnson was a small, gray-haired man who had been an accountant before giving his life over to the power of the grape, as he called it. He made his way quickly to the front of the cell. "I'd be happy to do so, Sheriff," he answered, in his usual self-effacing manner.

"Fine," the sheriff told him. "I'll let the commissioner

know. He'll be around for you later in the week, I'm sure."

"Thank you, Sheriff Harper," Weldon replied quietly.

"Thanks, Sheriff." Several others whose questions he had answered echoed the sentiment as he made his way back down the stairs.

With his hand on the outside door, Sheriff Harper nodded to the man handling the radio and telephone behind the counter.

"Have a good night, Ernie. I'll be around if you need anything."

"Good night, Sheriff," the dispatcher echoed back.

Sheriff Harper did not stay around to chat. Ernie Wilson was an able enough desk officer, one Harper had inherited from the last sheriff. He managed, most times, to man the radio and phones well enough, but like all his deputies, Ernie was always itching to be out in a car on patrol. It wasn't anything he could hang his hat on, the sheriff liked to say, but there was something about the man he never quite trusted. Good deputies were hard to come by, especially with what little the county could pay. Sheriff Harper couldn't always afford to be as particular as he would have liked in who he hired. He thought back to Milagro and her definition of *malicia* once again.

* * * * *

Task Force Agent John J. Brown bent over the blue aerial map, spread out over Sheriff Harper's desk. "Right here, that's where we've spotted suspicious growth in past years but we never could figure out a road in."

"You're right on the county line there," the sheriff explained as he studied the area indicated. "And there is no road in, not from either county."

"Then, how the blazes do --"

"Right here." Harper ran his finger down a squiggly line on the blue photographic paper. "The Fox River."

"You mean, they use the river as their roadway?"

"You're not from the country." It was a statement of fact.

"Chicago. Transferred down last year. Why?"

"Rivers were the first roads in this part of the world," Harper explained. "In some areas, they're still the only roads. No one lives up there, so it's not a particular problem. As kids, we canoed all through there. It belongs to the National Forest Service now. Roads still aren't a problem because the few who did live up there were moved out when the Forest Service took over."

"Even so, you know we have a problem with marijuana being cultivated in the National Forests and it gets to be a real hazard when tourists stumble in on those raising it. We've observed small patches up here in past years but didn't have the time or manpower to mess with it, but now we want it out of there. We've been ordered to take care of it and we're looking for your cooperation." He straightened up as he finished speaking.

"You've got our cooperation." Sheriff Harper pushed his hat far back on his head. "That's not a problem. Just what is it you need?"

John Brown grinned. "More than anything right now, I

need a guide. Sounds like that would be you."

* * * * *

"I can't believe they want to go in so early," Sgt. Roy Baker complained when the sheriff began explaining the plan to him. "We fight marijuana in this county every year, Dale, but in the summer time, once the plants are up and sizeable. What are they doing with it this early in the spring?"

The sheriff leaned back in his chair. "He said they've known about the marijuana patches up there for awhile, but they've got a heat detector now that's telling them somebody may be cooking methamphetamine up there as well. You talked to him the other day, didn't you?"

"Well, yeah, but our meeting was pretty short, all things considered. He said he wanted to talk to you and that was about it. I had no idea he was planning on something like this."

"Me either." The sheriff crossed his boots up on the top corner of his desk. "And I guess you really can't say he wants a lot right now. He did say the Fox River gets pretty busy with tourists in the summer and I couldn't argue with that. He says he's got another man he wants to take along and I told him to get in touch with Eddie Bluewater to get a couple of john boats. We'll just motor up there and see what there is to see."

"Be careful. I don't trust these guys. It's like you said, maybe they know what to do about drugs in the big city, but this is different," Sergeant Baker frowned.

"Well, that's not exactly what I said. What if he needs a little more help? You want to go along?"

"You know I do! Why didn't you say so before?"

"Sorry. Just wanted to see what you thought before I asked."

* * * * *

The next morning, the sheriff and the sergeant left early to drive out into the country where they met agents John Brown and Steve Walker at Petersen's Crossing, a low water bridge nearly thirty miles east of town. The other two had come in a sport utility vehicle with an attached boat trailer. The boats were already in the water when the two from the sheriff's department arrived.

"I see that Eddie got you all set up." The sheriff greeted Agent Brown.

"He certainly did. I told him you sent me in for a couple of flat-bottomed boats and motors for going up river, and he had them on the trailer and ready to go in short order. I was impressed."

"Eddie has always been a good friend."

"When you said something about The Bluewater River Emporium, I thought it was just the business name, but instead I found out Bluewater is actually his last name."

"Indian name, just like him," the sheriff replied. "He makes it work both ways. His is the best one around for canoes, john boats, fishing supplies, whatever you need on the river."

"I'll remember that," Brown added.

The sheriff noticed that while Walker was dressed in semi-military style lace-up boots and camouflage print pants, Brown was still in the light khaki pants and shirt and the knee-high black leather boots he'd worn the day before in the office. He wondered if it was Brown's get-up as well as his gung ho attitude that made Harper so uncomfortable.

As neither Brown nor Walker seemed anxious to run the boats, Sheriff Harper and Sgt. Baker took over the running of the small outboards. The smell of marine oil as it mixed with the water wafted into the air as they jerked the engines to life and headed northeast.

They made their way upriver and the forested woodlands quickly closed in around them. There were no buildings, docks, or other intrusions along the riverbank. The gray and brown tree trunks that lined the river were topped with the shimmering green of spring. They grew tightly down to the river's edge, giving the impression of what the river must have been like before the first white settlers intruded upon the area.

They proceeded in silence except for the whine of the outboard engines. The sunlight reflecting off the water made him squint but the gentle breeze was unseasonably warm, holding all the promise of an early spring. It was on mornings like these that Dale Harper counted himself a lucky man. While others made their living by punching a time clock, a computer or a factory press, he felt fortunate to find himself in a new and different situation on a weekly, if not daily, basis. On a morning like this, he had no complaints about his chosen line of work.

After twenty minutes or so, the sheriff suddenly stuck out his arm and brought it down swiftly as he cut his engine and pointed the bow in toward the bank. Baker followed.

They pulled up beside a brush pile at the edge of the river.

A second look revealed another boat, smaller yet similar to the ones they were in, tucked in next to the bank and obscured under a covering of loose brush.

Close inspection of the bank showed small steps cut into the dirt. The four men slipped up the dug-out path and silently followed the meandering foot trail that wound through the woods for nearly a quarter of a mile. They stopped just short of a small clearing that held a weathered cabin. A curl of blue wood smoke trailed from the stone chimney on the roof.

"I thought no one lived in the National Forest," Brown muttered to the sheriff as he stopped directly behind him.

"No one is supposed to," the sheriff responded softly. The other two slipped up behind them.

"Now what?" Baker gave voice to what they were all wondering.

"Now we find out who lives here and what they're up to," Brown growled. "Hello, the house!" he called out before anyone could stop him.

A loud grunt and the crashing of items inside the house gave Brown all the excuse he needed to run up to the front door, with the others in close pursuit. He pulled his Glock semi-automatic from his holster and the other officers did the same.

"Open the door! Federal officers!" Brown shouted as he pounded on the weak wood, but the only response was some sort of unidentifiable scream of terror mixed with pain and a crash, as if another door had been slammed shut. It was too much for Brown who kicked open the door and looked straight through the house to another door standing wide open on the opposite wall. A man's fleeing figure was already disappearing amongst the trees behind the house.

Glancing both ways, Brown and Walker ran through the cabin in swift pursuit. The sheriff looked about the scattered contents of the room. The smell of the unwashed, the cooking of some sort of wild meat on a small wood stove and the lack of ventilation hit him with a solid wall of stench. For a moment, he thought the man running out the back door was the cabin's lone inhabitant, and then a movement in the far corner caught his eye.

"Holy Hannah," he said, almost more to himself than to Baker, who was still close behind him. He took a long look at the trembling creature cowered in the corner. She braced herself against the wall, as if for a fight. Yet, at the same time, her eyes frantically searched for a way past the two men. The young girl's feet were bare and her matted dark hair hung loosely to her shoulders, half-covering her face. The tatters that clung to her thin frame could no longer rightfully be called clothing.

"Hey there, hang on now." The sheriff holstered his .38 and put his open hands out before him. "It's okay. We aren't here to hurt anyone. Let's calm down and--" He took a step closer as he spoke but her desperation only intensified. He stepped back, pulled up a wooden chair, and offered it to her.

"Come sit down, and we'll see what we can work out here."

She maintained her grip on the corner of the room.

"It's like nothing you're saying is getting through," Baker muttered, never taking his eyes from the frantic girl as he moved in a wide arc behind the sheriff, closing the back door.

"Yeah, I noticed that." The sheriff took another step closer and this time the panicked girl made a run for the door still standing open behind them. The sheriff grabbed her around the waist from behind as she ran past him. She immediately shrieked as if he had seriously injured her. She struggled, kicking and thrashing, as Baker slammed the other door shut.

"This ain't working, Roy!" The sheriff yelled above her screams. "I'm turning her loose, just watch the doors. Don't let her out of the cabin!"

He threw his arms open wide and she scurried back to her former place of refuge in the corner. She continued to stare wide-eyed at them, her tiny chest heaving, as she gasped for one panicky breath after another.

"She looks kinda like a bird you try to pick up on the side of the highway after it's been hit." Roy Baker stood far back as he watched her. "You figure it'll die of fear before anything else. How old do you think she is?"

"Who could say?" The sheriff answered as he continued to study her. "Eight or ten, maybe. Probably doesn't get much to eat." He nodded towards the still, simmering pot on the wood stove.

A gunshot outside snatched the men's attention in a new direction. "I'll go." Baker started towards the back door.

"No, if you open that door, she'll be gone, just like the bird you talked about," Dale Harper said. "Help me get her into a chair first, even if we have to tie her to it."

The sheriff tried again, talking in a soothing fashion the entire time as he moved closer to her but, once again, the terror-stricken girl bolted for the nearby door. This time when Harper grabbed her, he pinned her arms to her sides and turned towards Baker who helped him lower her to the waiting chair. Baker quickly cuffed her hands behind the chair but that did not even begin to restrain her. The sheriff continued to hold her physically in the chair, admonishing her to stay put, but to no avail. Baker grabbed a scrap of a bed sheet off the floor and twisted it into a rope. He tied her ankles securely to the front chair legs and brought the remaining end up over her lap to secure her firmly to the chair. Her struggles continued but with less vigor, and were replaced instead with strange wailing sounds. She hung her head so low she looked to be in danger of tipping the chair over forwards. Once she was secure, Baker started down the trail behind the house while the sheriff turned his attention to the young captive before him.

She was incredibly thin, almost wasted, and younger than he first thought. The wailing sounds continued, although they were softer now, and tears washed tiny clean trails down her dirty cheeks. There was no indication that she had changed her clothing or had a bath in months, maybe longer.

When she saw the sheriff looking at her, she quickly dropped her head to her chest. He noticed after a few seconds that she was unusually still as if she had stopped breathing. Harper looked closer and realized she was straining against the ropes and handcuffs with all her strength. The metal cuffs were already making deep red tracks in her wrists and she was closer than he liked to slipping through.

"Here, stop that." He spoke, not unkindly, and reached out to shake her shoulder. At his touch, she leapt so violently she nearly turned the chair over backwards and he had to grab her arm to keep her from falling. That set off a whole new round of wriggling, cries and attempts to break free from the captive chair.

"Good Glory, child," he admonished. "Calm down. No one wants to hurt you but you've got to quit fighting so!" He stood square in front of the chair and took hold of both of her shoulders. At that, she looked up into his face and spit on his cheek. She immediately took a deep breath and snapped her head sharply to the side, ready for the blow she apparently expected.

Harper moved slowly and deliberately as he released his grip on her shoulders and took a step away. He pulled a handkerchief from his back pocket and slowly wiped his face without taking his eyes off of her.

Sgt. Roy Baker burst, breathless, through the back door with shouts and a scramble coming close behind him. "Brown's been shot!"

Agent Walker half-carried his boss, Brown, who was hopping on one leg as they tumbled through the doorway. Baker and Walker eased the injured man onto the floor. He was pale, sweating and looking much less enthusiastic about this whole operation than just a few moments ago.

Baker ripped the pant leg and began to pull at Brown's boot on his injured leg.

"Hold it!" Sheriff Harper spoke up. "Don't take his boot off if you don't have to. Here." He eased the pant leg out of the way to reveal a nasty shotgun wound below the top edge of the boot.

"You're lucky," Harper told him, as he glanced around the filthy cabin.

Brown tensed as they worked over him. "Excuse me all to Hades and back if I don't feel so lucky!”

The sheriff jerked the sheet off the nearby bed, made of an old mattress and a slab of plywood balanced on crumbling bricks. He grimaced at its condition and then ripped several strips off the edge while he looked at Walker.

“You got a T-shirt on under that uniform?” he barked in his best military style.

“Yes, sir!” Walker answered, but the look on his face was one of confusion.

“Well, get it off! Your boss needs it!” Sheriff Harper ordered.

Walker quickly unbuttoned his uniform shirt and then skinned out of his undershirt and handed it to Harper, who ripped it in half. He folded the two pieces roughly and then stuffed them between the top edge of Brown's boot and his injured leg. He remembered his earlier thought about Brown’s boots, like what the man would do if he fell into the river in boots like those. Now, as he took a strip of the filthy sheet and tied it tightly around the top of the boot, putting pressure on the rough bandage and the leg wound, he was thankful the man had not worn more reasonable footwear.

"I should’ve known better than to follow that guy through his own fields. What are you doing anyway?" He squirmed at the sheriff's ministries.

"You're lucky," Sheriff Harper went on as if the injured man had never spoken, "because your boot caught a lot of the shot. If your boots were any shorter or he'd shot any higher---"

"He didn't shoot! That's what makes it even worse!" Brown spit out. "He was already gone. It was some kind of trap. He must've set it up beforehand." He hissed as he moved, trying to sit up, propping himself against the wall using his uninjured foot. "It was probably designed to keep people out but he led me right into it. I want it!" He turned toward the other two men. "I want that booby trap!"

"No, not now." The sheriff did not raise his voice but his tone left no doubt he would brook no arguments. "We've got an injured man and a girl we can't very well leave here alone. We have all we can handle at the moment. Sorry, Brown, you'll have to worry about your traps another day."

"But, the leg's not that bad--" Brown started to sputter.

"I'm not much on taking an injured man's word on how serious he's hurt. We're getting you out of here now! I told you, you're lucky the boot took what it did of that load, but it doesn't mean you can take your own sweet time about getting to a doctor."

"What about her?" Baker turned back towards the girl who had been watching them all in a sort of fascinated daze.

"I swear, I don't really know." Harper stood up slowly. "I'm not sure she even knows how to talk, or act like a sane person in a boat for that matter. I don't think we have time to find out. I'd say we take her like she is, chair and all. I don't like it much and we'll have to watch close that she doesn't throw herself and the chair both out of the boat or she'll drown quick. But as much of a fighter as she is, I sure don't want her dumping one, maybe both those boats. Water is awful cold this early in the season and I don't think Brown is up to swimming too far." That brought a partial smile from the man, still sitting on the floor.

It was a river trip, the like of which Sheriff Harper hoped never to repeat. Again, he piloted one boat and Baker the other, but this time, Baker's cargo included an injured man lying on the bottom of the boat with his leg propped up high, and the sheriff's boat carried a most unwilling passenger. The sheriff put Walker in charge of keeping the bound girl, still enough to travel, but her wailing reverberated off the trees and echoed along the river, like an animal mourning the end of its life. They left the boats and trailer at the site where they had originally met up with Brown just a few hours before. Walker rushed his injured supervisor to the hospital, while the sheriff and Sgt. Baker determined the best way to get the struggling child into the back of the patrol car.

“Let’s cut her loose and get her into the back seat,” Sheriff Harper told Sergeant Baker. “She can’t get out of there so let’s see how she does first. If we have to, we’ll try the seat belt or even the handcuffs, but I’d rather see if we can’t make it without trussing her up anymore.”

“Whatever you think.” The sergeant wiped his forehead with his handkerchief. “It’s the dangdest thing I’ve ever seen.”

She began by hanging on the heavy wire screen that was installed between the car’s front and back seats intended to keep prisoners out of trouble as they were transported. Earlier that morning they had decided to drive Baker’s car instead of the sheriff’s pickup, which they left behind for some routine maintenance.

“I’m sure glad we got your vehicle and not mine,” the sheriff commented as they put her in the back seat. “Can you imagine running down the road with her in that pickup truck?”

She watched the two closely from beneath her ragged mane like any other caged animal might have, but as the engine came to life and they moved out onto the highway, she curled into a tight ball on the back seat of the car. She peered warily out the window at the scenery flying past but was mercifully silent, except for the occasional sniffle.

While Baker drove, the sheriff radioed ahead to Wanda to alert the hospital to Agent Brown's condition and imminent arrival. He also told her to call Eddie Bluewater and tell him where his equipment had been left and why.

* * * * *

"What do you think we can do, Sheriff?" The director of the local child welfare department was practically whining as she edged towards the front door by the counter. "I don't know what you've got there or where you got her, but we don't have any foster homes that could take her on. I don't know what to tell you. Have you called Mental Health?"

"Do you think she's crazy?" the sheriff asked quietly.

"I don't know what she is," came the answer. "You don't know that she's not, do you? All I know is I can't help you. Call the Juvenile Division, maybe they can put her somewhere. I'm sorry. I've really got to go. I'm already late for a meeting."

Sheriff Dale Harper sighed as he turned from the door where the social service director had just disappeared. "Wanda," he called over the front counter. "Get me…I don't know. Who should we call now?"

Wanda shook her head. She walked in from the back and handed him a cup of black coffee. "You look like you need this. I don't know, Sheriff. I really don't. You know

Juvenile Division is not going to take her, and Mental Health, don't they have some rule about not taking a minor without having a parent's consent? What are you going to do about that? You don't know who she is, let alone who her parents are. I just don't...hey, where are you going?"

* * * * *

"I know my way down these stairs," Milagro told him as he tried to guide her down to the cell in the basement, the one everyone simply called the drunk tank.

"You do?" He was more than a little surprised.

"Yes, I was here once before. The night deputies did not tell you?" She stopped and then went on. "I thought you knew. I came to see a man who wanted to talk to someone about Jesus. It was late and he was drunk and a little crazy, maybe. I do not know, but he was also frightened and I think they were worried about him. They came and asked me if I would talk to him and they brought me in a police car one night right after I first came to town."

"Well, you just never know..." He let the thought die in the air."I don't know if you can do anything with what we've got here or not. I didn't know who else to ask. She's a sight, really. If you can't, I understand. You won't be the first one to say no."

He opened the door and they both stepped inside the dingy gray cell. The girl was tucked up in the corner on a mattress on the floor, much the way the sheriff and Baker had first found her in the cabin.

"Por el amor de Díos, pobrecita." Milagro dropped to her knees in the middle of the concrete cell floor.

The child's attention was riveted upon her. *"Mamá?"* The word was barely audible, but there was no doubt as to what she had said.

"*Niña, no ten miedo,"* Milagro continued in Spanish. "Don't be afraid." She held out her hands as she beckoned her to come away from the wall.

The girl peered out from beneath her stringy dark hair and looked tentatively at the woman but quickly fastened her stare on Dale Harper who was still on his feet. He moved back, away from Milagro, to stand near the closed door.

Milagro continued to call to her, softly imploring her to come and take her outstretched hand. Cautiously, the girl crept on all fours towards the woman seated on the floor. As she took her hand, Milagro reached out with the other, running her hand down over the matted hair as if she was petting a lost kitten. The child curled up beside her without uttering another sound.

Dale Harper swallowed hard at what he had just witnessed. "So what is it you want to know?" Milagro nearly choked on the words as she spoke to the still silent sheriff behind her. Without waiting for an answer, she bent over the child. In a voice heavy with both fury and heartbreak, she spat out her next words. "Tell me what I have to do to take her out of this terrible place!"

CHAPTER 4

A surprise snowfall had dropped three inches of white and taken the temperature down nearly forty degrees from where it had been the day before. Dale Harper buttoned his coat at the throat against the sharp wind as he and Sgt. Baker made their way upriver for the second time in as many days.

"I bet you had to do some fast talking to Eddie to get him to leave you another boat after yesterday," Baker yelled above the whine of the outboard.

Sheriff Harper grinned his answer. "Not bad," was all he said.

Eddie had understood once the circumstances were explained. The sheriff had also promised to come by and see him soon.

The world seemed a very different place than the day before, blanketed, muffled, and so much colder with an unforgiving crosswind. He thought of postponing the trip after the weather change but he knew, even after one day, there would be plenty of items missing. His suspicions were confirmed as fast as they pulled up beside where the brush pile had been the day before. He was not wrong to have come despite the cold.

"Hey, the brush and that other boat from yesterday are already gone," Baker noted, without any great surprise to his tone.

"Yeah, I was afraid of that."

"How did you know to stop here yesterday anyway?" Sgt. Baker asked as they climbed out of the boat. "Did you see the boat first?"

"No, I smelled the wood smoke first and that had me watching the bank. That brush pile, well, it was in the wrong place."

"What do you mean, wrong place?"

"You're not a river rat," Harper teased. "As a kid we were up and down the river, fishing, hunting, just growing up but you learned to watch the river and know what it does and doesn't do. Look up and down along this part of the river and you don't see any other brush piles, do you? The water moves through here pretty swiftly and it's deep enough that there's no logs sticking up from the bottom to catch anything. There has to be a reason for brush to collect in the first place. So I knew that brush pile wasn't put there by nature."

"Well, I never would have seen that," Baker admitted without hesitation. "What do you think we'll find up here?" They slowed their pace and approached the cabin with caution. One good look, however, told them much of what they needed to know.

Both cabin doors stood wide open, one of them moving

slowly back and forth with the breeze which was not nearly as strong as at the river's edge.

For the most part, the interior of the cabin looked the same as when they had departed the day before. Not that there was much worth salvaging, Harper thought to himself as he took a careful look around. Baker went through the back door to begin a canvass outside.

Harper noticed a thin chain around one leg of the pot-bellied wood stove. He reached underneath and pulled out the rest of it, which ended in a small cuff that looked like it had been taken off of a pair of old handcuffs. The chain, when extended its entire length, could reach the full width and breadth of the small cabin. Harper dropped it in disgust as he realized why it was there.

The old bed mattress had been flipped, sliced open, and anything once stored there was gone. A few other signs also spoke of a hasty departure. Mud tracked in from both doors told him whoever had returned had done so early this morning after last night's snowfall.

He found Baker outside, crouched at the end of a mound that lay beside the only outbuilding, a small three-sided lean-to. "Guess you better call those Federal boys back." Baker straightened up as the sheriff walked up beside him. "This is their land, and therefore their case, even if it is within the county, right?"

"That's right," the sheriff agreed.

"Well, they got bigger problems than just druggers cooking up here, and there's plenty of signs of that over there." He cast an arm in the general direction of the lean-to. "There's footprints everywhere and an old propane tank they used for a cook stove, but best as I can tell, it was only one person here to clean up. All the tracks match, only one set of boots, but look at this." Baker's gaze dropped back to his feet and with the toe of his boot, he pointed at what Harper first took to be a few scraggly dried weeds covered in snow. As his own boot tip touched it, Harper felt the resistance and then an unexpected shiver ran up his spine as he realized he was looking at three curled skeletal fingers pushing up through the snow.

"You know," Harper said quietly, still looking down, "I think I'm gonna quit taking river trips with you, Roy. They don't seem to be coming to no good."

The sheriff and Roy Baker had to make the return trip down river to reach the radio in their car before they could notify anyone. After thinking about exactly what to say and how to say it for most of the chilly boat ride back, Sheriff Harper surprised Sgt. Baker when they were off the water.

"Here's my best idea," Harper explained, once they were back in the patrol car and Baker had gunned the engine and turned the heat up to high. "Let's leave the boat here and you drop me off at Eddie's place. It's only a few miles up the road and I can use his phone to call into the office. That makes more sense than trying to tell them we've got a body up here when half the county listens in on scanners. We don't need the publicity right now."

Baker nodded.

"Leave me there and you go on back to the office. I'll have to wait for these Federal boys anyway and that'll give me some time to talk with Eddie. Somebody'll give me a ride back to town."

"And what about the boat?" Baker asked, as he started to back the car away from the covering stand of trees where they had parked earlier that morning.

"On a day like this…" Harper hesitated as he shrugged his shoulders forward and put his hands up close to the heat vent on the dash. "I figure the boat will be safe right there, just like I knew the car would be as long as we had it parked out of sight. This kind of weather keeps most of the mischief makers inside, especially along the river. Only ones out today are those who have to make a living and fool lawmen!"

* * * * *

"Dale, it's been too long!" The owner's booming voice and hearty handshake provided a warm welcome when Dale Harper walked through the front door of Eddie Bluewater's River Emporium. The pot-bellied stove in the back with its hot coffee and nearby checkerboard reminded Dale Harper he was truly coming home.

"You picked a good day." Eddie joined him beside the stove, coffee cup in hand, as he handed his friend an empty mug. "Yesterday the place was jumping with folks stopping in to get information, reserve canoes for the next few weekends. They start thinking about fishing tackle for the spring, but today, with this weather…" He shot a hand into the air in a gesture of disgust. "I even sent Gene and Natalie home today. There wasn't much going on so I told them they might as well take the day off rather than to just stand around here."

"Well, you know spring in this part of the country never comes easy," Dale Harper commiserated, and poured himself a cup of hot coffee from the old-fashioned metal pot on the stove. "I know it's rough out there. We left your boat tucked in the weeds down there at Petersen's Crossing, by the way. We're not done with it and I'll probably need another one or two in short order, if that's okay."

"Sure, no problem. What's up?"

Dale Harper contemplated the man before him, in his blue jeans and long-sleeved red flannel shirt topped with a leather vest, complete with rawhide strings. They had both grown up along the Fox River and survived all sorts of exploits together. Harper looked around the shop as he dreaded getting his old friend involved in the current business at hand. Eddie had decorated the place over the years with native wood, rock formations and small taxidermied animals such as a raccoon, a fox, birds and fish, each done up in a small part of its own natural habitat. "This place has come a long way, Eddie." Harper put off the unavoidable a few moments longer. "When you first said you were naming it The Bluewater River Emporium, I thought that was the silliest name in the world, but you've made it work."

"We started with gas, ice and canoes like everybody else up and down the river, but now we've got that and more fishing tackle, coolers, boats and motors for rent, cowboy hats and waders. It had to be something a little different. That's why I liked the word emporium. It speaks of something bigger and better than average but still a little old-fashioned, too."

"So what you going to do when those start to turn gray?" Harper reached over and flipped one of Eddie's long black braids. "You said you wouldn't cut your hair again once we got out of the army and you've stuck to it."

Eddie gave a matter-of-fact shrug and said, "Then they'll be gray. Remember when we first came back from Desert Storm? How we said we'd never wander far from the old Fox River again?" Eddie poked at his old friend and laughed at the memory.

"I remember two green kids who went and signed up with the U.S. Army looking for adventure, and ended up in a world of sand and supply lines. What we would have given for just the sight of a river or the smell of a pine tree!"

"That's why I knew I had to figure out a way to stay here and make a living at it, too," Eddie continued. "I'd had my share of fighting sand storms and government regulations. They didn't have to ask this boy twice if he was going to sign up again! And you weren't any different as I remember. I didn't see you re-enlisting when they came around with those papers."

"No, you're right. We joined together and we left together."

"So now tell me, what are you doing out on a day like today? I don't mind kicking old memories around on a snowy day but you said you were going to need more boats?"

"I had Roy Baker drop me off here so I could use your phone to call the office and not put what I had to say over the radio."

"Sure, no problem." Eddie got up and pulled a phone from beneath the counter. He fed out the line and set it on a small wooden barrel beside Harper. "I could get you the hand-held one from the other side of the store, but this sounds like official business so didn't figure you want that. I don't really know if people can listen in on those or not, but they say they can." He shrugged. "Hey, I'll leave you to it."

"No, it's all right. Don't go." The sheriff stopped him. "You might as well hear this from the beginning. Then maybe you can help out with anything you might be able to add."

Eddie stopped and sat down, more slowly this time, opposite the sheriff.

"Wanda, listen," Sheriff Harper spoke into the telephone. "Roy's on his way back in there to you and I'm out here at Eddie Bluewater's place. We found a body up there at the same site where we were yesterday. Yeah, where we found the little girl. It's been buried but we'll need to get the Feds back up here. It's on their land, so it's going to be their case, their mess really. Call the number we have for Agent Brown. I'm sure he's not back to work but try to talk to Steve Walker or whoever they've put in charge of this case. You can call me back here at Eddie's if they decide to come today and I can take them up there. Let me know what you find out. I'll call you later." He hung up the phone and looked up to see a very serious Eddie Bluewater watching his every move.

"A body? Where have you and Sgt. Baker been poking around? I don't like the sound of this. It certainly won't be good for business!"

"Hey Mr. Businessman," Dale Harper teased. "I can't say that's the first thing I thought of when Baker found three bony fingers sticking up through the snow!"

Eddie's expression remained unchanged for several seconds as he studied his old friend. "Geez, I can't believe I said that!" He shook his head from side to side. "The white man's business world has finally sucked me in all the way." Eddie grinned, robbing his words of any offense.

"Well, don't go posing for any Chamber of Commerce posters just yet. Somehow I don't see you on the cover of

Business World."

"Okay, my apologies. Forget my businessman's reaction to this body you found up there. Tell me, what's going on?"

Sheriff Harper took a deep breath. "Well, I don't know a whole lot more. You met that Federal agent, Brown, who came in and got the boats yesterday. Roy and I took him and another guy upriver to look at a place where he said they'd seen some marijuana patches in the past from the air. I showed 'em where they went in and out by river, with no roads in or out. He said they'd also noticed hot spots this last year and figured someone was cooking meth up there. He wanted to go up and take a look around. Baker kept saying it was strange to go so early for the marijuana but we found this little cabin up there in the woods. We lost the feller who was inside when he went running out the back door. Brown kinda went in like gangbusters, going after the guy. The next thing I know Brown comes hobbling back with his partner after he'd got himself shot. This old boy had rigged some kind of booby trap, and he managed to lead Brown right into it. He caught part of a shotgun blast in the leg but we got him back and he was still in the hospital last night."

"Yeah," Eddie cut in, "I got part of this from Wanda at least about an injured Federal agent when she called to tell me where the boats were. Thanks for that, by the way. You know some things have changed over the years but others haven't. It's still amazing how if you leave boats and motors out there overnight, they'll be gone or stripped by the next day. No one ever knows who or what. I've got my suspicions of a couple of guys, and that hasn't changed since we were kids, but go on with the rest of it."

Sheriff Harper stopped speaking while he stepped to the

stove to refill his coffee cup. “Anyway, as if that wasn’t enough, we found this little girl in the cabin. Eight or ten years old, I don’t know. I’ve lived here all my life, Eddie, and seen some pretty rough river rats, but I never seen anything like her. She was filthy, rags for clothes. Heaven knows the last time she’d seen a bath or even had her hair combed. She didn’t speak or seem to understand when we spoke. You should’ve seen me and Roy Baker trying to deal with her, now that was a comedy! We finally tied her to a chair and brought her and Brown both downriver yesterday afternoon, just trying to make sure we got everybody out as fast as possible, with nobody hurt any worse. She howled all the way down the river, too, like some kind of wild animal.”

“So you said Brown was still in the hospital. What became of the girl?”

The sheriff smiled. “I got lucky there. The new gal who’s running the old Main Street Mission agreed to take the girl for now. She came and got her last night and I haven’t even had a chance to check on them today yet, so don’t know exactly how that’s working out. I know Mrs. Smythe, the one who runs the state social service office, ran right back out the door when I showed her this little girl. Said she didn’t have a foster home that would take her and told me to call Mental Health!”

Eddie snorted. “And that surprises you?”

“No, not really, I guess. This girl was a mess. Anyway, Roy and I went back today, despite the snow, because I figured whoever was in that cabin would be back to clean out anything they could, and I was right. He’d been there, early this morning before we got back there. Left all kinds of footprints in the snow and took what he wanted, I guess.

While we were poking around, Roy goes outside to where they had a three-sided shed for cooking the meth. I have to say that kinda surprised me. Smarter than most, cooking it outside where the fumes aren't so bad. Most of them cook it right inside their own house or apartment where they live. The fumes make them nuts or they risk blowing themselves up. Anyway, there was a mound beside the shed and Roy shows me what I thought was a little bit of dead weeds at first, but it was definitely three skeleton fingers, sticking up through the snow."

Harper took another sip of the steaming coffee. "I'll tell you, that shot a chill all the way up my back to see them fingers there in with the dead grass and this year's buttercups just a-coming up through the snow. And that's all we know so far. Now, my question to you is, who do you know around here, someone new or strange that comes in for supplies that might fit into this picture?"

Eddie opened the door on the stove and stared at the dancing flames and then leaned back in the wooden rail chair, balancing it on the back two feet.

"Now that is a good question," he said, as he pulled gently on his braids. "I'll have to study on that one awhile, Dale. I mean, we see new folks in here all the time, tourists and others just passing through. They stop to buy gas, bait or a bite to eat, but someone who has come along in the last few years and who might have a wild girl with him, heh?" Eddie looked up as the sheriff got to his feet.

"Well, I don't think the girl would have been with him. I still can't quite figure her part in all of this except that I did find a long chain with a handcuff on the end which would be about the right size for her ankle. I'd say the girl never left the cabin, part of why she looked the way she did. My guess is that whenever this feller left, he just chained her up. Then he could come and go without worrying about her running off."

"Now that is creepy stuff!" Eddie shuddered and closed the stove door after adding another stick of wood. "A dead body in the back yard, a kid chained up in the house. This guy has got to be one very weird dude, Dale."

"Yeah, that's what we're looking for, Eddie. One very weird dude."

* * * * *

Hours later, Sheriff Dale Harper was back at the cabin site, having made two more trips up the river. He had gotten another boat from Eddie, which one of the new Federal agents on the scene had piloted, following him upriver. Then Harper had returned to bring up more men. Together, they hauled men, digging equipment, and a generator to the cabin site. He had to give the Feds credit that when they took over an operation, they brought more equipment in a car trunk than he could muster in his whole department. Eddie had promised he would bring up another boat at the end of the day to help haul the stuff and men back.

Once everything was delivered, there had not been a lot for him to do, so Harper scrounged behind the cabin and found half of an old metal barrel. It had a watermark on the side, like one that might have been retrieved from the river at some point. He was pleased to find the inside was clean with no sign it had been used in the meth operation. He pulled it to the back of the cabin, near the door, and threw a couple of armloads of kindling into it. Then he lit it with his cigarette lighter.

He had given up smoking years before, at Bonnie's request.

She kept telling him she didn't want to end up a widow without him. A sad little grimace crossed his face at the bittersweet memory. He still carried a lighter though. Every now and then it came in real handy. It wasn't long before he had a decent fire going which had all of the men stopping briefly as they went back and forth.

The sheriff had also taken time to look over what was left of the meth operation in the lean-to shed. It contained the usual trash he was getting way too used to seeing in these kinds of operations--chemical containers, two liter bottles, coffee filters, and enough tubing to set up a junior high science lab, all strewn about in a haphazard fashion.

How many people had he locked up in his jail in recent years, horribly addicted to this stuff, many of them clueless as to what was in it? He thought about the Truth in Labeling laws he had heard some politician on TV going on about recently and wished there was a way to show more people that their precious meth was made of drain cleaner, industrial acids, veterinary supplies and lantern fuel. He wondered how quickly they'd be willing to snort it up their nose or put it in their veins with a hypodermic the very first time if they knew that?

He looked over to where the men had been working all afternoon. They finally had the body out, or what was left of it. They were just tucking it into a plastic body bag.

It was nearly the end of the day and he was bone-tired. If they didn't quit soon, he knew they'd have the extra burden of trying to navigate the river in the dark.

"Lieutenant," Sheriff Harper spoke up as the new man in charge walked by. "We need to think about winding this up for the day unless you and your men want to spend the night up here. I need to get these boats back downriver before dark, and tomorrow, well…I can send my sergeant up here with you but I've got to be in court all day."

Lt. Russell Yancey glanced at the sheriff but continued walking as if he had not heard him. Then he stopped and turned back towards the fire.

"Is it too cold out here for you? You seem to be sticking pretty close to that fire," the lieutenant observed.

"Where are you from?" the sheriff asked.

"Wisconsin. Why?"

"Well, us southern boys, we ain't so fond of the cold as some." Sheriff Harper drawled out the words as he spoke.

"We won't be spending the night." Yancey returned to the original question. "We've got what we came for. The forensic boys can come back tomorrow or the next day if they need more than what we've collected for them. They can arrange to bring their own boats by then. Once they get this body loaded, we can get out of here."

Yancey held up his hand. "She had long hair," he said, as a few strands of black hair slipped from his fingers. "She must have been Mexican or Indian or maybe Polynesian. You got problems with any of those around here?"

It occurred to the sheriff that this was the most the man had spoken to him all day, treating him more like an equipment delivery boy than a fellow law enforcement officer. Still, the sheriff had said little in return, trying to convince himself that it was Yancey's youth and lack of knowledge about the area that had put him instantly on the defensive.

"Got problems with any of what?" was all he could think to say.

"Illegals, of course. Mexicans. Border trash. I imagine this town's got their fair share these days like everywhere else." Yancey snorted, as he dropped the strands of black hair he had been holding. The wind caught them and drug them across the rough ground.

Sheriff Dale Harper worked to keep his voice steady as he spoke. "We've got dairy farms here with owners who need help milking twice a day, seven days a week. We've got truck farmers who need crops picked. We've got restaurants and motels, all of which need people who are willing to work. Most of the Spanish-speaking types we got around here do just that. They work hard, mind their own business, keep to themselves, and fill jobs that nobody else wants. They don't cause us many problems. I expect we got some illegals, but that would be a Federal problem now. Immigration and all that."

"And you don't deal with that?" Yancey arched an eyebrow as he looked back at the sheriff.

"I try real hard not to, to be honest. Got more than I can say grace over in this county with the day-to-day business of husbands and wives and neighbors feuding, bad checks, drunks and drunk drivers, burglaries, this meth epidemic that is all but out of control, and then this sort of business crops up every now and again." He swung his arm wide over the area. "No, I don't go out of my way to get involved with immigration problems. They're fighting a losing battle. Even a country boy like me knows that. As for Indians, well, when we got the extra boats today, that man makes up half the Indian population of this county as far as I know. Ain't seen no Polynesians that I recall, unless you count the folks running the Chinese restaurant out on the highway. Then, of course, there's a family from New Delhi who manages one of the motels out there, too. That's about it. I took a look at the body over there earlier but what I saw wasn't too recognizable."

Lt. Yancey did a poor job of concealing a sideways smile. "You're right about that. Doubt that her own mother would recognize her at the moment. We'll let the lab techs tell us more in a week or so, at least about how old she is and how long she's been in the ground. I'm sure they can tell us if she's Tex-Mex, too." He turned and walked away.

Eddie suddenly appeared at the sheriff's side. "Wasn't sure if you were still coming." The relief was evident in Harper's voice, in spite of his words.

"Oh, I was just standing over there beside that tree, listening. You did a real good job of defending us, Bro'."

"Defending who?"

"Us. Indians, Latinos, people of color. I'd say he's not a fan."

Dale Harper snorted. "No, can't say he'll make a lot of friends around here. He actually makes me miss Brown, the one who was up here yesterday." He dropped his voice, lower muttering under his breath, "I'm thinking the wrong one got shot."

"Hmm, maybe so. So what do you think?"

"About what?"

"Who that woman might be? Who's been living up here, cooking this junk? All of this. I'm telling you, it's got me feeling creepy all over. I don't like people in my neighborhood doing this kind of thing. I like to think I got a nice little business out here in the woods, just the kind of place that city folks like to come to and relax and fish and float down the river. We don't need this! I mean, my father hasn't locked the front door on our house as far back as I can remember. I bet he doesn't even know where to find a front door key if he did lock it! Now, this kind of stuff makes me wonder if I don't need to rethink that whole idea."

"Geez, Eddie, that's quite a speech. I thought the Indian thing was to be the quiet, deep thinker."

"Well, you were always better at that part than I was. Even my father said so when we were kids. Remember?"

"Yeah, he did." The memory made Harper chuckle as he stared into the barrel fire.

"When we were kids, he always said you were more Indian on the inside. Said I took after my mother." Eddie shrugged with a grin on his face. "Maybe so."

"So how's your dad doing anyway? I didn't see him around at your place."

Eddie's demeanor changed quickly as he quietly answered. "He took a ride up north yesterday."

Dale Harper waited a respectful few seconds before he added, "And how is Albert?"

"Oh, he's doing okay, I guess. He writes that he's attending AA regularly and Prison Fellowship meetings. I hope so. Of course, if he'd done something like that before, he'd never have ended up there, but there's nothing to be done about that now," he finished with a heavy sigh.

"You're right about that. So your dad still goes to visit

him?"

"Once a month, like clockwork. Maybe I shouldn't let it bother me so much but it does. I'm not even sure why. I mean, what do I care if the old man wants to spend his time and money traveling up there? But he always comes home looking so tired after making that trip and it isn't just the time on the road, if you know what I mean? Just makes me want to kick my little brother's backside all over again."

"You've done that a few times, as I remember. Didn't seem to help much."

"Yeah, you got to break up a couple of those, didn't you? I forgot about that." He smiled in spite of himself. "But that's when we were both drinking. I got smart and quit. Just like you, right?"

Harper took a sharp breath and glanced sideways at Eddie who didn't seem to notice. "Right," he echoed softly.

"I just never could get through to my little brother to do the same thing. By the time the worst happened, he was also into drugs, too, meth, I'm pretty sure. If he'd have gotten sober and stayed clean, he sure wouldn't be where he is now and that kid on the highway, he'd still be alive, Dale." The emotion of all the painful years suddenly caught up with Eddie Bluewater.

"I know, Eddie. I know. Let's not go there just now. Come on. Maybe if we can get these guys packed up, we can get out of here and back to that nice, warm stove at your place."

* * * * *

Standing outside the renamed Foot of the Cross mission, Dale Harper looked up at the brightly lit neon cross of many colors. He wondered if it was too early to be bothering the folks inside but he knew this might be his only chance today to check on things.

“Good morning, Dale,” Martha greeted him, as he made his way inside. “Who might you be bringing us today?”

“Nobody today, Aunt Martha.” He smiled in spite of her tone. “Just wanted to find out how the little one I left off here with Miss Millie the other night is doing.”

“Oh, that one’s something else.” Martha shook her head. “Never seen anything quite like that before.”

“Me either, and I’ve seen a lot in this job, as I imagine you have in yours here. Is she causing you any headaches? Still howling like she was with us?”

“Oh, I can’t say I’ve heard any howling. Lots of giggling from the others but I haven’t heard a peep out of her. Just come on and you can see for yourself.” She led the way and he followed behind, hat in hand.

“Miss Millie,” Martha called across the back courtyard, and pointed to a doorway on the opposite side. “She should be coming right through there. I’ve got to get back to the front. I was supposed to be on my way to help in the kitchen when you came in.” She turned and left him on his own.

“Good morning,” Dale Harper called out as he crossed the courtyard. He could hear activity in different parts of the mission and the delicious aroma coming from the kitchen reminded him he’d had no breakfast, not even coffee, as yet.

"*Buenos días*, oh, I mean, good morning." Milagro corrected herself. "I forget, going back and forth." She had stepped out of the doorway with a hairbrush in her hand. She took a couple more strokes down through her curly, shoulder length black hair as she spoke.

"I'm sorry," he answered. "I don't mean to bother you. I just wanted to check and see how things were working out with that little girl. I'm glad to see you look like you're fine and that she's not making you crazy or anything."

Milagro smiled brightly. "Certainly not. Come, see for yourself." She led him down a short hallway and through a doorway into a small house that was actually located at the far end of the motel rooms where the mission's guests stayed. He had forgotten about the residence originally for the caretaker of the former motel from long ago. A quick glance around and he realized he was standing in her private quarters.

"So this is where you live?"

"Yes," she answered. "When I moved in they told me the previous director had refused to live here but I like it. There is no reason to live anywhere else, yes?"

"I guess that does work out pretty good for you."

"Look," she dropped her voice to a hush. She laid the hairbrush on a small table and reached out and took his hand so naturally it took his breath away. "Look right there." She pulled him forward to peek through an arched doorway into a bedroom where a young girl was sitting on a brightly colored mat on the floor. She had a comb in her hand which she was studying very closely as she held it up to her hair and then brought it back down again without actually pulling it through her hair.

Dale Harper contemplated the young lady with a Dutch boy haircut sitting quietly in a plain maroon dress. He noticed she had on socks but no shoes.

Milagro pulled him back, out of sight of the child, and raised her voice above the conspiratorial whisper. "Well, what do you think?"

"I think I'd like to know what you did with the girl you took out of the jail, 'cause that's a different one altogether!"

Milagro giggled at the compliment. "It was quite an interesting day yesterday. I believe she spent half of it in the bathtub."

"Only half?"

She grinned. "She slept the first night on the floor beside my bed where she is now. I did not try to do anything with her until the next morning. I checked her all over and was very surprised to find no bugs."

"Bugs?"

"No fleas or *piojos*. How do you call them, lices?"

"Oh, yeah, lice. I didn't even think about that but I guess she would have been a good bet for them, come to think of it."

"Exactly, but there were none so I got a couple of the other little girls to come into the bath with her. She is fascinated by the other children and she was happy as long as they were there. Of course, there was lots of splashing and playing. I was as wet as if I had been in the water, too, by the time we were done."

"But that hair! I figured you would end up shaving her head like a new army recruit!"

"Oh, no! I would never do that. You can do a lot with enough hair conditioner and just a little bit of the scissors." She made snipping motions with her fingers. *"Pobrecita.* She has been through enough, no?"

"Hey, what is that pobray—pobraysee?" he asked. "That's what you said the other night that brought her right out to you."

"*Pobrecita,* poor little thing. And it is true in her case. Martha helped me and we cut her hair some, but the rest we were able to save. She does not say anything, but she responds to the Spanish well, better than English. Her hair is dark but her skin is lighter. I mean, it is still brown, well, it is hard to tell."

"Not exactly like yours?" Dale Harper lifted one of her caramel-colored hands in his as he noted the contrast.

"Well, compared to yours, she is not so light. You Americans. So many different colors! Hers could change, too, when she gets enough to eat. Oh, to see her eat is a whole different thing!" Milagro rolled her eyes in an exaggerated fashion.

"I may know a little more about who her mama is, or was." Dale Harper told her briefly about the body found outside the cabin in the woods. "We don't know anything about her yet except where she was found and where this little one was. Oh, that reminds me, can you get her to come out here? Or can you get me up closer to her? I won't touch her, but I need to check on something. If you don't mind?"

Milagro went into the bedroom and returned with her new

charge, walking hand in hand at her side. At the sight of the sheriff, the child instantly drew back and hid her face behind Milagro's full denim skirt.

"*Está bien, está bien*," Milagro reassured her, pulling her gently from behind her. "*No hay que tener miedo*. Don't be afraid. *Maria, ven aca.* Come here."

"Maria? I heard that." He looked at the pair with more than a little amusement.

"We had to call her something. I did not want to keep calling her 'that little girl' like you do." Milagro found herself only slightly on the defensive. "Half of my world has Maria in their name. Maria Elena, Maria Teresa, Maria Milagro."

"That yours? Maria Mila-gro." He managed to pronounce the unfamiliar name for the first time.

She nodded. "So what is it you needed with Maria?"

"I don't see any shoes on her, just socks."

"Oh, we tried the dress first, because it is easier, you know, than pants and a shirt for someone not so used to clothes. We have a collection of clothes here for those in need. Even the socks she did not mind, but now shoes, those were a problem!" Milagro laughed out loud. "She did not like them at all! She started to cry. She made no sound, just tears running down her face. It was so sad. I decided we would wait for later for the shoes. She can walk around here like this. She might ruin the socks but for now, it is fine."

The sheriff made certain he stayed across the tiny living room as he pointed to her feet. "Can you slide those down or take them off?"

Milagro let out a little sigh. "I can, but what is under there breaks your heart." She spoke slowly with an emotion that reminded him of how she lashed out that night at the jail the first time she saw the child. While she continued to speak softly to Maria in Spanish, she slid her hand down to move the little lace-topped white socks down past her heels. The ugly dark scars around her ankles told the sheriff his earlier suspicions had been correct.

"That's all I needed. Thanks. She already looks so much improved from the little wild animal Baker and I brought down out of the woods, I can't believe it. You don't mind if she stays here awhile longer, do you?"

The sparkle was back in Milagro's eyes as she answered. "Not at all. She is doing fine. Oh, and Anna Mae, the one that you found her friend? She just adores her. She sat and read picture books to her yesterday afternoon. I do not know if Maria understood a word she said, but they both seemed very happy together. We have so many things to help her to catch up. She seems to have had almost nothing that other children would by this age. Even in El Salvador, the poorest of the poor are not usually as deprived as this little one."

The sheriff shook his head slowly as he continued to look at her. "I really appreciate you taking her on."

"It is like I told you before, this is why we are here."

"I can see that." He shifted his gaze from Maria to the woman at her side. "This seems to agree with you. I can't explain it but…"

Milagro held his eyes for a moment before turning her

attention back to Maria, smoothing out invisible wrinkles in her dress.

“Hey, I’m sorry to run off like this but I’m supposed to be working in court today, and if I’m late to be bailiff for Judge Billy Joe Randolph, he’ll not take it kindly.”

Milagro looked up with a smile. “Go, then, and know that we are fine. I have lots of helping hands here who are very willing to work on such a beautiful project.” She looked down at the little hand still clinging to hers. Maria continued to peer cautiously at the sheriff from behind the safety of Milagro’s full skirt.

“Goodbye, Maria.” He dropped his hand down low to wave at her and she ducked completely behind Milagro.

“Oh, do not tease her,” Milagro scolded him. “Not yet. Give her time.”

“I’ll do it.” he answered. “I’ll be back to see you both in a day or two.”

CHAPTER 5

It had been a long day in court. Serving as a bailiff often was, but at least in Judge Billy Joe Randolph's court, there was rarely much time to be bored. Working the court generally involved lots of standing around, listening to lawyers plead their clients' cases, escorting prisoners to and from the jail, and watching great volumes of papers shuffle back and forth. There was also the business of keeping an eye on who was coming and going at the back doors of the courtroom and making sure all who came in had a proper reason to be there.

A day in this judge's courtroom was all of that, but he never let things lag. Any lawyer who dawdled too long with his client conferences or his paperwork would only do so once in Judge Billy Joe Randolph's courtroom.

Judge Billy Joe, as the sheriff and a few others called him, was a tall thin man who looked taller yet in his cowboy boots and the large ten-gallon hat he always wore when he was not in his judicial robes. He was one of Serenity's own, a boy raised by his widowed mother who had spent summers working the ranches of west Texas to help put himself through college and law school. He liked to say his education had included lots of horse sense learned straight from the source. That kind of approach to life hadn't ended with his education, but rather had continued during his years as a lawyer, including time in the early years of the public defender's office. The end result was that Judge Billy Joe Randolph knew what it was to grow up poor. He did not accept that as an excuse for much of the misbehavior that ended up before him in the courtroom, but he also had no patience with lawyers whose treatment of their clients appeared to be based on their bank account.

The judge had already gone back to his chambers. As the sheriff took one last look around the courtroom before turning off the lights and locking the door, he thought back over the judge's rulings in court that day. He had treated them all the same, no matter if they wore a three piece suit or came into court wearing only three pieces of clothing.

The sheriff could hear the judge's clear baritone echoing down the hall in his best rendition of "Amazing Grace". At the end of a busy day in court, that was always a sign that Judge Billy Joe was in a good mood.

The sheriff stopped at the open doorway.

"Come on in here, son," the judge interrupted his own song. "Well, Sheriff, what do you think? Another day of good work behind us." The judge sat with his chair leaned back and his cowboy boots crossed, resting on the corner of his desk.

"Yes, sir, I'd say you're right."

"Of course, I'm right. Been doing this too long not to be." He laughed out loud at his own joke but kept his eyes carefully trained on Dale Harper. "I haven't had a chance to ask of late but how are you doing these days? I've been keeping an eye on you, you know, and I have a few other people who do that for me, too."

Dale Harper could feel his face start to flush at the unexpected concern even though the court clerks were already gone and they were the only two still in the building. "Now, Judge, I'm doing okay. You don't have to worry none."

"Of course, I have to be concerned. How would it look if the sheriff in the best county in my circuit were to come unraveled at the seams? Not that you don't have cause, mind you. When is that court date anyway?"

Dale Harper felt his stomach knot as he did his best not to let it show. "Next month. I guess it's going to full trial."

"I can't believe that fool of a lawyer, Walter Barrington, is letting it go this far. 'Course he's got a fool for a client in Sherwood, the son, so maybe that's all he can do. I'm sure his daddy is paying Barrington enough, that he ought to be able--." He stopped mid-sentence. "I'm sorry, Dale. That's no way for me to be talking, especially to you. You've got enough on your mind."

The judge sat up straight. "Just remember, I've been calling in the big guns on this one, son. There's lots of folks praying for you that this whole thing passes quickly, and don't you doubt it. I ask the Lord's blessing on you daily, Sheriff Dale Harper. You've got a heavy load to bear, that's a fact, but surely, before it's all said and done, Walter Barrington can get that boy to take a plea and let people get on with their lives. He's the highest dollar lawyer in this half of the state, so if anybody can do it, he can. Heaven knows he doesn't really want to take it to trial. There's no doubt the boy did it, and even pleading insanity, the best he can hope for is life in prison. He takes it to trial and that boy could easily get the death penalty. I imagine that's where you're at and I don't blame you, but..."

Dale stepped forward from where he had been leaning against the door frame and sat down in one of the two cushioned armchairs in front of the judge's ample oak desk.

"I know that seems like the most logical ending, but it's really no end at all. He'll sit on death row for at least another ten years, so I just don't know." He ran his fingers through his thick, wavy hair in frustration. "I know it's going to be miserable to get up there and testify, and I sure wouldn't mind avoiding it, but you know who I feel sorriest for?"

The judge let the question hang in the air for a minute as he closely watched the man in front of him.

The sheriff continued as if he had to get out what he was going to say quickly. "With all his money and such, I can't help but feel the saddest for Preston and Brenda Sherwood. I mean, I know they were never big fans of mine. Bonnie and me probably would've had some big fights about them if it hadn't been for the way she was about it all. She knew. She always knew that Preston done wrong by the way he raised Rodney, spoiling him so, dumping money on him, like one car after another, as fast as he wrecked them. And then once he started getting into serious trouble, Preston bought him out of that, too, every chance he got."

A heavy sigh escaped him. "We had at least two cases I remember over at the city police department that people refused to press charges when he ran through their property tearing up fences, a garage, other cars. But after Preston came along and spread lots of money around, no victims wanted to testify. And without a victim's statement, the prosecutor didn't want the case either.

"But now, the man had two children in life, a beautiful daughter and a spoilt brat son, and the son manages to kill his own sister. I mean, Bonnie had even told him he couldn't come to our house anymore because he was just crazy, ate up, as they say, on methamphetamine the last couple of times she talked to him. I mean, I know he was coming after me for locking him up but he managed to shoot both of us and kill her."

Dale Harper stopped speaking, his energy spent. He sat with his elbows resting on his knees, his hands extended, and his head bowed.

The silence in the room loomed heavy as the judge waited, saying nothing that might intrude on his friend's grief. "I just don't know what's right in this case, Judge," Dale Harper continued in a surprisingly steady voice. "For sure, this family has already suffered so terribly. Not that Rodney is worth saving, mind you. He wasn't before. Well, you know. How many times did you see his name on the lower court docket? He was headed your way, for sure, with that last case but when the lower court judge set the case with no bond, that meant Preston couldn't get him out of jail this time. Then, I had a problem. I couldn't very well keep my brother-in-law in my own jail. I shipped him out, one county over. I told Mitch Johnston, the sheriff over there in Chisolm County, that he was a handful and to keep an eye on him but he got away from their midnight jailers, and….you know the rest of the story. He come after me and managed to kill his own sister."

"That's what I'm saying to you, Dale." The judge leaned forward. "I got to make sure things hold together here, but most of all, I've got to be sure you're holding together, for your sake, first of all. The county, well, it's important but it comes after that, if you follow my lead."

The sheriff squirmed under the judge's scrutiny. "I'm okay, Judge," he answered quietly. "I just want to get this court thing behind me because all this waiting and thinking, it ain't good for anybody."

"I'd say you're right there. So who's going with you, up to court, I mean?"

"Going with me?" Dale lifted his head and looked at the judge.

"Yes, going with you. I know you're a man who's used to walking into tough situations, but this is different. It ain't work, it's personal. It's a change of venue three counties away." He snorted, "Like that makes any difference. The whole state has heard plenty about this but it's the best they can manage under the circumstances. Even so, you should get somebody to drive you up or at least ride along with you."

"I hadn't given any thought to that."

"Well, give it some! I might drop in on a day of it up there and if I do, I don't want to see you there all by yourself. Is that clear?

"Yes, sir." A little smile appeared on Dale Harper's face despite the seriousness of the discussion. "I'll take care of it."

"Good. Now on to more pressing matters."

"Sir?"

"What are you going to eat for dinner tonight?"

"Well, I can't say."

The judge cleared his throat, as if he were still on the bench waiting on a reluctant lawyer. "Seems to me that's the problem with you of late, Sheriff Harper. Got to take care of the important details. What I'm saying is I think you better come with me out to the country club and have a steak tonight. I'd say it's probably been way too long since you've had a decent dinner and it won't do you a bit of harm. You're looking thinner than I am, and that's not easy to do." He laughed again as he pulled a cigar from his inside pocket.

He pressed it gently under his nose, savoring its aroma. Then he put it back in his pocket.

Dale Harper remembered that Judge Billy Joe had been instructed by his doctor to give up smoking his beloved cigars. Harper seized the moment to change the subject.

"Judge, I was wondering if I could ask you about one of the boys I got over there in jail?"

"Certainly. Who or what are we talking about?"

"It's Freddy Ganst. I'm sure you remember him and all three of his brothers. They're through here on a regular basis but with Freddy it's always been the drinking, one way or another. He's no angel but he's not a bad sort either, when you get right down to it. This time when the state patrol picked him up, he had a sizeable quantity of meth on him. He says he has information that would be valuable to us, as to where he got it and who's supplying folks around here, but of course, he wants to deal for it. So I was just wondering…"

The judge pulled out his cigar again and stuck it between his teeth as he gazed at the ceiling for a moment.

"Sheriff, if you can get anything that is of any true value to you in this war against the devil's own concoction that they call meth, you get it, any way you can. You rest assured that this member of the bar will back you in whatever needs to be done to make that happen. Does that answer your question?"

"Yes, sir, I'd say it does. Thank you."

"Good enough." He popped to his feet as if he'd been shot out of his chair. "What about that steak, son? Let's get to it. Come on. Ask anyone, only a fool says 'no' to a good steak and a free one at that!" He pulled his buff-colored cowboy hat off the rack by the door, and settled it gently in place on his thick gray hair. He picked the sheriff's gray felt hat off the same rack and stuffed it into his hands. He clapped a firm hand on the younger man's shoulder and hustled the sheriff out the door before he could refuse his offer.

* * * * *

Despite the steak dinner, Dale Harper slept fitfully again that night. Nothing unusual about that, he thought as he watched the first light of dawn creep over the horizon on his drive to work. Even so, he got to the office early because he remembered he still had a paperwork mess to tend to before he could get anything else done.

He picked up the empty box he had left beside his desk a few days before with the intention of simply piling the various files back inside. That is when he realized by the weight of it, there was still more there than the box itself. He pulled the last manila folder out of the bottom of the box. It was empty but beneath it was a flat black pistol in a heavy clear plastic bag. The sheriff picked it up gingerly, turning it over in his hands without opening the bag. He looked for a serial number but found none.

He stepped over to his desk, opened the middle drawer, and rooted in the back for a moment before coming up with an old-fashioned handheld magnifying glass. He hated to admit it but reading glasses were probably not too far in the future. For now he managed, using the magnifying glass, provided no one was around to notice.

The place where the numbers should have been was covered with scratches. Not the sort of thing he would have expected from a kid like Rupe Jensen. Of course, once again, he thought back to his father's greatest complaint about this case. "None of it was what anyone would have expected out of Rupe Jensen."

He flipped the gun over again and peered at the back of the business card that was also tucked in the bag. It was one of his father's cards, the kind he used to hand out during the elections, but penciled on the back he read: "Found March 25, 1988 in Rupe Jensen's right hand." The word 'right' was underlined and those long loopy letters of his father's handwriting suddenly reminded him of how much he missed his dad. He swallowed hard and tried to think of something else. He laid aside the unopened plastic bag with its intriguing contents and gathered the files into a neat stack. He deliberately sought out the case narrative and positioned it on top.

As he placed the entire stack back in the box, an extra long tail of yellowed paper caught on the corner of the box. He pulled it free and glanced at it to try to determine which folder it belonged in.

Eunice Dunstan, he read across the top, and he started to look for her folder. Then he looked again, more carefully this time. It was a dated receipt for a biological sample delivered to the State Crime Lab. It had a receipt number and words in that same long, loopy handwriting. "Taken from under Eunice Dunstan's fingernails at crime scene." He laid the receipt in the middle of his desk, something to look into a bit later. He set the box with its files on the floor behind his desk.

While he worked, his mind replayed a part of the conversation he had shared the night before with Judge Billy Joe. Once he had finally turned the judge's concern away from his own state of mind, he asked him what he remembered about the Dunstan case.

The judge had let out a low whistle between his teeth. "Whoa, son, that's one we'd all like to forget and likely never will. It was quite the thorn in your father's side, I remember that."

"How so?"

"Well, you know, just in general. She was a harmless old lady who had never been any bother to anyone. Her husband had died a few years before in a traffic accident. Now he was the hard-headed one, Carlton Sr. He would argue with anyone over just about anything. He and old man Jensen, the neighbor, had gone a few rounds over land squabbles. As I recall, Jensen wanted to buy part of Dunstan's land, as Jensen's dairy herd was growing and Dunstan wasn't using his land for much, except cutting hay. Dunstan would have none of it though. The two men got into some real shouting matches but the women folk remained friends and told the men to keep their fight amongst themselves. Anyway, once Carlton died, everybody figured Miz Dunstan would go ahead and sell to Jensen but that never happened. Her daughter, Carol, and the son-in-law had done well by her, to help her keep up the place. Carley, the girl's twin brother, had run off to

California several years before and had finally turned back up a few months before. Everybody knew he was about as worthless as a milk bucket under a bull calf. The sister, Carol, on the other hand, was as good as gold. Your dad didn't talk about it much but I believe he was still taking a real hard look at that shooting about the time he died. He couldn't prove anything but he was not convinced the kid did it."

"Oh, I know he wasn't."

"You do?"

"Yes, but I'll tell you about it later. Please go on, and tell me the rest of what you remember first."

"There isn't much more to tell," the judge continued. "Your dad just kept listening and waiting, hoping something else would turn up that would tell him more."

The sheriff nodded in between bites of steak and baked potato. "Sometimes that's the way you have to deal with an investigation, even when you're sure you already know the answer."

"Exactly." The judge gestured with his fork while he was talking. The sheriff had to keep his head down to hide the smile that threatened to cross his face at the wrong time as the judge continued. "You see, your dad had more than just his own suspicions going for him on this one. It turned out that the reason Miz Dunstan didn't sell her land to the Jensens is because it was right around this time that the highway department come calling to buy land to put through the new section of Highway 57 out there. Talk was that she was signing all the money over to her daughter, Carol, and leaving Carley out in the cold. Who could blame her? He hadn't been around and nobody had heard from him in years, but instead, she died. So the highway department paid the money to Carol and Carley, even split."

"And what did the sister say about it all?" the sheriff inquired after a few moments of silence. As long as he had the judge going strong on the subject, he figured he might as well learn all that he could.

"I'm not sure. I know your father was hesitant to even bring it up to her. She was already so upset at the death of her mother, and God bless her, she never did say a bad word against Rupe Jensen through it all. I mean, it made no sense really. The Jensens and Dunstans had been neighbors for years even though the men didn't always get along. You know, Virgil, the oldest boy, he's just like his dad, got more temper than is good for any one man. I think your dad was taking a real hard look at him, too, thinking maybe he did something in a fit of anger. Rupe, the kid, he was always over there, helping out. It just didn't make any sense the way it looked.

"And that Carol, now she gave folks something to think about. The day after her own mother's funeral at First Baptist, Carol came to Rupe's funeral at our church, St. Mary's Catholic, and held Rupe's mother's hand through the whole thing. Now, people can talk about this one or that one being a good Christian but I'm here to tell you, this town never saw a better example of it than that. I don't think your dad even knew how to bring up the subject of her mother's killing with her, if you know what I mean."

"Oh, I do." The sheriff sat back from the table. "There are times in this job you find yourself having to ask questions you'd just as soon not. I can still remember my mother used to say, 'Never ask a question if you really don't want to know the answer.' Then she'd look at my dad and smile. As a boy, I didn't have a clue as to what she was talking about but you know years later, thinking of her as a sheriff's wife.

"I remember my dad really going on one night about this case, swearing it couldn't have been Rupe Jensen that did the killing. I was just a kid, upstairs in bed, and it was like he and my mother were arguing about it downstairs. But then later I realized she wasn't arguing back. It's just that she saw a whole different side of his work."

"How is your mother?" The judge shifted back to the present. "And where is she?"

"Oh, she's fine. She's still in Florida. She moved there with her second husband, Bill. You remember him, the real estate man. He was into all that golfing and such at the retirement village where they moved. He died last year but she's got her a group of friends out there, so she says that for now, she's just going to stay where she is."

And with that, the conversation never came back to anything else to do with Eunice Dunstan and her family. Still, Dale Harper continued to sift through all the bits and pieces in his mind as he picked up the bagged gun once more. He turned it over in his hands before laying it back down on the corner of his desk.

A stir in the outer office brought him back to the business at hand. He strolled up front to find Wanda and Roy Baker sharing the various events of the last two weeks with Jimmy Henriquez on his first day back from vacation.

"So how was your trip?" the sheriff joined in.

"It was good," he said, with only the slightest trace of a

Spanish accent. "But it is good to be home, too. If I had stayed any longer with my mother's cooking, I would not fit in my uniforms!" He patted his ample belly. "It sounds like life was not boring here while I was gone."

"No." The sheriff drawled out the word. "You know, things rarely seem to get that way around here." He squinted at Jimmy unexpectedly. "Maybe it would be nice if they did sometimes."

Jimmy laughed good-naturedly. "Oh, Sheriff. You would not like it. You only think you would!"

"Maybe you're right. I don't know. Sometimes, I think I sure wouldn't mind trying it for awhile." The sheriff turned his attention towards his chief deputy. "Hey, Roy, didn't I hear a highway patrol trooper telling you the other day about a new process for finding serial numbers on guns when somebody has tried to remove them?"

"Oh, yeah, Bryan Arthur from up at Troop Headquarters." Sgt. Baker made a check mark in the empty air. "He said their lab was having real good luck with it. Why?"

"There's a gun in a plastic bag back there on the corner of my desk, a Walther PPK. It's from an old case and might not come to much but get it up to him, will you? We'll let them see if they can do anything about pulling up the serial number on it. Looks like somebody scratched it off years ago but I'd sure like to see if we could come up with a number on it, especially with this newer method." The sheriff turned back to Jimmy.

"Hey, while you were gone, Carley Dunstan was in here with Dickie Ravens."

At the mere mention of their names, Jimmy rolled his eyes

toward Wanda who was still seated beside him at the front desk. She cleared her throat and muttered something better left unsaid as she turned back to the ringing phone at the desk.

"Carley introduced himself to us like we didn't even know him. Said his name was Carlton Dunstan now, and Wanda says he's got him some sort of new insurance office on the other side of town. She said you'd stopped in there a few weeks back. Know anything about what he's up to?"

"Yes and no," Jimmy answered with a smile as he shifted to face his boss. "You know, Sheriff, I have had my troubles with insurance since that fire at my house last year. So, yes, I went there to see if he had something that would help, but I could make no sense of what he said. He showed me pamphlets on this and that kind of insurance program but nothing that would really help. He had nothing that was cheap, you know? All of it was from far away and too much money, so, no, I do not know what he is doing really, because you know, he did not seem like he had much business. I just went back down to County Mutual and I am paying their prices. Not so good but at least they would take me, and lots of the companies do not after things burn up. It does not seem to matter that it was electrical wiring in the mobile home."

Jimmy smiled and shrugged despite the heavy sigh he let pass. "*Así es.* That is just the way it is."

"Thanks, Jimmy. Sorry about the insurance in general. I was just wondering what Carley is really up to."

"I really do not know." Jimmy's usual sunny disposition was back on track. "But I do not think he is so good at the insurance!"

"Hey, speaking of Carley and his cousin, the commissioner," Sgt. Baker chimed in with his own question. "Have you heard anything about Commissioner Ravens going back into farming big time?"

"What do you mean?" The sheriff raised an eyebrow in his direction.

"I don't really know," the sergeant conceded with a shrug. "Somebody said he's thinking about plowing up and planting those fields above his house out there in the back country. I mean, they were his dad's, and I guess years ago he planted up there, but I've never known them to be anything but hayfields that he had somebody cut and bale each season."

"Yeah, that's all true," Dale Harper nodded. "Wonder what's gotten into Dickie Ravens that he's wanting to do all that work? Doesn't sound like him, to be honest."

"No, it doesn't," Baker agreed. "That's why I was asking. Guess you ain't heard anything about it."

"No, can't say that I have. Something to think about. Maybe if he's on a tractor now and then, he won't be in here haunting our door quite so much."

"Now there's something nice to think about," Wanda added with a smile and a big bubble of gum which snapped loudly when it burst

* * * * *

The gold letters on the glass door were eye-catching, outlined in silver and red **Carlton Dunstan Enterprises**. Dale Harper pushed the door open and found himself in a small but plushly furnished waiting room that was as ornate as the sign on the door. There was no receptionist, but a distinct, yet discreet, buzzer sounded as he entered. Before him were two overstuffed upholstered armchairs, a heavy wooden desk, and an ornately carved wooden door opposite the glass door he had just come through. A rack on the wall was neatly filled with insurance brochures and even some maps and information on nearby tourist locations, just like Jimmy had described. The sheriff absent-mindedly fingered through one or two of the insurance flyers.

Carley Dunstan came through the carved door from the back area with his head down and in a hurry. He was taken aback to find the sheriff standing in his waiting room.

"Why, Sheriff Harper, what a surprise! How nice to see you again." He attempted to regain his composure while he stuck out his hand in not quite as formal a handshake as the sheriff remembered a few days earlier. This time, the sheriff took his hand and began to talk to him about the brochures on the wall.

"They tell me you're in the insurance business these days and it's something I've been meaning to look into," Dale Harper began.

"Look into? Whatever do you mean?" Carley continued to battle to regain his salesman's balance.

"Oh, you know, the county's insurance is all right but I was thinking I might need something more in terms of health insurance and such." The sheriff chatted on, paying no notice to the other man's discomfort.

"Well, uh, we have a variety of programs we can set you up with, as you can see." Carley stepped closer to the brochure rack. "Exactly what did you have in mind?"

"Oh, I'm not really sure. I mean, they are paying off on my big medical bill from last year, but I'm just afraid they're going to come back at me with something different pretty soon. Hey, do you suppose we could go discuss this somewhere else? Do you have an office that is a little less public?" The sheriff nodded his head towards the glass door. "I really don't need to be discussing this too openly, if you know what I mean."

Carley was totally confused now but was also unwilling to refuse the sheriff's request for privacy. "Well, I don't know, Sheriff. To be honest with you, I was on my way out. Would you like to make an appointment to come back and discuss this at a later time?"

"No, I really don't need to do that. I just thought you might be able to line out a thing or two for me, but if you don't have the time, I understand." He started to turn towards the front door. "Maybe I'll just read up on this stuff and then, if you could just answer a question or two?" He looked again towards the outside door, as if he seriously dreaded being seen by anyone.

"Well, uh…" Carley took a step towards the glass door just as someone suddenly yanked open the wooden door from the other side.

"So did you want--?" The workman coming through the door stopped so quickly he almost hit himself in the face with the door. He froze momentarily and the sheriff recognized the look on his face as one he had often seen on a man who is debating whether to run or stand his ground.

"Hey, George." The sheriff stepped forward and stuck out his hand. The man before him was blackened and oily as if he had been working on vehicles, but the sheriff still recognized him. "I didn't know you worked here."

“Yeah, I’ve been here a couple weeks is all.” He looked down, pulled a rag from his back pocket and began wiping off his hand before taking the sheriff’s.

“I thought you worked over at the Feed and Seed with Virgil Jensen and those boys.” It was a statement but with more than a bit of question in the sheriff’s tone.

“Oh, you know me, Sheriff.” The young man before him would have dug his toe in the dirt if he hadn’t been standing on carpet over concrete. “I work a little here, a little there. This is a good thing for me, I think, working for Carley.” He caught himself. “I mean, Mr. Dunstan, and all. Suzie is working at the Four Leaf Clover now, did you know? She really likes it. Together, we can really make something. We even bought a house over on Polk Street and…”

George was suddenly aware of Carley Dunstan’s presence and the distorted look on his face. “Oh, I’m sorry. I thought you was alone, Mr. Dunstan. I gotta get back to work.”

He turned to go but not before Sheriff Harper managed to stick his foot in the door before it closed behind young George.

“Come on, Carley, oh, I mean, Carlton. Give me just a minute or two on these insurance questions and I’ll be on my way. What do you say?”

Dunstan passed by the sheriff, who still held the door open with his back, his hands filled with insurance brochures. He led the way back across an open work area that looked more like a commercial garage than anything attached to an insurance office.

“So what are you doing back here?” the sheriff asked in his

still overly-friendly tone. "You got all kinds of businesses going on under one roof?"

"That's why the sign says Carlton Dunstan Enterprises." Carlton once again assumed his more formal tone. "This is a small operation I took over some time ago. We're repairing mobile homes, so it is related to the insurance business in that we repair the ones that have been damaged in transit and that sort of thing."

"Now that makes sense, I suppose." The sheriff pushed his hat back on his head as he tried to determine if the man before him might actually be in a legitimate business after all.

"Of course it does." Carley Dunstan gave the sheriff a terse business smile. "The man you just saw, he's one of the welders, a new hire. Apparently someone you know?"

"Oh, yeah, George. Just a kid I've seen grow up around here, on the poor side of town really. He's always been a good one though. Now he's got him a young wife and I just hope he'll make a go of things."

"I see. He just started here, so of course, I know next to nothing about him. He doesn't seem to be afraid of a little hard work, though, and I appreciate that. Not to sound like all the old timers, but good help really is hard to find." The sheriff watched Carley carefully as he chattered on nervously, making explanations the sheriff had not requested.

"Well, now about those insurance questions…"

Carley stepped back to a small, much less prestigious office than the one out front. Boxes of various parts lined the walls and the overwhelming mountain of paperwork covering the small single desk made the sheriff feel pretty good about the condition of his own desk. Two small glass ashtrays on the desk were overflowing and the sheriff snatched them both up and stepped outside to a nearby trash barrel in the garage where he emptied them quickly before he sat down.

Carley Dunstan stepped behind the desk and sat in the meager chair that was held together with duct tape in several places. He indicated the nicer chair in front of the desk for the sheriff.

"Carlton, you seem like a man who has been working way too hard. I won't keep you, but it looks to me like you've got to slow down a bit." He set the ashtrays down on the desk, drew out his own lighter, and began to pat his pockets as if looking for something. "Oh man, I guess I left my cigarettes in the truck. Can you spare one?" He turned to Carley, who immediately drew a pack from the desk drawer and tapped out two. He offered one to the sheriff who promptly lit it and then leaned back to take a long drag before continuing.

"So this is what I was wondering and kind of worrying about. With these insurance companies, when they pay out a big claim sometimes, say on a house fire, then they don't want to cover you anymore. Or if they do, it's going to cost you a fortune, you know what I mean?"

"Well, Sheriff, you know insurance is a business like any other," Carley began to politely defend his industry. "We have to be able to cover costs and make ends meet. When a big claim is paid out, it may seem like the insurance company immediately rules against the little guy, but that's not the way it is overall. But you haven't had a house fire, so why does that concern you?"

"Oh, not me. One of my deputies, Jimmy Henriquez, he had the house fire back a couple years ago. The wiring in his house trailer all fried. Seems like nobody really knows why. The fire marshal ruled that it was not arson or anything he or his wife did. As a matter of fact, she was smart enough to get out quick and shut the power off at the pole when she smelled the smoke. The whole thing never did actually burst into flames, but now he can't hardly get insurance on his current mobile home and…"

"Sheriff, sheriff," Carley put out his cigarette in frustration and quickly lit another. "I'm really sorry for your deputy's problem. He and I discussed it and I told him what we could offer, but what does that have to do with you? I thought you said you had an insurance problem."

"Well, yeah, I do." The sheriff took another draw on his cigarette and then went on. "You see, what I'm wondering is this. If that's the way they do after, say, a house fire, maybe the insurance company the county has will be looking to do me in a similar way now that I've had this big medical expense. You know, I was in the hospital for nearly a month last year and I had to have a nurse come to my home for another couple weeks after that. I've never seen a bill on it all but I know it had to be a major chunk of change. So here's what I'm thinking…would a feller like me, in my kind of job, would it be wise to buy some kind of extra insurance now, in case they decide that I'm too big a risk and they don't want to continue to cover me? And then there's the whole thing with the commissioner's office. Well, you know about that, with Ravens being your cousin and all. I'm sorry. I'm just a little worried about the money end of it, the insurance part coming back to get me. Does that make sense? Do you see what I'm saying?" The sheriff stubbed out his cigarette in the empty ashtray that Carley had not used. He pulled a clean handkerchief out of his back pocket and made a light cough that he covered instead with the crook of his elbow.

"Sheriff, I don't think you have anything to worry about." Carley Dunstan gave Sheriff Harper a smile that never reached his eyes. "First of all, it's two different kinds of insurance. Real estate versus medical insurance. I really don't think you have a problem. As a county office holder, you are completely covered by the county government. Secondly, even if you weren't, there are policies available to you through organizations like the state sheriffs' association. I mean, I hate to run off business but I don't think you need to---" The distinct buzzer that the sheriff had heard earlier when he had first entered the office sounded again.

"Oh, excuse me just one moment." Carley Dunstan stood up from the desk and made his way to the other door. The sheriff finished with his handkerchief and quickly tucked it back into the pocket of his blue jeans.

He stood up and walked away from the cluttered desk in Carley's office. He was nearly to the wooden door when Carley Dunstan stepped back inside from the outer office as the glass door buzzer sounded again. The sheriff did not see who had come in or gone out.

"Hey, Carlton, I really appreciate your time." He grabbed the surprised man's hand and pumped it quickly as he headed towards the outside. "You said you had some place to go and I don't want to hang you up. You answered my question real good. You seem to know your stuff on this insurance, and if you say I got nothing more to worry about, then that's good enough for me. I'll let you get back to your business and I won't worry about this insurance any more. Thanks a lot!" The sheriff glanced back over his

shoulder once more but the young workman he had seen earlier was nowhere in sight. He was happy to find himself out in the sunlight of the parking lot.
Before climbing into the pickup cab, he carefully pulled his handkerchief out of his pocket and laid it gingerly on the seat beside him.

Carlton Dunstan returned to his office, still somewhat baffled by the sheriff's unexpected visit and even more by the unexpected insurance questions. Maybe he was a better insurance salesman than he had ever given himself credit for. He did not notice that one of the two ashtrays on his desk was once again empty.

CHAPTER 6

"Well, here's what I'm wanting to know," Sheriff Dale Harper inquired over his office telephone. "I've got a receipt here from your lab from twenty years ago." He laughed at his listener's response. "Yeah, I know. My question is, do you still have what was sent to you on this case, and if so, can you run one of those DNA tests on it? I know it's a long shot if you even still have it, let alone if it's in good enough shape after all this time. Still, I thought it can't hurt to ask." He laughed again. "Give me a fax number and I'll send a copy of this receipt to you, and then we'll go from there. Meanwhile, I've got another sample I just picked up today that I'm going to send up to you. I'd like you to take a DNA sample off of it, too. Thanks, thanks a lot. Listen, just call me back at this office if you find that twenty year old sample, okay? Thanks again." The sheriff hung up the telephone.

He got up from his desk and wandered to the next office.

"Hey, Roy," he began slowly, still thinking about his last phone call. "I spoke to Judge Billy Joe last night about Freddy Ganst. I told you that Freddy's claiming to have information that might help us catch up to the source of that meth he had when he was stopped. The judge says he has no objection to us making a deal with Freddy. So what do you think? Want to get him down from the cells and see what he has to say?"

"Sure, no problem." Sgt. Roy Baker practically jumped out of his office chair. "This paperwork stuff is making me crazy anyway. You know I'd rather be doing something, anything, even be in a fight, rather than do paperwork." He brushed past the sheriff on his way to the jail cells as he finished speaking.

* * * * *

"You know I want to help in the worst way…" Freddy Ganst was practically whining as he squirmed in his seat in Sgt. Baker's office, "but I really don't know these guys' names."

"Come on, Freddy." The sergeant raised his voice in irritation. "I thought you told Sheriff Harper you wanted to deal. You expect us to believe that you're getting this stuff from guys you don't even know? Maybe I should just take him back upstairs, Sheriff. He's just wasting our time."

"No, no, I'm not." Freddy turned quickly to face the sheriff who stood leaning casually against the doorway of Sgt. Baker's office. "Sure as the world, I can get 'em for you, Sheriff, I swear. I just need a couple of days on the street and then I'll know all their names."

"You'll know all their names then, heh?" The sheriff looked across the top of Freddy's head at Baker. "And what do you call them now, Freddy? Who are these fellers?"

"Well, you know how it is with a lot of the different ones, they have street names. One of 'em goes by…" A nervous giggle escaped him as he hesitated. "Well, we call him Booger, 'cause that's how he looks. I mean, he's bad, you know. And the other, well, he's some businessman really, at least that's how he always looks to me, not like a regular meth cook, and then there's a couple of others. Everybody works for the businessman. I can find out his name for you, Sheriff. I know I can. I won't be long at it, you know me. I can be really fast when I need to be." The chatter had such a childlike innocence to it, Harper turned away and feigned a cough into the crook of his elbow to cover the fact that Freddy Ganst always made him smile. If ever a boy was caught in a man's body.

Sheriff Harper stood looking at the man in orange for a long moment before he finally spoke. "Here's the deal, Freddy. I'll give you three days and that's it. You be back here with the information or so help me. You know that I know everywhere you might run to ground. I know your mama's house and your sister's, and where all your brothers live who ain't in prison at the moment. There won't be no running and hiding. You better turn back up here in three days with the information or you'll wish you'd never left. Do you get my meaning?"

"Yes, sir, Sheriff. I get your meaning just perfect. You can depend on ol' Freddy. I'll get your information and then you'll make it all right with Judge Randolph, won't you? You can do that, sure as the world. If anybody can, you can."

"Freddy," Sheriff Harper interrupted the babbling man. "Judge Billy Joe Randolph is the one who is allowing me to let you go for these three days. Don't you mess this up or he'll put you back in jail and throw away the key. You got it?"

“Yes sir, Sheriff. I got it.” Freddy, expectant and quivering with excitement, stopped speaking but continued to nod his head like a soundless little bird.

“All right then.” The sheriff shook his head. “Go back up to your cell and sit tight. Don’t go gathering up your things or nothing until the jailer calls, you hear? We’ll get you downstairs right after lunch and get you out of here, but keep it under your hat as to just what you’re up to! You go babbling upstairs about getting out, and the word will be on the street before you are that you’ve cut a deal. You better look as surprised as a two-headed jack rabbit when the jailer calls you downstairs after lunch!”

It was late afternoon when Dale Harper finally escaped the office for the day. Many times like today when he had too much on his mind, he would just get in his truck and drive around what he had long thought of as “his” county. He’d considered it that long before he was elected sheriff. It really went back to the time that he and Eddie had spent in Desert Storm when he made a promise that if he could just get home safely, he would never go wandering far again. And he never had. He had been happy to come back and now that he had a job that said he was responsible for the whole of it, he considered it “his” county all the more. Still, the weight of that kind of responsibility did grow heavy, especially when there were questions that seemed to have no answers.

He cruised along the back roads, just outside of town. He noticed how many of the trees were starting to flower. Service berry, shad bush, and dogwood, were all covered in white blossoms complemented by the bright lavender sprigs of the redbud trees. Together, they dotted every hillside for as far as he could see. He found himself on the road that led down past Fleming’s dairy farm and thought about the day he had come out here last week to bring Lou Ann into the Main Street Mission. Foot of the Cross Mission now, he reminded himself. He didn't want to insult Milagro but he wasn't sure he'd ever get that name change straight in his own mind.

He pulled up in front of the dairy farm's wooden gate just as the school bus stopped to discharge its load of several young Flemings. They eyed him curiously as they ran towards the gate.

"Hey Sheriff, what's up?" the oldest Fleming teenaged daughter asked as she reached the gate.

"Hey, yourself, young lady," he answered cheerfully, hoping to cover the fact that he couldn't remember any of their names. "I just needed to ask your mama a question or two about a lady who she came to visit the other day. Nothing serious. If you're going in, do you mind to ask her to come out?"

"Oh, you mean Miss Anna Mae Cunningham. Mama took us in to meet her and she's been here for dinner, too. She's really nice," the daughter answered as she held open the gate for her younger brothers and sister who scrambled in behind her. "I'll get Mama for you, Sheriff." She stopped and turned back. "Miss Anna Mae, she's all right, isn't she?"

"Sure, she is." The sheriff nodded. "No problem. Not to worry."

"It's just that I was just thinking, she is kinda old, you know, and Mama's been so happy to see her."

"No, she's fine." He reassured her again and she turned back towards the house.

Lou Ann came outside, wiping her hands on her large white apron. "Sheriff, what are you doing out here? Come on inside where I can at least get you something, a cup of coffee, a glass of buttermilk?"

"Oh, that sounds good, Lou Ann, but no thanks. I just need a minute, and I didn't want to ask a lot of questions with the kids around. Could I ask you something about when your brother was killed? Can I ask you about Rupe?"

"Well, certainly, Sheriff, although I don't know what I can tell you. I didn't even get home all those years ago until after he was dead and buried for two weeks. I felt awful about that at the time. I didn't call home as often as I should have back then, and you know."

"That's how we all did when we were young, Lou Ann. I did the same thing. Ran off to the army and I think my mother thought I was never coming back." He laughed, trying to help ease her past her own long-held guilt.

"Thank you. You're very kind. I suppose that is true of most of us when we're younger. That helps, you know."

"Lou Ann, what I need to know is, do you remember if Rupe was right-handed or left-handed? It may seem a funny question at this late date but…"

"No, it's not a funny question, as much as it has a funny answer." She smiled and looked down. "Rupe was both. You remember, I imagine, that Rupe wasn't like other kids. They called him slow or worse, but he was still so dear in his own ways. He started out at the Catholic School like we all did and at that time the nuns tried to teach the left-handed ones like Rupe to be right-handed. I guess they thought it would make life easier for them in a world that is mostly right-handed. So Rupe was one of those who learned to write one way and did everything else the other. What I mean is, to use a pencil at school he wrote with his right hand, but to do anything else--use a hammer or a saw, pitch horseshoes or shoot a gun--my brother was left-handed."

"Shoot a gun?"

"Like every other country boy in this county, by the time he was eight he was off hunting with the big boys and in that way Rupe was no different than anyone else. He went deer hunting and turkey hunting with Daddy and his big brothers, but he was always a lefty. I remember because my oldest brother, Virgil, is too. The oldest and the youngest but all the rest of us Jensens are right-handed. That's who you ought to talk to, Sheriff. Virgil pretty much stepped in and handled everything at that time. He was already thirty years old when Rupe was killed, and Mama and Daddy, well, they were just destroyed by it all. I talked to Virgil after I got home. He told me what all he'd done, making the funeral arrangements and all, because they just didn't seem able to do it. I know he's the one who talked with your dad, the first Sheriff Harper, about things. Virgil felt like he was really going to look into things more, you know. To try and see if there wasn't more to the whole story somehow, but then he died, and the next sheriff…Well, I guess, according to Virgil, he just wasn't too interested in what he saw as something that was all cut and dried. I know Virgil went in and talked to him a couple of times but nothing more ever came of it. Then it got to the point where we just had to get on with life, don't you know." She squinted into the sun as she looked up at the sheriff. "It sure didn't mean we didn't miss Rupe something fierce, but Daddy had a stroke not too long after that and there was just the business of living to be taken care of."

"I understand. I really appreciate you talking to me about this."

"Can I ask you a question now, Sheriff?"

He nodded, although he knew what it would be before she spoke.

"Why are you asking about this now? Is it on account of Anna Mae's visit?"

"I'd have to say, her showing up like she did is what got me to thinking about it again. I don't know that there's anything there that will change, but it just seems to me there are some unanswered questions. If I can find out anything, I will, and I'll let you know. How's that?" He put his hand on the top of the gate to open it for her as she went back inside.

"That would be good." She laid her hand over his for a brief moment. "I really appreciate it. Anything I could tell my mama, even after all these years, would ease her mind considerably, I'm sure. Talk to Virgil, Sheriff. He'll be getting off work at the feed store in another half hour or so. He can tell you anything more you need to know."

"I'll talk to him. Understand, there's no promise here that I can do anything more than that, but if I can, you know I will." He turned towards his truck when she called him back.

"Did you know that tomorrow night is Anna Mae's last night? She is leaving the day after to go back home to Kentucky."

"Well, I'm glad you two got to have a nice visit over the last few days."

"Oh, I am, too, and it's all because of you." Her gracious smile touched him and reminded him of why he did like his job most days. "We are having a little get-together tomorrow night over at the mission. Miss Millie said to bring the whole family, but I'm thinking that might be kind of overwhelming for all of them, especially Anna Mae. I might take my oldest daughter with me, though. Will you come, Sheriff? I know Anna Mae would love to see you again. We're just going to have a little gathering outside in the patio area and share some snacks and sing a few songs. You know, to remember the old days we have to sing a little since that's how we met and what we used to do on the road. Please say you'll come join us, at least for a little while?"

"Well, I'll see. Maybe I'll stop by for a minute or two, if you think that'd be all right."

"I think we'd all like to see you there. Don't forget now. Tomorrow night," she called after him.

"I'll remember," he answered as he climbed into the pickup. She waved goodbye from inside the gate as he drove away.

Sheriff Harper managed to catch up to Virgil Jensen as he was leaving the Crossland County Feed & Seed for the afternoon. They walked down the block to the Four Leaf Clover, Jack and Doreen Walton's café, where they sat in a booth far from the front door, the sheriff's favorite, each with a cup of coffee.

The sheriff sat quietly, contemplating the man before him. Virgil Jensen was a bull of a man who used his size to his advantage every day, tossing feed sacks and moving salt blocks the way other men might move shoe boxes or file folders. He barely fit in the restaurant booth they shared at the moment.

"Sorry to pester you with sad memories, Virgil, but I just had a question or two about when Rupe died. You know Lou Ann's friend who came to town recently, that is how she remembered where to find her by recalling the shooting. It got me to thinking and I wanted to ask you a couple of things if you don't mind?"

"I don't mind." Virgil smiled as he leaned back in the booth. "I tried to get that worthless excuse for a sheriff that came in after your dad died to look into it more, but he never would. Lazy son of a gun, he was. What do you need to know, Sheriff?"

"Hey, before we get to that." The sheriff turned the conversation unexpectedly. "Didn't George O'Brien work with you at the feed store?"

"Yeah, he did." Virgil took a sip of his coffee. "But not no more."

"I know. I just saw him at his new job. What happened with the job, with you all, if you don't mind me asking?"

Virgil Jensen shrugged. "I really don't know. He worked for us about six months or so and he was great. Always early to work and worked hard and steady. Never had to worry about him punching out early, and then the last month or two, it's like he was somebody altogether different. Every time you needed him, you'd find him smoking out on the loading dock rather than doing what needed to be done. He started coming in late, making excuses to leave early."

Virgil leaned back in the cramped booth. "I even tried talking to him, just talking, you know, asking if there was some kind of problem at home, something that was bothering him. He just laughed at me and said things had never been better. I don't know what it was, but finally, instead of showing up late, he didn't show up at all for three days in a row. That was enough for most of us over there, including the boss. Is he in some kind of trouble?"

"Oh, no." The sheriff shook his head. "I was just curious as to why he switched jobs. It probably doesn't mean anything. What I really needed to ask you about was Rupe. I was wondering, can you tell me, was he right-handed or left-handed?"

Virgil chuckled and gave an answer similar to Lou Ann's, explaining that Rupe Jensen was both.

The sheriff smiled back. "That's just what Lou Ann said. She mentioned that he pitched horseshoes left-handed and went hunting the same way. So tell me, hunting would have been with a long gun. What about a pistol? Do you remember that?"

"I remember I took him target shooting with a .22 revolver from time to time. That's what I had, and I let him use it when I was right there. He was a lefty with that, too, just like me."

"A .22 pistol," the sheriff repeated. "So where do you suppose he came up with a Walther PPK?"

"I honestly don't know, Sheriff. It wasn't anything Rupe was likely to have. If he would have had a gun at all, I'd imagine it would've been a .22, a revolver. He wouldn't have had any interest in that, what was it, some kinda James Bond spy gun? That wasn't anything Rupe would have. I'm sure of that."

The sheriff saw Doreen approaching, coffee pot in hand, from behind Virgil's back. He waved his hand down low, just below the table, and she turned the other way. He did not want to interrupt their conversation at this point.

He had always sensed a gentle honesty in the man before him, despite his reputation for a bad temper from time to time. With that in mind, he decided to ask him straight out what was really on his mind.

"To be honest with you, Virgil, I still have questions about the whole thing. No matter how I try to put the pieces together, I just can't make it work the way the report says it did. It just isn't anything like the kid I knew Rupe to be. I know there was half a feud between your father and old man Dunstan over the land but other than that, I always thought you all did all right as neighbors. Was that wrong? What do you think happened that day?"

Virgil hunched his big shoulders forward, dwarfing the coffee mug in his mammoth hands. "Sheriff, I've asked myself that a million times over the years," he spoke quietly. "Rupe was a funny kid in a lot of ways. Most people could only see what he couldn't do. He didn't do well in school, or at least not in the public school. He did all right in the Catholic School, as the nuns kinda took extra care of him, you know? But once it closed, he didn't have no choice except the public school, and frankly, he couldn't think and talk fast enough to keep up. If anybody went to teasing him, he was pretty much lost. He'd get flustered and upset and that was that. But he come as close to anyone I've ever known to having a true heart of gold.

"He loved that old woman, Eunice Dunstan, and why wouldn't he? She always spoiled him like he was her own. Yeah, my dad and old man Dunstan had their problems and

I have to say I was surprised after her husband died that she still didn't want to sell us any land. I was pretty upset about that at first, and then I figured once he'd been dead and gone awhile she might change her mind especially if she started having money troubles. Her husband always worked a job in town, and once he was gone, you know, she had a lot less to live on. I thought once she'd calmed down, maybe she'd change her mind. I couldn't really get mad at her over it all, although I think my dad still held a grudge, but he never said. None of us knew nothing about the highway deal. I don't even know how long she knew before it happened but, as it turned out, she sold to them instead and she might as well. They were going to get what they wanted one way or another. You know how those government deals go."

He stopped speaking for a moment and then went on. "I swear I don't know what happened over there that evening with her and Rupe. I don't understand it but I do know this. I'll go to my grave believing my little brother did not kill that dear old woman and sure as I'm sitting here before you, he didn't kill hisself. Jensens don't do that! Now anything more than that, I can't say, but that much I do know!"

He dropped his full weight against the back of the booth, and it creaked in protest. The sheriff noticed with deep regret that all signs of his earlier affable manner had disappeared completely.

* * * * *

Sheriff Harper began the next morning with hopes of a routine day of phone calls and paperwork. There were still a few bases he wanted to touch before he boxed up and put away the Dunstan case once and for all. Much as he would like to give Lou Ann Fleming and Virgil Jensen satisfactory answers to their lingering questions, he knew the chances of that were about as good as the average grasshopper surviving a tornado. Still, over the years he had seen some strange things happen before, after, and during tornadoes. His plans for a quiet day, however, were rudely sent packing before he had worked his way through the first pot of coffee.

"You better come up front." Wanda's tone was ominous when he picked up his desk phone on the first ring. "There's a Federal man up here, says his name is Yancey, and he doesn't seem too happy at the moment."

"Be right there." Harper sighed as he stood up. He ambled up front, refusing to give Yancey the satisfaction that he had once again come running at his first call.

"Lieutenant Yancey, what can we do for you today?" The sheriff thought he might as well start things out with his best foot forward.

"You can start by telling me why you failed to mention you took a witness out of that cabin in the woods last week?" Yancey's tone was all business, just short of being rude.

"A witness? Well, I don't remember any witness." The sheriff was caught by surprise.

"I was talking to Brown yesterday. He was back in our office and he said you and Baker brought a girl out the same day he was shot. You didn't say a word about that the whole time we were up there in the snow. I want to know what she had to say about the man we're looking for. I want a chance to question her, and furthermore..."

Sheriff Harper looked straight at his boots, but that didn't completely conceal his smile. “The girl? That’s what’s got a burr under your saddle? Well, if that’s all it is...” He reached over and lifted the breakaway counter while shaking his head. “Come on back. Grab yourself a cup of Wanda’s excuse for coffee.” He waved in the direction of the coffee pot and its ample stack of styrofoam cups. He grinned at Wanda who tried to look irritated, but the relief on her face at the turn of events won out.

“It’s a sight better than what you can make,” was all she said.

“Now that’s probably true,” the sheriff admitted, as he headed back to his office with a confused drug enforcement agent following a few steps behind.

“So what else did Brown say? How is he, by the way? I kept meaning to get by the hospital and see him. I got by there late one night, but it was nearly midnight, and he was already sound asleep. The nurses told me he was on the mend and that was all I really needed to know.”

Yancey’s mood was still frosty as he answered. “He seems to be doing all right. He walks using an orthopedic cast and a cane at the moment, of course, but he says he’ll be back to work at a desk soon.” Lt. Yancey settled himself into one of the round caned chairs in front of Harper’s desk. He dropped his jacket across the other.

“Brown told me that you and Baker escorted a young girl downriver and you never mentioned her the day we went back up there. She’s a material witness to this case and I need to know--”

“Escorted?” Harper interrupted. “Is that what he called it? I’ll tell you this. I’ve escorted a lot of prisoners in my day and I hope to never have to do another one like that!” He leaned back in his barrel chair as he savored the moment. "As I recall, that day up there in the snow you didn't ask me much except to tote that barge and lift that bale. You didn't seem much interested in what us country boys knew. I thought the best thing was to let you take care of your investigation the way you wanted and when you got around to it, you'd come ask what you needed to."

The lieutenant's jaw tightened as he watched the sheriff take a slow sip of coffee. "And now?"

The sheriff was aware he had made his point. "I'll tell you what." He let Yancey off the hook. "You tell me what your lab boys found out about that woman's body we found up there and then I'll tell you everything we know about this girl you're so interested in. How's that?"

"All right," Yancey responded slowly, observing the sheriff with more regard than before. "They tell me she is Hispanic and has probably been tucked behind the lean-to there for a year or so. She was approximately thirty-five years old, and must have had her left arm broken badly at one time because there was a metal pin in her elbow. There are no fingerprints for us to run, so we're going to have to depend on dental records if we can figure out where to begin to look for those. The same with any x-ray records of that broken bone. If we don't even know where to start to look, it's going to make identification pretty difficult. So far, that's all we know."

The sheriff sat silently for a moment or two after he finished. "Sounds reasonable," he nodded slowly. "Now as for the girl she's a little girl, maybe eight to ten years old, tops. I don't even know if she's that old. When we got her, it was hard to tell the difference between her and a large muskrat. Ask Brown or Baker, if you don't believe me. She doesn't talk at all, and the only response we've gotten is when a friend spoke to her in Spanish, which makes sense if that was her mother buried out back of that cabin."

The sheriff continued, "One thing is sure. Nobody, including that old boy that Brown was a-chasing when he got shot, has taken any care of this girl for a long time. She was filthy, unwashed, hair so matted, clothes were pure rags. Looked like she hadn't changed them in months. Smelled that way, too, to be honest. I never seen the like and I've been doing this kind of thing with all kinds of people for a long time."

Yancey listened but persisted. "I still need to talk to her and see--"

"What part of this are you not understanding?" The sheriff sat straight up to his desk. "She can't tell you anything. She hasn't spoken a word to anyone as yet in English or Spanish. I've been checking and I'll keep checking. If I find out anything different, I'll be sure and let you know but meantime, believe me, there is nothing she can tell you."

"So where is she?"

The sheriff's eyes narrowed as he looked across his desk at the Federal officer. "Some place safe. Some place that can take care of her far better than you or me."

The lieutenant stood up and dropped his now empty foam cup in the trash can at the side of the sheriff's desk. "You know, if the mother was an illegal alien and we have no idea who or where the father is, that makes the child an illegal, too. Maybe the simplest thing is to notify Immigration and be done with it, if she's of no use in the case." He picked up his coat and strode towards the front door.

The sheriff sat, staring after his departing figure for several seconds, as he thought about the implications of Yancey's last words.

CHAPTER 7

While Dale Harper had not really planned to attend the gathering at the Foot of the Cross mission that Lou Ann had mentioned, he realized now he would have to go by and speak to Milagro about this latest development. He didn't like it much, but he liked nasty surprises even less.

The bright lights of the cross reminded him of days gone by when the previous cross had lit that side of town when he was a teenager. The multi-colored glow was different now, and yet that light in the same familiar place warmed his heart in a way he couldn't explain.

"Good evening, Dale." Martha bustled by as he came in the front door. "Come on back to the campfire, or at least that's what I call it." She led him to the back courtyard which was surprisingly full of women, children and a few men. They were all the regulars at the soup kitchen, the sheriff realized with a quick look around. Still, there were others he recognized, a couple of social workers, one of the Bible teachers who volunteered at the jail regularly and one of the new public defenders. It certainly looked like Milagro and her brood were making all kinds of new friends.

In the center of the courtyard area, several large rocks had been arranged in a circle and a cozy fire burned in the middle. Hay bales had been arranged in two semi-circle rows around the fire, making inviting benches where almost everyone was already seated. He was standing in the shadows when Milagro scooted past him. “Hey, lady, don’t you know there’s an ordinance against burning inside the city limits?”

She jumped so violently he realized she was completely unaware of his presence until she heard him.

“You started me so!” Her words all ran together as both of her hands flew to her face. “You should not start a person that way!”

Once again she had made him smile as soon as she spoke. “Startle,” he told her.

“Startle?” She looked at him and blinked, uncomprehending.

“The word you want, I think, is startle. Not start.”

“Start? Startle? Oh, you are right. You see, you startle me so, I do not even know the right word! Can we really not burn a fire here? I did not know. I made them put two big barrels of water close by. Do you see?” She pointed to a pair of fifty-five gallon barrels, sitting just to one side of the fire.

“No,” he laughed. “I’m only messing with you. It’s not a problem.”

“Oh, I never know when to believe you! But I am glad you came. Lou Ann said she invited you.”

“I wish it was all good.” He decided he might as well get

the worst over. “How is the little one doing? Maria?”

“Look for yourself.” She turned and pointed to the front row of hay bales where Maria was perched, beside Lou Ann’s daughter and Guadalupe Alvarez along with a young man with his arm in a sling.

“Has she said anything yet?”

Milagro shook her head. “No. She watches and listens to all of us, but like a puppy, you know? With her head to the side like you are very funny when you talk.”

“Well, I can understand that,” he grinned at her. “Some of you around here are pretty funny when you talk.”

“Oh, you know what I mean to say!”

“Yes, I do. I’m sorry. So what do you think? How is she really?”

“I really do not know what to think. She is quiet but not unhappy. Oh, and today she is wearing shoes. Do you see?”

Dale Harper looked again and spied little pink rubber sandals on her feet, buckled over the white lacy socks.

“Why, yes, she is.”

“It just took a little time before she was able to do that. I think that is the answer to many of your other questions, too.”

“Pink shoes?”

“No, more time. With time, she will talk. We know that she can. You heard her that night at the jail, yes?”

"I could swear I heard the word 'mama' that night," the sheriff nodded. "Still, for her to learn to talk so anybody can understand her…The problem is we may not have that kind of time." He sighed and told her about Lt. Yancey's visit to his office earlier in the day.

"Can he do that?" The look of horror on Milagro's face made Dale Harper wish he had never said a word. "She is only a child. Who will take care of her there? What will happen to her?"

"I'm sorry. I'm not sure," he stammered. "Maybe I shouldn't have said anything but I just didn't want to have it come as a big surprise in the next couple of weeks. Maybe he won't do anything at all."

She bit her lower lip for a moment as she looked away. Then she turned back with a smile on her face. "Then that is what I shall pray for. That he does nothing. If we have a little more time I think we shall find her to be a wonderful treasure. She has already surprised us a couple of times."

"What do you mean?"

"Because she does not talk it is easy to think she is not smart, but that is not true," Milagro began to explain. "She knows things, things about how to live."

The sheriff frowned. "Like what?"

"Like today in the kitchen, someone gave us two chickens, whole chickens with all the feathers. Our cooks, they are younger mostly and they only know about chickens from the supermarket, yes? But Maria, without talking, she walks over to the stove and takes off some hot water for tea and pours it on the dead chickens and begins to pull off the feathers. And then she takes a knife and she had that chicken in pieces like *uno, dos, tres*." She snapped her fingers as she spoke. "The cooks, women, all grown, they look ashamed at how quick this little girl takes care of what they just argue about."

The sheriff began to chuckle as she told the story. "Well, I can't say that surprises me, seeing, like I did, where she was living. If that man shot a turkey or stole a chicken now and then, I'd say she'd know how to take care of it. Looked to me like eating was not at the top of the list of what they did out there, though."

"Oh, *pobrecita*. Just the same, she knows how to clean a chicken, which it seems to me, many people do not."

"I can't argue with you there. I never said she wasn't smart. It's just kinda hard to tell with what we've had to deal with so far. I guess for now just keep working with her, if that's all right with you?"

"*Por supuesto*. Of course."

"And we'll just have to wait and see about the other with Immigration, I guess."

"I shall pray. God has taken care of Maria this far. He will not forget her now."

Sheriff Harper shook his head with a smile at her steadfast faith.

The melodious strumming of strings interrupted their conversation as Anna Mae stood before the group with a mandolin in her hands.

She smiled shyly at the gathering and they quieted as she began to speak. "You all have been so kind to me during my stay here and I wanted to say thank you. So before I go tomorrow, my friend Lou Ann and I want to share some of our music with you. We hope you like it." She turned to Lou Ann, who was seated on a hay bale to her right with a guitar across her lap. Anna Mae began to strum the mandolin as Lou Ann accompanied her on the guitar, and together they sang a snappy chorus.

"Three men on a mountain, up on Calvary, and the man in the middle was Jesus, He died for you and me." They continued, telling the story of Jesus' crucifixion and the two thieves who hung on each side of him.

"Fear not, fear not this earthly death, before this day is o'er, You'll be with me in Paradise, On Heaven's golden shore."

To Dale Harper, bluegrass music was as common a part of life as green grass, tall trees and blue skies. Maybe that was why he was so surprised when he saw the tears streaming down Milagro's cheeks as she stood at his side.

"Are you all right?" he asked softly.

"I do not know this music," she whispered in an unsteady voice, "but it touches me." She reached into her skirt pockets and came up empty-handed.

"Here." Dale handed her a clean white handkerchief.

"Thank you. I am sorry."

"You don't have to be sorry." He had become accustomed to seeing her in complete control. This was something new. "I was just a little worried about you, that's all." He smiled. "You will miss her when she goes, won't you? The old woman, Anna Mae?"

"Oh yes, she has been so kind to everyone here. So many people, they come with their lives broken. Anna Mae is one who came whole, to help others. She has been a gift from God these many days. She has stayed in the far room, over there." She pointed to the corner opposite her own cabin, closest to the street. "I shall be sad to see her go." She wiped her eyes again but still held onto the handkerchief. "And Guadalupe, do you see her there with her son, Juan Carlos?"

"The boy with his arm in the sling?" he asked.

"Yes, he is out of the hospital now and they have bus tickets for tomorrow. They are going home to California."

The group broke into applause as the duo prepared to sing another, this time an old ballad about star-crossed lovers, followed by another gospel tune.

"Someone else here knows how to play guitar and sing, too," Lou Ann said as their song ended. She stood up and looked across the crowd directly at Milagro. "Play one for us in Spanish, Miss Millie, please." Milagro shook her head in protest but the others called after her. When she glanced sideways at Dale Harper, he grinned at her and made a sweeping gesture with his arm toward Lou Ann and Anna Mae that left her little choice.

"I should not have played for you today," she hissed at Lou Ann as she took the guitar from her, but Milagro's smile took away the sting of her words. "Now I will have to think."

She sat down and ran her fingers across the strings. "In my country, each town has its own song. You have that here, too, for some cities, like Kansas City and San Francisco, yes? In El Salvador, there is a song for San Vicente and

Cojutepeque and San Miguel and for many different towns. One of my favorites is about going to the beach at El Tamarindo," and she began to play in a minor key, *"Con mis amigos, ya me voy a El Tamarindo, El Tamarindo es un bañario encantador, Llega la gente a bañarse los domingos, bellos pasajes de mi tierra, El Salvador."*

The children quickly caught the rhythm of the song and began to clap along. The sheriff continued to watch from where he stood in the back. Now it was his turn to say he did not know this music, but he particularly enjoyed the lilting high, clear voice of the guitarist and the joy the music brought to her face. Then he caught a glimpse of Maria.

At first she seemed almost mesmerized, then quickly she got up to twirl and dance in front of the others as they continued to clap and call out to encourage her.

Milagro kept playing as the little one danced in front of her, twirling and spinning, as if her tiny spirit had been suddenly freed by the music.

"Maria, *¡qué bien! ¡qué bonita!"* Guadalupe exclaimed, as she reached out to pat the little dancer on the back when the song ended. Maria's shy nature quickly returned and she ran to a hay bale and threw herself down beside Anna Mae, hiding her face in her lap. Milagro laughed out loud as she began another song.

"You all know this one, just with different words. *"Cristo me ama, me ama a mi, por la Biblia dice así. Niños pueden ir a él, Quien es nuestro amigo fiel.*" As she played the familiar strains of *Jesus Loves Me*, Lou Ann led the others as they joined in.

"Thank you so much," Lou Ann told her. "Who knew we

would get dancing tonight as well? I have another song here," and with that Lou Ann began a solo. Milagro reached over and tickled Maria until her silent smile returned and then walked back to Dale Harper.

"I have to bring some things from the kitchen. You can help, yes?"

He trailed along behind her through the labyrinth of halls that led past the nearly-built child care center, a classroom or two, and out to the old skating rink kitchen. Two large aluminum kitchen trays on one of the empty tables held tidy stacks of chocolate bars, boxes of graham crackers and bags of marshmallows.

"Wait one minute," she said, and disappeared into the darkened kitchen. When she returned, she had a small white bag in hand. "If we go out there with all these like this," she said as she began shoveling the chocolate bars into the bag, "they will all be gone *en un minuto*."

Dale Harper grinned, watching her. "I may not speak Spanish but even I understand that one."

"Take this." She handed him one of the two trays while she hung the plastic sack from her arm and picked up the other one to lead the way back to the patio area. She set hers down on one of the hay bales close to the fire, and turned to take the one the sheriff was carrying.

"Now I think I see where you're going with this," he began.

Martha stepped up behind Milagro with a handful of green branches already cut to size and sharpened on the ends.

"Another time and place, I remember you were pretty handy with a hickory switch, Aunt Martha," Dale Harper drawled as he surveyed the sticks in her hand.

"Another time and place, as I remember it, you needed the business end of a hickory switch more than once," she answered him smartly. "You and Eddie, I swear. When you weren't in the river or the woods, you were into ten different kinds of mischief at once. It's a true miracle neither one of you ended up in jail."

"Well, actually I do spend a lot of time there."

"Yes, but on the right side of the bars, thank heavens. I asked one of the men to get these for me earlier today so we'd have them for tonight. I had to explain to Milagro exactly what s'mores are."

"She tells me they are marshmallow sandwiches. Is that right?" Milagro wrinkled up her nose at the idea but the young ones around her quickly lined up for the sticks, marshmallows and chocolate bars as they were being passed out.

"Marshmallow sandwiches. Yeah, that pretty much describes 'em," Dale laughed as he nodded.

After another song or two, Anna Mae and Lou Ann joined with the others in toasting marshmallows around the fire. Dale Harper leaned back against a wall, far from the fire and simply watched the laughter and the sharing of the sweet treats in front of him. These were probably the poorest people in town and yet, at the moment, he had no doubt they were some of the most joyous. He tried briefly to remember the last time he had been part of such a happy group. He even laughed out loud at the look of total surprise and awe on Maria's face as a warm toasted marshmallow passed her lips for what he thought was probably the very first time in her life.

"Adíos, Sheriff." A shy voice at his elbow turned him in another direction. Guadalupe Alvarez stood beside him, her arm hooked through her son's uninjured one.

"My mother told me you brought her to this place and to *Niña Milagro*," the young man at her side began to explain. "My name is Juan Carlos Alvarez and we are very grateful, sir." He slid his arm from his mother's grasp and held his hand out to the sheriff, who was impressed by the polite manner of the teenager.

"Well, it is mighty nice to meet you, Juan Carlos Alvarez," Sheriff Harper responded. "Glad to see you out and about. I know your mother was pretty worried about you that first day," he added with a smile.

"I was pretty worried that first day!" Juan Carlos added, laughing. "When I saw that big truck coming down on top of our car, I could not imagine that we would both ever make it back to California!"

"And I hear that is where you are going tomorrow."

"Yes, sir, tomorrow. Everyone has been very kind here but we must go home. It is time."

"Well, I'm glad I got to meet you. Your mother makes a mean chocolate cake, by the way."

Juan Carlos grinned and his mother waved as they headed towards the seats by the fire.

Sheriff Harper went back to watching the group from a distance when another familiar voice interrupted his reverie. "I know it has already been said, but one more time, let me say thank you, Sheriff." Anna Mae stepped forward. "Thank you for helping me to find not only my friend, but some joy in life again."

Dale Harper smiled down at her but said nothing.

"After my Roberta died, it was as if there was nothing left to live for. I have no idea why I thought to come look for Lou Ann, except for the grace of God. Perhaps that is exactly why I did come, at His direction. But I might never have found her if it hadn't been for you. I just want you to know, you've made an old woman feel like life is worth living again, and that is no small thing."

"Well, I agree with you on that last point, ma'am." He looked down, caught off guard by her kind words. "But you give me way too much credit. I was just doing my job. I do appreciate what you said about losing your daughter and not being sure life is worth living anymore, though."

She stepped closer and gave him a quick hug and then looked up at him, her old eyes full of life's wisdom. "Oh, it is, Sheriff. Believe me, it is. It's just that down here on earth sometimes, we lose track of that in our comings and goings. The Good Lord, He never forgets. Turn back to Him, if you've lost your way. He'll show you. I promise He will. He brought me to you, back to Lou Ann, and to all these kind people here. Now I can go home, back to Kentucky, and know that I'll be fine.

She turned around and picked up her mandolin. With no announcement, she struck up the familiar chords to *Amazing Grace.* Within moments, most of those gathered were singing along.

* * * * *

"What a wonderful last song for a beautiful night," Milagro commented as she walked alongside Sheriff Harper outside.

The colors of the bright neon cross sparkled in the reflections off the hood of his gold pickup truck.

"It was a very fine evening," Dale Harper agreed. "Haven't done anything like that in a long time."

"I am glad you came to be here with us tonight."

"Me, too." Dale Harper was surprised to hear himself say it, but even more so, to realize he meant it. "Thanks." He swung quickly into the driver's seat of his parked truck. "You best get back inside now," he admonished her through the open driver's side window. "Nothing personal, lady, but you know, you don't exactly live in the best part of town."

"Oh, I know," she smiled at him, "but it is the best part of town for me."

"Get inside, girl," he grinned. He hesitated, not pulling away until he saw her open the door and step inside.

Sheriff Dale Harper drove slowly up and down various streets as he made his way back to the jail. He knew he wouldn't sleep for some time yet if he went home, and going back to work held no appeal either.

The full moon overhead had already bathed the entire countryside in its beautiful pale blue light. It would be a good night to simply cruise the back roads, surveying, making certain everything was as it should be. He did that on occasion, just to put his own mind at ease.

Despite the arguments he had heard over the years from experts who claimed the full moon did not have any particular effect on people, the only thing he could figure out is that those experts had never worked in a jail. There was something about a full moon night that often lent itself to an extra measure of noise, stress and upset and in this business that translated into major mischief-making.

On full moon nights, he liked to drive around to do his best to make certain none of it was going on in his county. He had driven for over an hour and seen absolutely nothing out of the ordinary, except for a meandering skunk or possum and, of course, the always dead-on-the-side-of-the-road armadillos. Live ones were the rare sight indeed. He decided to go back through town and loop around the blocks close to the jail. If all remained quiet, he would head for home. He had heard very little on the radio tonight from the evening dispatcher, which was another good sign. Cruising through town was as uneventful as driving the back roads. Everything was perfectly quiet, as if all the world, except for him, had long since gone to bed.

For no particular reason, he turned the pickup once more towards that glowing cross on the west end of town. He coasted silently past the Foot of the Cross Mission. Due to its construction, half a dozen different buildings pulled together, it had a sad, bedraggled look on the outside that certainly belied the warm welcome waiting inside, Harper thought.

At the last moment as he passed by, he noticed an older utility truck tucked in behind the building. It was the kind the local secondhand furniture places used for deliveries. He had not seen it earlier in the evening and he found himself wondering just what it was doing there as he reached his turn a couple of miles further on. Instead of cutting through the woods towards his own home, he made a sudden U-turn and headed back towards the mission.

His heart leapt as he rounded the last curve before town and saw the flames running across the far corner of the roof of the mission building.

"Dispatch, this is 365." He broke the silence of the night on his radio. "Get the fire department down to the Main Street Mission, flames visible on west end of building. I'll start evacuation of residents. Tell 'em to move it!" He flipped on his light bar, threw down the radio mike and jumped out of the truck.

He ran to the front door first, but it was locked tight. He pounded away, calling out loudly, but there was no response. He couldn't afford to wait. He whirled instead past the flaming end of the building and jumped the roadside split rail fence. Scrambling through the field, he found himself desperately trying to remember the exact location of the back door to Milagro's cabin. As best he could determine, the part of the building that was on fire was where Anna Mae was staying. He stumbled and fell to his knees and cursed his clumsiness and the fact that he had not grabbed the flashlight from the pickup truck. As he struggled to his feet, he glanced back over his shoulder to where that utility truck had been just a few moments before. The spot in the field shone clear and empty in the pale moonlight.

He found the steps and a wide porch and half ran, half fell up the stairs. He pounded on the door, yelling, and with a hard twist, wrenched the doorknob and the door flew open.

"Milagro!" He cried out as he crossed her small living room in two strides. All at once, he brought up his hands and grabbed her by the shoulders to keep from colliding with her in the darkened room.

"What! What is it?! *Por el amor de los santos*, Sheriff Harper, you give me such a start!"

"Quick! You've got to get everybody out, especially Anna Mae and people on that side of the building! Grab the little one and come with me! Your place is on fire!"

"Fire?! *O, por favor, no!"* She stopped in shocked surprise.

"Come on! Move NOW!" He turned her around and pushed her towards the bedroom as Maria came wandering out towards them, rubbing her eyes.

"Here!" He snatched up the child, shoved her in Milagro's arms, and pushed them both down the hall and out into the courtyard ahead of him.

"Get her and Anna Mae and any of the others out by the front door! I'll be here!"

He turned and grabbed a bucket that was sitting beside the barrels of water she had brought in for the campfire. He noticed the ashes still smoking slightly in the center of the rocks in the middle of the courtyard, but he was quite sure they had nothing to do with the blaze before him. He plunged the bucket into a barrel and ran towards the flaming roof of Anna Mae's room. He followed that bucketful with another and yet another. He saw Milagro scurry by with Anna Mae as well as Lou Ann, who had apparently been spending this last night with Anna Mae. He saw the others also run for the Main Street door exit as Milagro shepherded them all to safety.

In short order, bucket after bucket, he was soaked with both the water and his own sweat as he continued his fight against the flames. Even so, they were spreading across the roof to the next set of rooms away from Milagro's cabin. Suddenly, she was there beside him, a bucket in her hand as well.

"Where is everyone else?" he managed to ask her as she filled her bucket and ran after him, handing it to him to throw at the most advantageous place.

"They are all out!" she panted, scurrying behind him. "Everyone is safe. Anna Mae has Maria but I came back to help you!"

He smiled in his heart as he looked back at her with her hair all scrambled damply around her face in a sort of moonlit halo. She had on a long, now wet, cotton nightgown, and her feet were bare. As fast as he threw the buckets of water, she snatched the empty pails and ran back to the barrels. He knew they were losing the battle, and it was then that he heard the sirens of the approaching fire trucks. It would soon be out of their hands.

The firefighters attacked the fire with water hoses on the inside and out and quickly stopped the fire's spread, but not before a portion of the roof fell in on the now empty motel rooms. As they brought the flames under control, he and Milagro stood to the far side of the courtyard.

"Are you okay?" he finally thought to ask, glancing sideways.

"Yes, I think so." She pushed her bedraggled hair back from her face. "But our poor mission---" The words caught in her throat as her tears suddenly welled up. She closed her eyes and took a deep breath. "*Lo importante…*" She stopped and began again. "The important part is to remember it could have been so much worse than this." She finished in a whisper and quickly made the sign of the cross across her chest. "God was watching over us. There is no doubt."

"I'd say He surely was."

"What were you doing here in the night?" The lady-in-charge voice he was accustomed to from her was back.

"Well, that's kind of an interesting point," he acknowledged. "Normally, I would've been home in bed by now, but it just seemed a good night for driving cross-country, so to speak, and taking a good look around. And that's what I've been doing. After that, I drove past the jail and even back down past here once and then…well, it's that one last time that got me wondering. Hang on."

The sheriff stepped forward to meet the fire captain as he walked toward them. The thin white-haired man was all energy, even as he kept an eye on his firefighters while he spoke. "We've got 'er just about out, Sheriff. Quite a mess for these folks, I'm afraid."

"I'd say you're right about that one." He looked over his shoulder to where Milagro had been standing but the spot was empty except for the wet footprints she'd left on the concrete. He turned back to the fire captain.

"What can you tell me about what caused this, Jay?" The sheriff was all business now that he was certain their conversation was not being overheard.

"I'm not sure who but we can still smell some kind of accelerant and see the signs of its use. Not positive, but my guess would be a mix of diesel and gas. That's what the forestry boys use when they burn fields and that's sure what this smells like to me. The fire marshal will be here to start a proper investigation tomorrow morning, but for now I'd say somebody tried to burn these folks out tonight. I'll leave the figuring out of the rest of it to you and the fire marshal."

He touched the brim of his fire helmet and turned back

towards his firefighters as they began the cleanup.

Milagro reappeared coming from outside where she'd been to check on the other mission residents. She'd also apparently been back to her quarters long enough to grab a pink terry cloth robe, which she now wore over her damp gown.

Although shaken from having been awakened in such a fashion in the middle of the night, all were mercifully uninjured. A fireman escorted the bewildered little group to the kitchen area, where Milagro quickly had them all seated while she instructed a couple of the girls to begin making hot chocolate for everyone. She and Lou Ann began moving mattresses onto the dining area floor from a large storage closet at the far end of the room. That was where the sheriff caught up to her, counting out blankets and pillows.

"They've got the fire out and tomorrow, of course, they'll be back to begin an investigation and--"

"Investigation? Investigate what?" She stopped what she was doing to look directly at him.

"Well, what caused the fire, for one thing," he said. "Milagro, I don't mean to always be the one bringing you bad news, but this was no electrical fire or anything like that. Don't know who or why yet but somebody started that fire tonight."

"What? Someone put us on fire on purpose?" she hissed at him as she pulled him into the storeroom with one hand while her other hand still held its place in the stack of blankets she had been counting. "Who would do a thing like that? Try to burn what? Children, some old men and women who have to struggle not to drink too much, an old lady from another place and her friend? That is crazy!"

"I agree. It's crazy and I don't know any more than that now, but I guarantee I will before this is all over!" The grim determination in his voice made her stop counting a second time to look at him again.

He was usually more careful than that, he thought even as he spoke. He didn't make promises he couldn't keep but somehow he knew he would find a way to keep this one.

"I really do not understand." She turned in frustration back to her blankets, pulled out the stack, and handed them to Lou Ann as she came up behind him.

"Hello, Sheriff." Lou Ann seemed mildly amused to find him still tucked in the closet with Milagro. "What are you doing here?"

"It's kind of a long story," he answered with a crooked half-grin on his face as he stepped past her out into the open.

Milagro followed him and turned back to Lou Ann. "I will be right back. I want to thank the firemen and get them something to drink."

After they had moved a few steps away, she reached out and tugged at his elbow. "You never told me exactly why you came back. Why do I not understand what is happening here?"

He turned to face her, speaking quickly in a hushed voice. "I don't have any answers for you yet, but believe me, I'm going to be working on that tonight yet, and tomorrow, for as long as it takes. I drove back past this way tonight, figuring to cut through the back woods towards my own house, but I saw something, a truck parked at the back of your place. It took me a minute to realize it was out of place. So at the dirt road I turned around and came back, and that's when I saw the flames on the roof. Now that's all I know for sure. That and the fact that in the ten minutes it took me to get back here, that truck was gone."

He took hold of her shoulders to make his point. "Give me some time, girl, because investigate is exactly what we'll all be doing tomorrow. Meantime, not a word to anyone, do you hear me? Everybody will have way too many questions tomorrow and in the days to come as to what caused this. You know nothing. Do you understand? It's the only way to keep you and yours safe!"

His intensity frightened her and she took half a step back. "Oh, Sheriff, now I am really worried."

He grinned at her. "Don't do that. Do that other thing you always mention. I think that'll do more good for all of us right now."

She looked at him, uncomprehending for only a moment before a smile spread across her face. "Yes, I shall," she said. "I shall pray."

"Good. Let's go see if those firefighters are ready for some hot chocolate, and maybe you can get these folks bedded back down for at least a part of the night. What do you say?"
Her expression brightened at the thought, and she followed him out to the fire trucks where the men were rolling hoses and putting their equipment back on the truck.

CHAPTER 8

The dawn's light found Sheriff Harper squatting beside the field where he had spotted the truck the night before. He located the place in the barbed wire fence close to the corner of the lot where it had been cut and laid. Examining the tracks in the grass, he could see where the truck had been backed in and then driven alongside the building. He stood up and walked out to the highway to look back at the partially burned building. Thinking about the height of the truck he had seen in that quick flash as he drove by, he realized a man standing on top of the back would be at just the right level to spray the roof with something to set it on fire. If that was the case, then that took care of the how. But it was the why that had kept him awake most of the rest of the night. At least now he had a theory worthy of discussion when the fire marshal finally arrived in town.

He wandered around towards the back of Milagro's cabin and stopped at the place where he had fallen in the dark. The impression made by his knees in the dirt was still clear. He noticed both knees were more than a little stiff when he rolled out of bed that morning. He glanced across the grass to gauge the distance to her porch steps.

"Good morning, Sheriff." He heard her voice but did not

see her until he walked closer. She was wrapped in a quilt, tucked in a wicker rocking chair in the corner of the porch and partially hidden behind a blossom-covered dogwood tree.

“Good morning, yourself.” Sheriff Harper answered. “Did you get any sleep? I’m surprised to see you up so early.”

“I am always here at this hour. It is a good way to begin the day, yes?” She held up the book she had in her lap and he realized it was a Bible.

“Oh, I didn’t mean to interrupt.” He stopped at her porch steps.

“It is all right. I am mostly finished. It has been a morning of prayers of thanksgiving for what we did not suffer last night more than one for reading.” She closed the book but left it in her lap.

“That don’t look like the Bible my mother used to read,” he commented with a grin.

“It is the same on the inside.” She pulled the quilt up closer. “On the outside, too. *Santa Biblia*, Holy Bible. Is that not what yours says?”

“I suppose it does.”

He stood in silence for a moment before he asked, “So, how are they all in there?”

“Most are still asleep, I think. It was so much excitement last night. I did not know if I would ever get Maria to calm down. She would not stay in her bed last night after we came back here. She slept with me in my bed which means, of course, I got no sleep.” She shrugged with a smile that said she really did not mind. "I looked at the cabins a little bit this morning. What a *relajo*!"

"A what?"

"I am sorry. What a great big mess! All wet and black and well…you know. After breakfast, I guess we shall see what we can save and what is just trash."

"Oh, hold on." He came up the steps towards her. "I know you're anxious to start cleaning up, but for now you've got to leave it until the fire marshal can take a look at it all and make his determination."

"You mean we cannot even clean--"

"No, not until after he's been here. I know it's a pain in the neck, but believe me, it's the only chance we have to figure out who is behind this."

"Oh." She slumped back in her chair and was quiet for a moment. "Do you know this flower?" she asked, and reached out to gently finger one of the crowned blossoms beside her.

"Yeah, dogwood. They're everywhere at this time of year."

"They are so beautiful. Anna Mae was telling me a *leyenda*--how do you say? a legend about them. She said that the story says this is the same kind of tree that was used to crucify Christ. Back then it grew large like an oak tree, but the tree was so sad for the terrible suffering of the Savior that afterwards He changed the tree. He said because the tree had pity for Him it would never again grow large enough to be used for such a cruel purpose. The flowers were changed, too, and that is why the petals have this little mark here at the edge. It is for the nails in His hands and feet. See? It is like the mark left by a nail. The crown in the middle is for the crown of thorns that He wore. This way, all who see the flowers will remember the Savior. That is a beautiful story, no?"

"Yes, it is." He found himself watching her as she spoke, gently caressing the blossom during her retelling of the dogwood legend.

"The old stories, they help us, you know, just like the ones here," she said as she laid her Bible on the small table beside her chair.

He lifted his eyes from the blossom still in her hands, up to her face.

"You said before, 'the Bible that belongs to your mother.' You do not read the Bible?"

His eyes narrowed, trying to read the meaning in her question. "Not in a long time," he answered after a moment's hesitation. "Can't get my mind around a man that sat three days in the belly of a whale or that a man was raised from the dead by another man just calling him out. Things like that."

"Oh, I see," she responded as she considered his answer. "*Jonás y Lázaro*...how do you call them, Jonah and Lazarus, yes?"

"Yeah, that's them, I guess. There's a few others." He wondered how deep he was getting in as she continued.

"You have been there, no?"

"Been where?" Just about the time he thought he knew which direction she was headed, she took a turn he was not expecting.

"In the belly of a big fish."

He laughed in relief. "No, I've been a lot of places but I can't say I've been there."

"Oh, yes, you have," she continued lightly. "We have all been there at some time. We are stuck in some place where we do not want to be, all because we did not listen to where God was trying to send us in the first place. You wake up and find yourself in some terrible place like the belly of a fish and you say, how did I get here? What did I do to deserve this? And then you begin to think back to when you knew you should have chosen a different road, but at the time it seemed too hard or too frightening. You try another way, because you thought it would be easier. And all because you did not have enough faith."

Visions of sandstorms, supply lines and khaki uniforms danced, unbidden, through his head.

"The best way out of such a place," she continued, "is to pray and ask God to show you the way to go. Sometimes that is what we do. Sometimes we try to fight harder and then it usually gets no better, maybe even worse."

He had never heard a Biblical story interpreted like that.

"And surely in your work you have seen a man come back from the dead?" She did not wait for an answer. "You see, sometimes people get confused and they think the Bible is just a collection of old stories. They even get into fights about which ones could be true and which ones could not. And it is so silly. The stories in the Bible are still going on today. We have all been in Jonah's shoes, trying to run away from what we know we must do and it only gets us into more trouble. The important part is not did the stories happen two thousand years ago? The important part is that they are still happening today. By reading this book, we know we are not the first to face those kinds of times and places. We know we are not alone."

He stood silent, marveling at her simple explanation of what he had always regarded as a particularly thorny portion of the faith issue.

She continued happily as if she did not expect a response. "I love the old stories from your country and mine, because many times what is before us in this life, it is not easy. The old stories, they lift us up so we can continue even when the road is very hard." She shifted her gaze from the flower and held his eyes for a moment as he wondered why it was that this woman made him feel as if she could see right through him.

A stirring at the door revealed Maria, standing shyly watching them both from behind the screen door.

"Someone is looking for you," he said with a smile. "And I need to get back to checking on things around here. The fire marshal should be along soon. We'll come find you when he gets here, if that's all right."

"*Hola, mi amor*," Milagro greeted Maria who smiled silently in response but made no move to open the door. "Certainly." She turned back to the sheriff as she stood up. "I shall be here. Look for me when you are ready."

"She still doesn't like me much, does she?" Dale Harper grinned and backed down the stairs as Milagro opened the door. Maria stayed put keeping a careful watch on the sheriff's movements.

"We are working on that," Milagro told him as she stepped inside. "As soon as I can, I want to start taking her for walks outside the mission so she can learn more. But like I said--" She cut herself short in mid-sentence. "*Por el amor de Díos*, was it only last night we were talking about this?" She shook her head in disbelief. "It will take time. Oh! Did I tell you? She said a word last night after we got back to bed."

"She did?"

"Yes. She was half asleep, but she said *fuego* several times just before she fell asleep. *Fuego.* It is Spanish for 'fire'. At least we know she still remembers how to talk, yes?"

"Yes, you're right. That's a good sign. Maybe it is like you said, it will just take time with her and now," he jerked his thumb towards the burned-out corner of the mission, "for you as well."

I just hope we have the time, Dale Harper thought as he walked away.

* * * * *

It was two days later that he let his mind drift back to that conversation on the porch. His days since had been filled with discussions with the fire marshal and the stench of wet, burned material as they dug through the charred remains of the damaged mission. It was definite, according to the fire marshal. The roof of that part of the building had been sprayed with diesel fuel to make it burn faster.

"See the way the wood here has turned a blue color?" The fire marshal showed him later that morning. "And look how the burn mark here is a straight or slightly curved line. A regular fire burns in a jagged kind of pattern. This wood was sprayed to make it burn faster. Sorry, Sheriff, but we've got more work to do now, and so do you."

Once again, he turned over the pieces of the puzzle in his mind as he drove. He had looked all over town for the utility truck he'd seen the night of the fire but to no avail. Probably brought in from out of town, he told himself, or already repainted.

It was late in the afternoon on a rainy spring day. He had another kind of search he knew he'd have to begin soon as well. This time it would be a search for Freddy Ganst who had not reported in as he had promised. First, however, he decided to stop by the mission to see how the cleanup work was progressing.

"Miz Anna Mae, I didn't expect to see you here." Dale Harper spoke to the woman behind the counter when he came through the front door. "I thought you were going back to Kentucky."

The diminutive old woman's face was lit from within. "Yes, well, after the fire, I decided not to go right away," she told him. "I thought I better stick around if somebody thinks I'm important enough to try and kill!" Her eyes widened dramatically at the implication of her words.

"Is that what you think?" The sheriff had tried to push that thought from his mind every time it arose, but he had to admit it fit with the evidence.

"Well, it was my roof someone set fire to, now wasn't it?" Her smile belied the serious nature of the situation. "I'm just contrary enough that if they want me gone that bad, I'm gonna stick around to see why." The twinkle in her eye was unmistakable.

"Now, Miz Anna Mae," the sheriff began slowly. "You be careful who is around when you say such things. We don't know who's involved yet and it could be even more dangerous to you and others."

"Oh Sheriff, I'm not discussing this with anybody. I'm just listening. I hear a little bit here and a little bit there and I'm putting it all together. I just told Lou Ann and Miss Millie I wanted to stay on a bit longer to help out with Maria and all, and they were fine with that. They have their hands so full, don't you know, they're happy to take a little extra help, even from an old lady. We took Guadalupe and Juan Carlos and put them on the bus the morning after the fire, but I just decided to stay a little longer."

The sheriff grinned at the wise woman before him. "I should've known you'd be more careful than that. I am glad you are still here. Just keep an eye out for anything that doesn't fit in, if you know what I mean?"

She smiled broadly. "I'd be glad to, Sheriff, and if I come across anything, you'll be the first and only one I tell."

"That'll work." He gave her a thumbs up sign and started to ask about Milagro and Maria when his words were cut off by a thunderous explosion outside. "What in the name of--"

He ran out the front door and saw a black cloud of smoke rising above the roof tops a couple of blocks away.

He jumped in his pickup, calling in on the radio as he flipped on the lights and siren, and headed towards the smoke.

"Explosion on Polk Street, 400 block! Get the fire department rolling. I'll tell you more in a few minutes!"

For the most part, the small older homes on the west end of town had seen their best days long ago. Many were rental houses now and others looked older than their true age. The occasional well-kept house shone like a jewel in this part of town, but the majority of them were in various stages of neglect. At the moment only one, however, was fully engulfed in flames, much of its roof blown off. Sheriff Harper pulled up short in front of the house and saw two bodies lying on the front lawn, halfway between the house and the curb.

He ran to the first man who was starting to moan as he attempted to roll over.

“Stay still!” the sheriff cautioned as he reached out to touch him and then drew back. Much of the man’s clothing had been burned away and what was left continued to smoke and smolder. The skin on his right arm and the side of his neck looked like dripping candle wax as it barely clung to his frame.

“Sheriff? Sheriff Harper?”

Dale Harper cringed as he recognized the voice, husky with shock and pain.

“Freddy, boy, what have you got yourself into this time? Don’t move, I tell you. I’m calling for an ambulance. There will be more help here in a minute or two. Don’t you even breathe hard, you hear?”

The sheriff tore back to his truck and called on the radio for an ambulance. He grabbed a wool blanket off the back seat that he kept for all sorts of emergencies, and laid it as gently as possible over Freddy who was lying face down in the grass.

"Freddy, you keep talking to me, boy. I want to hear something out of you."

"Well," the voice was weak but unmistakably Freddy as he drawled. "I guess you ain't real happy with me about now. I should've come and talked to you like I promised, I suppose. Maybe if I'd done that, I wouldn't be here right now." A muffled chuckle escaped him that ended in a painful groan. "Good God Almighty," a coarse whisper followed. "What have I done to myself, Sheriff? What smells so awful?"

The sheriff couldn't tell him it was his own burned flesh that was filling his nostrils. "Freddy, just take it easy. Talk to me about something easy. What day is it today? Do you know? What year is it? Who is the President? Keep talking, Freddy. I'm listening, but I got to check on this other man."

The sheriff looked up from where he'd been attending to Freddy to see the other man was on all fours and unsteadily making it to his feet. "Hey, hold on there!" Sheriff Harper was also on the move. The other man, whose clothing was still smoking, gave a quick look over his shoulder through stringy dark hair and began to scramble towards the back of the burning house. Harper took a few running steps after him, but then thought better of it and turned back to Freddy. He had seen enough of the fleeing man. He would not be hard to find later.

"Freddy, are you still talking to me?" Harper asked as he slid on the grass to once again sit next to the prone figure.

By now, others from the neighborhood were gathering on the sidewalk to stare at the burning house and at the injured man, who was twitching uncontrollably under the blanket. "Get him some water or something to drink with a straw if you can," Harper barked at one of the neighbors who asked what he could do to help.

The ambulance and fire trucks rolled up in a cacophony of sirens, and the crowd broke into clusters around the edges of the activity as men and women in uniform jumped from the emergency vehicles. The Emergency Medical Technicians ran towards Freddy and Harper carrying a collapsible gurney.

“He’s in pretty bad shape,” Harper breathed in a low voice to the first EMT. “Take care of him and try to make sure that he’s not feeling too much pain. He was a good boy down deep.”

“Was?” The young female EMT was taken aback by the sheriff’s words.

Sheriff Harper gave her only a sharp look in reply as he stepped away to direct the local police who began to cordon off the area with yellow tape. He gave a brief description of the man who had run off to a couple of other officers who drove away to canvass the neighborhood.

Despite the frantic activity that demanded his attention, he kept an eye on the ambulance attendants and their cargo as they prepared for transport to the hospital. He stepped up close once more just before they lifted Freddy into the ambulance.

Freddy’s eyes were now swimming wildly as he shifted his gaze, looking for something.

“Sheriff!” He cried out in a near-panicked voice. “Sheriff!”

“I’m here, Freddy.” Harper stepped up beside the gurney. “Calm down now, and let these folks get you to the hospital so they can get you some help.”

"Oh, I will, Sheriff. I will. I just wanted to ask, will you do something for me?" From beneath the sheets, Freddy's nearly melted hand reached out.

"If I can, Freddy, you know I will. What is it?"

"Will you pray for me, Sheriff?" Freddy asked in a hushed voice. "Will you pray for me, 'cause I think that's the only thing that's going to get me through this."

Harper caught his breath, thinking back to the conversation with Milagro on her porch only a few days before. "Yes, I will, Freddy," he answered quietly. "I'll do that, and I'll pass the word."

"Okay, Sheriff. Thank you. I'll talk to you later."

The ambulance attendants finished bundling him into the vehicle and eased out of the emergency traffic to make their way to the hospital. The sheriff turned back to what was left of the house before him. The firefighters continued to pour water onto the charred rubble on the right side of the house. Half the house stood as if untouched, and the other side, the kitchen side, the sheriff assumed, had apparently blown up. Harper had no doubt these boys had been cooking meth and they had made a costly mistake. Fortunately, the force of the blast had gone up and out towards the front, not seriously involving the houses on either side. Roof shingles were scattered into the street and across the yards of the neighboring houses. The mess reminded him of the debris left behind after a tornado.

A uniformed policeman pulled up and motioned the sheriff over to his car. "Got a message for you," the officer called out over the noise of the firefighting equipment. "The boys wanted me to let you know they picked up your guy a couple of blocks over. They're taking him over to the jail right now. Just thought you'd want to know."

"I appreciate that," the sheriff told him above the din. "I really do."

Once things were under control at the explosion site, the sheriff made his way back to the jail. They would have to bring in specialists to examine the house remains and clean up the toxic chemicals he suspected would be found in the ruins after it cooled down completely. This meth business was not only heart-rending, it was budget-breaking. This county, like most of its neighbors, was not prepared financially for what this evil epidemic was costing in hard cold cash, not to mention in terms of human suffering.

Back at the jail it only took one look at the prisoner, still in charred tatters, to confirm what Harper already knew to be true. He had never seen this man before today in the front yard of the house on Polk Street.

"Is he hurt or burned so as you could tell?" The sheriff asked Sgt. Roy Baker and the jailer on duty who was manning the dispatch desk.

"I don't think so, Sheriff," Baker answered. "He seems pretty much out of it, and he smells terrible, all chemical-like, but I didn't see any real burns on him, other than his clothes."

"I figured I'd get him a shower pretty quick," the jailer spoke up. "I'll get him out of those things, and then if he's hurt anywhere, we can get him over to the emergency room, but I haven't seen anything to indicate that he is. Lucky son of a gun, I'd say!"

"Maybe," Sheriff Harper responded. "Get it done as quick as you can but get yourself one of those masks like the painters use. There's some up there on the shelf in the back closet. He's pretty well contaminated, so wear the mask and those heavy rubber gloves that are also back there. Save his clothes. Put 'em in the exercise yard for now, and make sure it's locked so no one can get at them. Once they dry out good, put them in one of those plastic evidence bags, label 'em, and lock 'em up."

The sheriff took a step or two towards his office and then spun around on his heel. "Hey, do either of you know where George and Suzie O'Brien moved to? George used to work at the feed store, but he's been working for Carley Dunstan lately. I heard they bought a house over on Polk Street but I wasn't sure of the address." The sheriff looked back at the two men at the front counter as he asked.

"Yes, sir." The jailer flipped up the page in the typewriter that held the daily log. "It's right here. 402 Polk Street, the house that blew up today. Is that the one you mean?"

"Yeah, that's the one," the sheriff let out a long, slow breath as his heart sank. The jailer began to move towards the back closet.

"So what do you think, Roy?" the sheriff asked.

"Some days, I try hard not to!" Baker replied in exasperation. "I think we're lucky nobody else from that neighborhood got hurt. Where do you suppose George and Suzie are? And how are they mixed up in this? We've never had any trouble out of them before."

"I know, but this is different. Get the paperwork going, will you? I want a search warrant for Carlton Dunstan Enterprises. George has been working there lately. That's our next stop. We might get lucky and pick him up there but I wouldn't count on it."

"I'll get right on it." Baker turned back towards his office and then stopped. "I heard Freddy Ganst was in on this, too. I guess we should have thought twice before we turned him loose."

The sheriff sighed. "Freddy may have made his last wrong move. From what I saw today over on Polk Street, I can't imagine that he'll live through this."

CHAPTER 9

The chilly, wet mornings of early spring slipped away into warm days of balmy breezes and dappled sunshine. It was mid-morning on such a day when Sheriff Harper walked towards the front of the office to refill his coffee cup and heard Wanda exclaim, "Well, look at you!"

He stopped to see an older man in a wheelchair being wheeled in the front door by a short, round, middle-aged nurse. Wanda scampered around the counter and gave him a hug.

"Ho, ho, ho!" The man sounded like Santa Claus, Harper thought. "Haven't seen you in a long time, girl!"

"Earl Walton, as I live and breathe. It's so good to see you!" Wanda squealed. "You look good. You really do!"

"I have to agree with her." Harper stepped around the backside of the counter.

"Hey, Sheriff." Earl stuck out a hand, and Harper grabbed it in a firm handshake.

"I hope I look a sight better than the last time you saw me!" Earl bellowed good-naturedly.

“That you do,” the sheriff laughed softly.

“Here, let me make my introductions. This here is Emma Jane, my girlfriend. She also happens to be my nurse at the Veterans’ Home, so that works out well, don’t you know.”

The plump lady behind the wheelchair smiled shyly and nodded her head in greeting.

“So tell us, Earl, how’s it all going? Did you say the Veterans’ Home?” Wanda was full of questions.

“I did. I’m staying out there awhile since I’m still on the mend, but doing lots better than I was. After I went off to that mental hospital that the sheriff sent me to,” he gestured at Harper as he spoke, “they got me squared away on a bunch of stuff, including the fact that I got diabetes. It means I got to eat better and no more drinking, but then that’s not all bad. Still a little weak in the knees some days. That’s why I use this chair if I gotta go very far. But I sure feel a lot better than I did.”

“And it shows!” Sgt. Baker came in the door behind him. “Earl, you old son of a gun, how are you?” He shook Earl’s hand and thumped him on the back as he stepped around him. “You look like a million bucks!”

“Well, I don’t know if I feel quite that good!” Earl answered, enjoying his moment in the sun, “but close.”

“You ain’t shooting at nobody these days, are you?” Baker teased.

“No, no,” Earl laughed. “No guns, none of that.”

Emma Jane leaned close to whisper in Earl’s ear and he answered, “Oh, sure, sure. Hey Sheriff, can I sit here a few minutes with you while Emma Jane runs up the street on an errand?"

"No problem, Earl. You want to come back to my office? Let me grab you a cup of coffee. You still drink that, don't you?"

"Sure. Make it a big one and black. Don't go messing up good coffee by dumping stuff in it!"

Earl maneuvered his chair, rather expertly, Harper thought, as he watched him move around and under the breakaway counter that Wanda held up for him. The sheriff filled their coffee cups and followed Earl back to the office.

"Now that brings back some memories," Earl remarked as he rolled in and cast a long gaze up at the large wooden sheriff's department logo on the wall. "I remember the day I hung that up for the first time for your dad. He wasn't going to put it up, you know."

"Really?" Harper handed his old friend one of the steaming cups. "Now I didn't know that."

"Nope. He said it looked too much like bragging. I reminded him that it was a friend who'd carved it. And all because he was so proud of him for getting elected sheriff in the first place. He just had to put it up or at least let me do it for him."

"That's funny, because I pretty much told Bonnie the same thing after I came in here. But she was the one who said it was my dad's and he'd served proudly under it, and there wasn't any reason not to put it back up when I came into office."

"Ol' Oscar Jensen, the Swede, we used to call him, because

he still spoke with the accent from his old country. He's the one who carved it and gave it to your dad." They sat in silence for a few moments, both lost in their own thoughts.

"What's this stuff?" Earl's sharp eyes caught the name on the end of the box that held the files on the Eunice Dunstan shooting. "I haven't seen that name in a lot of years, son."

"Oh, it was just something that came up in conversation, you might say." Harper went on to explain Anna Mae's arrival in town and the subsequent events, including the fire at the mission. "You still worked here at the time of that case, didn't you?"

"Oh, yeah. Your dad went out to the original call but I helped him what I could on the investigation that followed. He never did believe that Jensen kid did it but he couldn't prove any different. That was Oscar's youngest grandson and it just broke the old man's heart. He didn't live too much longer after that, as I recall."

"What else do you remember?" Harper sat down behind his desk and leaned back, ready to glean any new details. "Look through that box, if you like, and see if anything there jogs your memory. It sure can't hurt."

"Are you trying to re-open the investigation after all these years?" Earl inquired.

"I don't know just yet. I don't have anything right now that I can really hang my hat on, but if I did, yeah, I'd be willing to go at it, just to give the Jensens some peace of mind, if nothing else."

"I'd say they could use that." Earl proceeded to dig through the box. "Oh my, I remember this little baby. I think it was one of the things that bothered your dad the most because no one could come up with a sensible answer as to why a boy like the Jensen kid would have a gun like this in the first place."

"Yeah, that's part of the reason why that file box is even still in here. I just got it back from the highway patrol. They've got a newer process now than they did back then for pulling up old serial numbers off the guns. The number had been scratched off of this one but they got most of it to come back up in their lab."

"And did that help?"

"I don't know yet."

Earl stopped digging and looked directly at Harper. "What do you mean?"

"Well, I've sent the number off to the state capital for them to comb through their old records, the ones before they started putting everything on computers, and see if they can come up with anything. I want to see if they can tell me who owned, bought, or sold that gun back around the time of the shooting."

"That'd be good, if they could tell you that," Earl nodded his head thoughtfully.

"I sent the same request out to California."

"California? You think the youngest Jensen got this gun from California? He was just a kid, maybe thirteen or fourteen years old at the time, I think."

"That's right, but Carley Dunstan had just come back from California around that time and--"

“You think Carley Dunstan did this?” Earl leaned forward excitedly. “Boy, howdy, I’m telling you--”

“Hey, Earl, I don’t know. I don’t have any evidence that says so. It’s just a funny feeling.”

“Oh, I know, I know but don’t you see? Darrel, your dad, he had the same feeling. He told me that once but he swore me to keep it a secret, and to this day, Dale, I always have. Did he ever say anything to you?”

Harper snorted as a grimace crossed his face. “No, he never did. I wasn’t much older than Rupe Jensen. I was only fifteen when Dad died. He didn’t share the details of his cases with me. Used to make my mom mad, because he had so many things on his mind sometimes, but he wouldn’t talk about much of it. He used to tell her it was for her own good. He said it would keep her safe and keep her happier if she didn’t know, but that didn’t set well with her neither. They had more than one good row about it when I was growing up.”

“Well, all I remember is that Carley Dunstan was just as worthless as an armadillo, dead or alive!” Earl blurted out. “He ain’t still around here no more though, I don’t believe. Haven’t seen him in years.”

“Oh, he’s back,” the sheriff continued. “Calls himself Carlton Dunstan now and fancies himself some sort of insurance salesman, but it’s still him.”

“Well, that’s real interesting.” Earl leaned back in his chair. “Hey, you’ll keep me posted on this, won’t you? I mean, if you find out anything from California or something else?”

“Have I got your investigator’s nose a-goin’ again after all these years?” Harper laughed suddenly. “How are you doing really, Earl? Tell me about this girlfriend."

"Oh, I'm doing good, Dale. I really am. That day out there at the shack when you found me, that's as low as I ever wanna go, boy, I'll tell you. When you start shooting at your friends, that ain't never a good thing. I never got a chance to thank you, by the way."

"Thank me?"

"Yeah, for bringing me a bottle, just like I asked. Not that I ever got a taste of any of it. And I forgot something important your dad told me about you a long time ago."

Dale Harper stopped shuffling the Dunstan paperwork on his desk as he looked up at his old friend. "What's that?" he asked.

Earl Walton set his coffee cup down, enjoying the fact that he had his listener's full attention. "You know you've never been near as big as your dad. Even as a kid, you were built pretty small, but your dad would always look at you and smile and say, 'Yeah, but it ain't the size of the dog in the fight, it's the size of the fight in the dog,' and you sure reminded me of that a few weeks ago with that hit up aside the head." He rubbed the right side of his forehead as if it still ached.

With a burst of laughter, Earl continued. "Truly, I'm glad you came that day. It was a terrible day, but every one since then has just been getting better. And that Emma Jane, she's a peach, ain't she? She's had her troubles too, and we ain't doing nothing serious, but it's good to have someone, you know? Somebody who cares if you wake up each morning and someone who is there when you close your eyes at night. She's there 'cause she works there, but it's lots more than that. We'll just have to see where it goes from here, but things is lots better than they were. I've sworn off the bottle, and I can see that has helped, too, much as I hate to admit it. How about you?"

"How about me what?" The turn in the conversation pulled Harper up short. He was still feeling slightly guilty about hitting Earl, despite his friend's attempt to make him feel better about it.

"How're you doing?" Earl asked. "In general, how's the Sheriff of Crossland County feeling these days?"

"Oh, not bad, not bad," Harper answered with a shrug.

"You finally over the worst of it from that shotgun blast to the ribs?" Earl asked more specifically.

"I guess so." He finished the last of his coffee and set the empty mug down on the back corner of the desk.

"Well, it's the pain underneath those ribs you got to watch out for," Earl stated flatly. "Be careful, will you, boy? Don't let yourself get to the point that this old man did, ya hear?"

"Okay." The younger man grinned as he looked up. "I'll try to be careful, Earl."

"Good, good. You watch yourself now." Earl seemed satisfied with the warning he had passed on. Emma Jane appeared at the office door, guided to the back by Wanda.

"Hey there," Earl greeted her. "All done? It's time for us to be moving along, Sheriff. This young lady keeps me hopping, that's for sure."

The sheriff and Wanda followed Earl and Emma Jane back

up to the front counter. Before they could get out the front door, Milagro opened it from the outside and stepped in, accompanied by a shy, dark-haired little girl in a yellow sundress and bright pink sandals.

"Are you out for a walk around town?" Sheriff Harper greeted Milagro.

"We are," she returned with a bright smile.

The sheriff introduced Milagro and Maria to Earl and Emma Jane. Maria extended a tiny hand for a proper handshake when prompted by Milagro and then added a very soft, "'ello". Sheriff Harper's eyes met Milagro's at that, and she gave him a small but triumphant smile at the definitive sign of progress. Even so, Maria's wary manner remained unchanged, and her face held its usual serious countenance as she kept a watchful eye on all of the adults before her.

"This is the first time we have the chance to walk a little," Milagro shared as she stroked Maria's hair lightly. "We are just taking little steps right now."

"That's the way it goes when you are coming back from hard times," Earl added. "I appreciate that a lot more these days." He grinned as he waved and started to roll towards the front door.

As Earl moved forward, Sheriff Harper caught a movement out of the corner of his eye and realized there was a prisoner in the visitation booth at the far end of the room, talking with his lawyer. In and of itself, that would be a routine occurrence in most county sheriff's offices that are short on space and long on prisoners. This particular prisoner, however, had just taken exception to what the lawyer had to say. He struck the small table in front of him sharply with both fists as he jumped to his feet with a defiant roar.

The disturbance caught everyone's attention, and the sheriff immediately began to move in that direction to quell the problem when a strangled little cry behind him made him swing around the opposite way.

The bone-thin man with the dark stringy hair was on his feet but he was no longer interested in his lawyer. Instead, he was staring through the glass at the little girl who had just uttered the terrified squeal. Maria also stood transfixed but only for a moment. She shot past Earl's wheelchair and hit the glass door in front of her with both hands as she shoved it open and bolted out.

"Maria, *esperate*!" Milagro cried out behind her, but the child was already gone.

"What's that all about?" Earl tried to roll the chair back but promptly ran into Emma Jane, who was also struggling to get out of the way. "Harper?"

The sheriff was already around the counter, opening the door of the booth. He clapped a hand on the prisoner's shoulder and had him out of the booth in one smooth move. He jerked a pair of cuffs off the back of his belt and cuffed the man's wrists quickly behind his back.

"Are you all right?" The sheriff directed his question to the young bespectacled public defender before him who, though visibly shaken, nodded his head silently.

"Fine," the sheriff said, and roughly moved his prisoner toward the stairway to the downstairs solitary cell. "Jailer!" he yelled up the stairs toward the majority of the cells.

A uniformed officer appeared and the sheriff handed over the prisoner. “Take care of him. He goes downstairs and stays there until I say different!”

The sheriff turned towards the front door. “I’ll talk to you later, Earl,” he called out as he scooted past him following Milagro who had already run out in search of Maria.

“Go, go!” Earl waved him on. “See you later!”

Outside, Sheriff Harper found Milagro standing on the courthouse lawn looking up and down the street.

“*Por el amor de los santos---”* She turned towards Dale Harper as he caught up to her. “She is gone. I do not know which way to go, which way she goes!” Her voice caught, and he grabbed her by the shoulders as she nearly collided with him when she turned around.

“Calm down, we’ll find her. She’s a little girl. She can’t have gone far. She doesn’t know her way around here so let’s just look a little…”

He cast a glance down the block. Both directions offered a fairly unobstructed view, and he could not imagine the child had gotten that far in the state of panic he had seen on her face.

He took a few steps and then stopped and turned back to motion to Milagro to be quiet but to follow him. A pair of tiny, bright pink sandals lay at the base of the largest of the half dozen huge maple and catalpa trees that graced the courthouse lawn. The gnarled broad trunk gave way quickly to a large fork, which then extended into a virtual explosion of emerald leaves that extended over much of the green lawn below. Slowly, the sheriff circled the tree peering up into the lush green foliage, and in just a few seconds he spied what he was looking for. A bright sundress with a tiny girl inside was pressed tightly against the trunk of the tree nearly thirty feet above the ground.

He took hold of Milagro's hand, pulled her close and pointed to Maria's small still form.

"*Santa María*," Milagro whispered as she made the sign of the cross. "How do we get her…"

"Down," the sheriff finished the sentence for her. "Good question. What's your pleasure? I can climb up there but no fonder than she's been of me in the past, I'm not sure but she wouldn't jump right out of that tree rather than to deal with me. You can try to talk her down if you think that would work and she would listen. Or I can get one of the fellers over here from the city with a cherry picker, a truck with a bucket on an extended arm. But I sure don't want to scare her or have her jumping around up there if bringing in any kind of equipment is going to upset her more."

Milagro nodded and moved cautiously around the foot of the tree without ever taking her eyes off the child. "Let us begin slowly," she half-whispered to Sheriff Harper, "and then we shall see what we must do next."

He nodded and stepped back as she moved to a point where she could see Maria most clearly.

"Maria," she called, barely loud enough to be heard. *"Maria, no ten miedo. No hay nadie aquí que te hace daño. Por favor, hay que bajarte ya. Me da miedo a tenerte alla en un arbol tan alto."*

The child bowed her head to look at Milagro standing on the lawn more than two stories below. With the grace of a woodland creature, she turned and sat down on the branch where she had been standing. She looked down at the two below, her legs dangling gently, her hands at her sides, resting easily on the branch where she sat.

"*Ay, no puedo mirar.*" Milagro looked away for a moment and then turned her head back.

"Well, did you see that?" The sheriff's tone of wonder did not impress Milagro. "What did you say to her?"

"Yes, I saw it!" she snapped at him. "It nearly gave me *ataque de corazon,* how do you call it? A heart's attack. I told her to come down, that no one here was going to hurt her, and that she was making me scared up there in such a big tree."

He laughed at her choice of words. "Why? Did you see her? She moves around up there like a cat, like she was born to it. She ain't scared and I imagine that's what's going to keep her from getting hurt. My guess is she's spent quite a bit of time climbing trees to keep herself out of harm's way. She seems to know what she's doing, that's for sure." He shoved his cowboy hat back further on his head as he watched the little one with new respect. He looked down long enough to poke the toe of his cowboy boot at the pink shoes on the ground.

"Don't guess those were too helpful in climbing trees, so she left 'em behind in her hurry."

Milagro did not share his appreciation of the girl's skill. She snorted slightly at his change of attitude and began anew to cajole the child to come down. Maria, for her part, simply continued to watch them both from her perch on high and made no effort to leave her safe haven.

"So now what?" Milagro turned to the sheriff.

"I'd say," he began as he looked down at the ground for a moment, "that the fear is gone out of her for the moment. She seems to know she is some place safe, at least to her way of thinking. She don't seem inclined to move from there so the next step would be to do something that convinces her she needs to." With that, he stepped up and lifted himself into the fork of the tree and climbed up a few feet.

Maria took instant note, scrambling to her feet, one hand resting on the tree trunk, the other poised in the air. For a few moments they remained in their two positions, the sheriff venturing no further for fear she might climb even higher.

Milagro continued to call to her, pleading with her to come down. After several seconds of contemplation, Maria leaned into the trunk of the tree and began to scramble down the branches. The sheriff heard Milagro's quick intake of breath as the child seemed to streak towards the ground. When she reached the sheriff, he stepped back, searching carefully for safe footing, and reached the ground at the same time as the girl.

"Maria, Maria," Milagro's voice was as scolding as it was relieved. *"¿Qué te pasó? ¿Qué pensaste? ¿Por qué huiste así?"*

"Take it easy, Mama." Harper chided her. "She's back on the ground, safe and sound, but if you're asking her why she did what she did and you get an answer, I'd like to know that one myself. Seems to me it was the sight of that big ugly guy in there that did it. If you two are doing all right, I think I'm going to go have me a little talk with that feller and see if I can get some answers."

"That would be fine with me." Milagro straightened up

from where she had been on her knees, her arms wrapped tightly around Maria, who now proceeded to put her shoes back on. "I think we have had enough excitement for one day. We are going home." She took hold of Maria's hand and started back down the sidewalk.

"I am sorry." She turned back towards Sheriff Harper, who had stopped to simply watch her walk away. "Thank you for helping to get her back safely. I was just so frightened, and…"

Harper broke into a grin. "You don't like heights, do you?"

She shuddered as she looked away, almost in shame. "No. No, I do not," she answered softly.

"It's okay," he said, stepping towards her, reaching out to cup her elbow. "They don't bother me but I know they do some people. Do you want me to get the truck and drive you both back to the mission?"

"No, it is not necessary," she assured him. "We started out to walk, and we shall finish our walk. Thank you for your help. And you will tell me if you learn anything more, yes?"

"Yes, I will." The sheriff touched the brim of his hat as he turned towards his office. "You bet I will."

Back inside, he assured a curious Wanda, Earl and Emma Jane that the little girl had been found unharmed and that she and Milagro were headed back to the mission.

"What do you suppose got into that young 'un?" Earl asked Harper as they started towards the door once more. "Baker here was telling me what kind of a state you found her in up there in the woods on the Federal land. She sure looks a sight better than what he described!"

"Oh, she is much better than that day like a different child altogether." Harper laughed as he recalled the day of their harrowing boat trip. "She still doesn't talk, only a word or two, and I just found her prancing around up in one of those big courthouse maples in a fashion that would make any mother squirrel proud. She is quite a little character, there's no doubt. Still, it strikes me that there is a whole lot she might tell us, if only she could." He looked past Earl to the visiting booth at the end of the front counter once more.

"Earl, it was good to see you. I'm glad you're looking so fine." He shook his old friend's hand one last time.

"Sheriff, it was good to be seen, I don't mind telling you. And you look like you're doing right by yourself, all things considered. And, hey," he held onto Harper's hand, pulled him down close to his wheelchair, and whispered in his ear, "don't be buying no more bottles of R & R, ya hear? Don't matter who asks for that stuff. It just ain't worth it, boy. You know what I mean?"

Harper stood up straight, a bit startled by the unexpected advice as he grinned in embarrassment. "Yes, Earl, I do know what you mean."

Sheriff Harper called for a jailer to bring in the prisoner who had caused all the earlier commotion. Once the tall, rawboned man was seated at the table, the sheriff stepped inside the booth where he stayed on his feet.

The prisoner kept his eyes downcast, staring at the table before him with his hands resting on his knees below the table.

"Your lawyer went home." The sheriff opened the

conversation. "Seems you upset him with whatever was going on earlier. Those lawyers are good to have in court but, you know, if you get violent with 'em or yell at 'em, the younger ones especially, they get scared and sometimes they just don't come back."

The prisoner shot the sheriff a sideways glance, startled by the lawman's revelation.

"Of course, if he don't come back and they never get around to setting you a court date, that means you could be sitting here a very long time. I've had some boys sit in jail a year or better before they ever really got to court, what with delays and continuances and such." Sheriff Harper leaned against the back wall of the booth and studied the ceiling as if he had nothing better to do with his time.

The prisoner shuffled his feet, making the ankle restraints he still wore clink against the metal table leg. "Wh--what," he stammered, and then stopped. He took a deep breath and tried again. "What do I do now?"

"Well, you could start by being a little more cooperative around here." Harper spoke softly, almost as if he was speaking to a child. "You could start by telling me your real name, and not that fake one you gave the drug agents. They tried that in the computer and it came back with nothing as in 'doesn't exist.' I suspect there's a reason for that."

The man's head stayed bowed, his eyes still fastened on the table.

"Let's see, you've been in here what, about two, three weeks? That's time for enough of that junk to get out of your system so that you can begin to think a little, not much maybe, but a little. I'm not sure what all you've been up to, but it's clear to me you aren't running this operation and that whoever put you up to it is happy enough to leave you to take the blame. Meanwhile, there's a man over there in the hospital who, by the grace of the Heavenlies, is still alive. I'm not sure how, but he is and that's good. At least for you, 'cause if he dies the prosecutor can have you up on murder charges in addition to the dope charges."

The sheriff stopped speaking for a moment to let his words sink in. No sound came from the prisoner but the sheriff noticed that he was beginning to shake as if he were chilled.

"Now, I just seen something a few minutes ago that gives me a whole new set of circumstances to start thinking about. I saw you look at a little girl that we found up on Federal land at another drug lab site. And more important, I saw the way she looked at you, which had her running right out of this place and climbing the highest tree she could find. Now what do you suppose that's all about?"

The sheriff continued as if he did not expect any kind of answer. "It makes me think that we need to go back and compare some of the fingerprints and other evidence we found up there in the woods to what we've got on you. And if I find what I think I will, it sounds to me like the Federal boys could be lining up drug, and maybe even murder charges on you for the body they found up there. As a matter of fact, I think maybe I better go make me a couple of phone calls while I'm thinking about it..." The sheriff started towards the door of the booth.

"Wait." It was barely a whisper but the lone word was clear. "Bo, Bo Kroll."

"Bo Kroll?"

"Bo Kroll, that'd be me. Don't need no trouble with the

U.S. government." Despite his words, he still did not look up or change his position.

"Well, that may be, Bo, and I can't promise nothing, but what else can you tell me? For instance, who is the girl and what can you tell me about her? And whose the woman we found in the ground, behind your cabin?"

He shook his shaggy, dark head side to side as he answered. "Her name is Maria, Maria Cecilia, after her mother."

"Her mother?"

"That's who buried in the back, but I didn't kill her. She just got sick, and then she died, last year. I put her there 'cause I didn't want no trouble but I didn't kill her. She come to me when her last old man threw her out. Years back now. The girl's his child, not mine. I just took care of Cecilia the best I could. Not good enough is all. She still died."

Harper watched the man before him closely. Harper still found himself surprised at his own reactions when a man made admissions of his wrongdoing. Generally, he found he had little sympathy for the ones who did what they did for financial gain or to satisfy some personal score. Occasionally, however, he found himself moved by the most unlikely of prisoners.

"Doesn't look like you've done much about caring for the girl. I found that chain in the cabin you used on her and she doesn't look like she's had any care at all--"

"I did what I could!" The prisoner finally spoke up in his own defense. "What she'd let me! I don't know nothing about taking care of no girl-child. Wasn't my place to go taking off her clothes, trying to wash her or none of that. I only put that chain on her to keep her safe because she'd go out in the woods and wouldn't come back! But she's as crazy as any coyote. I was afraid she was going to chew her own foot off the way she carried on with that chain. After awhile, I give it up. If she gets lost in the woods, it ain't my lookout." He pulled his hands up and set his elbows on the table. He dropped his face in his cuffed hands.

"How long you been out there on the Federal land?" Harper changed his line of questioning as he took a step closer to the table.

"I dunno, maybe three, four years. Move in and out so they don't notice me so much. Started out just growing and then last year started cooking."

"Whose idea was that?"

The shaggy head wagged side to side again but no sound followed.

Harper tried a different turn. "What were you doing over there on Polk Street when things went wrong? Did you lose your touch? What caused the explosion?"

The head kept shaking but the answer caught Harper off guard. "The man said to do something about that boy. He said he talks too much, make him be quiet."

"And who is this man?" Harper asked again.

More head shaking, and the big man went totally quiet.

Sheriff Harper decided not to push any more today. This one might talk again later if he was handled carefully.

Harper stepped back and Bo Kroll, sensing the interview was over, stood up and turned towards the door.

In a rough whisper, Sheriff Harper called the name Freddy Ganst had given him weeks ago.

“Booger.”

The prisoner turned back immediately.

“That is what they call you on the street, isn’t it?”

The prisoner dropped his eyes again but not before Harper had seen the light of recognition. Bo Kroll nodded without saying anything more.

“Remember what I said,” Harper concluded. “Whoever this man is, he is happy to let you go to jail while he continues to walk free. Don’t fool yourself into thinking he’s going to rescue you. If he was going to do that, he’d have done it already.”

The sheriff called for the jailer and watched silently as the prisoner was led away, back upstairs to the main battery of cells.

“Find out anything worthwhile?” Sgt. Baker looked up from the report he was struggling with at his computer as the sheriff walked by.
“I don’t know,” Harper answered thoughtfully. “A little, maybe a lot. Just not sure yet. Think I’m going to take a ride.” And with that he closed his office door and headed past the front counter and out the door.

CHAPTER 10

The afternoon sun found the sheriff relaxing on the back porch of Eddie Bluewater's River Emporium. Unlike the snowy day when he had last found his way here, the only white to be seen outside today were the snowy bits of catalpa blossoms, decorating the towering, twin trees immediately behind Eddie's store. The sweet air of early summer was comfortable, yet heavy with humidity and floral pollen. The front door of Eddie's place faced the highway and parking lot but Harper preferred the back porch with its view of the tree-covered Ozark hills. Eddie walked out of the door with two cold bottles of Coke and handed one to Harper.

"You picked a good day to come by, Bro'," Eddie commented as he dropped his weight into a rocking chair formed from bent saplings that was identical to the one in which Harper was relaxing. "Middle of the week lull. I like that. Weekends have already been plenty busy not that I'm complaining, mind you." He leaned back and took a long pull on the bottle in his hand. They sat in silence for several minutes, simply contemplating the greenery that rolled away before them.

"So, you going to tell me what's on your mind, or am I going to have to torture it out of you, question by question?"

Harper gave him a sharp, sideways look, taking his eyes from the green valley before them.

"Is that the only reason you think I come out here?"

"To be honest, since you became sheriff, yeah, it really is. We used to take time to go fish or just hang on the river all day, but the last few years…"

"I got married, Eddie, and then, I *did* get elected sheriff."

"I wasn't going to bring up the marriage thing. I didn't want to sound like I was complaining about that. Besides, Bonnie never objected to you going fishing, did she? I don't remember if she did."

Harper grinned at the sweet memory. "No, Bonnie never complained about that. She just always made me promise to bring home what we caught, remember? That girl loved fried fish."

"That's right," Eddie nodded thoughtfully. "We did have to clean more fish once you two were together. And then the next thing I knew, you were running for sheriff. I never did ask, but I've wondered. Whose idea was that, yours or hers?"

The sheriff leaned back in his chair, tipping it nearly to its limit. "Well, now that you mention it, I guess she was the first one to put the idea out there. She pointed out what a poor job of it Sheriff Hayes was doing. I mean, as a city cop, we all had a pretty good idea of what he was up to, but once I got into office, I found half a dozen little ways he was slipping money or goods into his pocket. Not that I could prove most of it but it sure left us a mess to clean up when I took office. Made more than a few people mad, too, when they found out things were not going to continue the way they had for so long." He let out a long sigh as the rocker came back forward.

He grinned again. "Made some folks mad, but I have to say, it tickled Bonnie all over. I guess she always knew, one way or another, with her dad being the businessman he was. So, I guess you could say it was her although I never really thought of it that way. Once she got to talking about it, I decided it wasn't a half bad idea. Make more money for still being a cop. If I'd known what it would cost us, what it would cost her…" His voice trailed off.

"Hey, Bro', don't go there. Did they ever find out anything more in the investigation? You go to court in another week or two, right?"

"No, we don't know anything more. If Rodney has told his lawyers anything about why he did what he did, the prosecutor hasn't been able to get it out of them." Harper leaned forward, letting his elbows rest on his knees, still holding the soda bottle in front of him. "Sometimes I wish I knew what made him do it. Other times, I think maybe there's something to that old phrase, ignorance is bliss."

He was quiet for a moment before speaking again. "Hey, that reminds me. Judge Billy Joe says I need to take somebody with me when I go to court. His idea, not mine, but he was pretty insistent. Even said he might come by and check on me." Harper let out a snort. "You gonna be busy the week after next or can you get away? Not that I expect it will be a real fun day for any of us. The whole thing starts on Monday of that week, and I'll be up there every day, of course, just to watch, but I figure by about Thursday is when I'll have to testify. I'd appreciate the company if you can spare the time."

"Not a problem." Eddie rocked slowly and rhythmically in his chair. "I'll get my dad and Gene to watch this place. You got to go, what, three counties over?"

"Yeah, Miller County, change of venue. They couldn't do it here, of course, what with all the publicity and the influence the Sherwoods have in town."

"Sure, we'll go. Ain't no fishing trip but at least it'll get us out on the road, right?"

"Yeah, on the road. Thanks, Eddie." Harper stayed hunched over. "I got another question for you."

"Shoot, I'm ready."

"Remember some years ago, that woman your brother, Albert, was with for awhile? She was from down on the border, wasn't she? What was her name?"

"Oh my gosh. Ceci. That's what Albert called her. Strange woman. She was Mexican but I guess she spoke the world's worst Spanish. Her English wasn't so hot either."

"What do you mean?"

"Oh, I just remember one night when we all got into it. She and Albert were both drunk and I ended up having to call the Sheriff's Department. You were still with the police department back then but Jimmy, the deputy from Arizona, came out and when he tried to talk to Ceci in Spanish, she couldn't hardly understand him. He told me later, she couldn't really speak Spanish. Her English sounded like she should but she really couldn't speak either one. Why you asking about Ceci?"

"Ceci. That short for something? Like Cecilia? What happened to her?"

"What?"

"You heard me. What happened to this Ceci?"

"Oh, she and Albert couldn't quit drinking and fighting. They had a big blowout one night and she fell and broke her arm. I had to take her into the emergency room, and they put a pin in her arm 'cause the bone was broke so bad. Just shattered, the doctor said. I remember I pushed Albert pretty hard on that because he's the one that told me she fell. I wondered if maybe he was the cause of it. Anyway, it wasn't long after that, she was gone. Albert said she went back to El Paso or somewhere down there, where she was from. That's about the time I figured out Albert was doing more than just drinking, so I was glad she was gone because he was enough to deal with."

Eddie's eyes narrowed as a darker realization began to take hold. "Now I've answered your questions. What about mine? Why are you asking?"

"Well, I think I figured out where she went and it wasn't back to El Paso." Harper and Eddie spent the next several minutes tracing the time line back.

"You really think she was the one they found buried up there?" Eddie's face paled.

"That's exactly what I'm thinking, and that business about her broken arm, it all fits. There's more," Harper went on. "This old boy we got in jail says when he met up with Cecilia, as he calls her, she was already pregnant. He says the little girl, Maria Cecilia, is not his child. Don't know any other way to put it, Eddie, except to say that little girl living at the mission with Milagro may be Albert's daughter, your niece."

"Holy smoke." Eddie let out a long, slow whistle from between his teeth. "Who would have thought? I mean, I don't even know what to say. I guess my first question is how do we find out for sure? And then what?"

Harper leaned back. "Well, there's a couple ways to go. With Ceci's full name, I can get her medical records from the hospital where they treated the broken arm and give those to the Feds to check them against the body. It sounds pretty likely though. Then, as far as Albert goes, if you think he'd be willing, they do DNA tests now to prove fatherhood. They're pretty routine. We have a lab tech come into the jail every now and then to get a sample to prove paternity in this or that case for child support. If Albert is willing, it won't take long to find out. They just use a swab and run it along inside his cheek. That's all."

"Holy smoke," Eddie repeated, this time lost deep in thought as he began to rock slowly once more. "Looks like I might just have to make a trip up north with my dad to talk to Albert about all this."

"That would sure make things easier here," the sheriff nodded. "I've got to send Kroll's fingerprints off to the Feds, and Ceci's X-rays as quick as the hospital can lay hands on 'em. I don't suppose you remember her last name, do you?"

Eddie grinned and shook his head. "You know, it's been what? Eight, nearly ten years? I'm surprised I remembered her first name, but somehow when you asked, it came right to me."

"No matter." Harper stood up. "I can find what I need at the jail through the records of that fight, when she and Albert both got arrested. It won't take long, now that I know who I'm looking for. Hey, Eddie, thanks for the Coke and the info. Don't know if I ever told you, I mean, I know I make fun of you as the big businessman but you got a nice place here. You've done well by yourself." He turned to go.

"Well, thanks yourself, Sheriff," Eddie responded in mock seriousness as he followed him off the porch. "You ain't done so bad yourself for a lawman."

"I'll see you next week."

* * * * *

Sheriff Harper spent the next few days confirming what he and Eddie had discussed. Everything was falling into place just as he had suspected. The call came from Lieutenant Yancey on Monday morning of the next week.

"Harper, we got that stuff you sent up here. The fingerprints are a match on the man. He was definitely the one in that cabin, and it looks like this may be the woman. How did you figure this out?" His voice crackled and skipped in Harper's desk phone, telling him that Yancey was calling on a cell phone from somewhere on the road.

"Good old-fashioned detective work, what else?" Somehow, Harper could not let his guard down with this Federal agent.

"I see. Catch a break, did you?"

"You could say that." Harper smiled in spite of himself. "Got a joker in jail here for a meth lab in town and it just seemed to fit. When I started asking him questions, he pretty much told me the rest."

"Well, however it happened, I'm glad we got the information. The lab boys up here had basically decided, from what they could tell that she died of natural causes. Pneumonia is their best bet. Still, we got him for the meth and the illegal dumping of a body."

Harper wadded up a paper he had been sketching on with a pencil and tossed it at the trash can, making a perfect basket. "Pneumonia would go along with what this old boy Kroll told me. He said she just got sick and died. He's got big legal problems here anyway. His last meth lab didn't go so well. He blew up a house and another guy with it. That one's still in a coma in the hospital. Either way, I'd say he'll be in jail for quite awhile."

Yancey gave a short laugh. "Well, that's the main thing. I'll keep you posted if we come up with anything else."

"You do that," Harper responded. "Thanks for the call." He hung up the phone.

Harper put his elbows on the desk and rested his forehead in his hands for a brief moment.

"You look like you just lost your best friend," Wanda cracked as she came around the corner with the day's mail in her hand.

"No, not quite." The sheriff sat back up straight. "Just got to go deliver some news to a friend that may not be too welcome." He sighed and reached for the large manila envelope that she held out to him.

"I've already been through all the junk and advertising for the day," she explained, "but this one's marked 'Lab Results' from the state capital. Were you waiting on something? I don't remember you saying so."

The sheriff opened the envelope carefully, without saying a word.

"Afraid of what you might find in there?" Wanda asked as she waited.

Sheriff Harper read over the single sheet of paper.

"Well, whatcha got?"

"This may be the answer I've been looking for." Harper looked up with half a smile. "Don't know for sure, but it looks like it to me."

"What are you talking about?" Wanda's curiosity was starting to get the better of her patience.

"Nothing I can discuss now." Harper's boots slapped the floor. He pulled his cowboy hat off the coat rack pole by the door. "Catch ya later, Wanda. Gotta go."

Before she could ask anything more, he was out the front door with the yellow lab report folded into his front shirt pocket.

* * * * *

Dale Harper listened to the echo of his own steps as he walked down the long hospital corridor that led to the rooms just outside the intensive care unit. The window blinds stood at half-mast in the room where he stopped just as they had every other time he had been here. They let in enough light to brighten the walls, yet shaded everything in a way that lent a quiet reverence to the lone bed that stood in the middle of the room.

Freddy Ganst looked the same as the last time he had seen

him, 'resting comfortably' is the way the nurses described him. He slept like he spoke, Harper noted, with more than a hint of the innocence of a child. He did not move except for the barely perceptible lifting and falling of his chest. After a week in the intensive care unit at the hospital over at Montgomery City, the doctors had determined there was nothing more they could do for him that could not be done in his hometown, and they sent him back to Crossland County Hospital.

Freddy had been in a coma now for over three weeks. Dale Harper was beginning to wonder how long he might remain that way. As a lawman, he wanted to know what Freddy knew, but Harper also found himself wondering about Freddy even more as someone who had watched him grow up. He had never found anyone else here visiting when he stopped by. All at once, he remembered his promise to Freddy that day on the lawn of the burning house as the paramedics prepared to take him away. He pulled off his hat, dropped his head and tried to remember the last time he had prayed about anything.

"Is everything all right?" A soft female voice behind him interrupted his reverie.

"Yes, I just stopped by to see how Freddy was doing." The sheriff quickly pushed his hat back into place and turned to face the young nurse who had come in behind him.

"He's doing a little better." The nurse stepped forward and picked up the chart at the end of the bed. She flipped through it as she spoke. "He is still in a coma, of course, but his vital signs are all good and strong. He seems to be holding his own."

"No signs of his coming to any time soon?" The sheriff could not help but ask what was really on his mind.

"Nothing that would indicate any changes like that." The young nurse shook her head. "Many times, we don't get any signs ahead of time. They just open their eyes one day and they are back with us." She smiled, a sweet but professional gesture, Harper thought to himself.

"All the same, if he does any time soon, have you got it written down somewhere for them to call me?"

"Yes, sir, Sheriff Harper." The woman replaced the chart. "Those are our instructions at the front desk to notify you immediately of any significant changes in this patient's condition."

"Fine, I appreciate that." Harper turned to go. "I just hope…" He stopped.

"We do, too." She finished the thought for him. "We hope he comes out of it soon, very soon."

* * * * *

The mood at the Foot of the Cross Mission was a definite improvement over what he had felt at the hospital. As fast as he stepped inside, three young children streaked past the front counter in a fast game of chase. There were shrieks of delight and mock distress as the little boy doing the chasing almost caught up to the two girls. It was then that Harper noticed that one of the girls was Maria. She was running hand in hand with a little girl with thick blond curls. It was the other two children who were squealing and calling out to one another but the broad smile that spread across Maria's face spoke louder than any words.

"Oh, hello, how are you?" Milagro was a few paces behind the children and surprised to find a visitor in the lobby. "Outside, outside with all of you. *Fuera, fuera,*" she added as she looked directly at Maria and waved her hands in front of her. "You should not be running inside here anyway." She clapped her hands and the children quickly obliged.

"Our little miss looks like she is having a good time," Harper grinned at Milagro as she turned back from shooing the children out of the room.

"Every day she is doing a little better. I was not so sure after the other day at your office but it is like she has forgotten about it for now. Did you find out anything more from that man? You never called to say."

Sheriff Harper looked at his boots for a moment. "Yeah, I did, and that's why I came by today. Sorry not to let you know sooner but I didn't want to say anything until I was pretty sure of what I was talking about."

She ushered him towards the small couch in the empty vestibule. "Come and sit," she encouraged.

Dale Harper followed her with some reluctance, trying to gauge her possible reactions.

"After you left the other day, I went back in and talked to Kroll. Bo Kroll, that's what he told me his name was and when we checked him out in the computer, it came up with an old misdemeanor record and pictures that could be him. Hard to tell with all that hair. No fingerprints on file but his fingerprints match the ones we found at the cabin. He admitted to being the one up there on the Federal land and he said your little friend's name is Maria. You guessed right, Maria Cecilia. It's her mother who was buried out back. I'd seen her a time or two, years ago, but I'd just heard her called Ceci back then and I didn't connect her with the body we found. Kroll says he's not Maria's father, so I did a little more checking and if I'm right, the good news is that you won't have to worry about Immigration deporting her."

"You mean, you know who her father is?"

"I think so, but the bad part is that it's not anybody who is going to be able to take care of her any time soon."

"What do you mean?"

He took a deep breath. "It looks like Albert Bluewater might be Maria's father. He's Eddie's younger brother and he's in prison on a DWI charge that involved a traffic death. I don't have any idea how long he'll be there, and to be honest, even when he gets out. I mean, he and Eddie and their father, we're talking about a bunch of old bachelors. What they know about raising a little girl, you could write on your thumbnail and have space left over."

He saw an unexpected sparkle in her eye as she reached forward and took his hand.

"What are you so worried about? If I understand, you are saying that Maria has a father who cannot take her away. To know who she is and to know she is safe, to stay here with me—I mean, with us. It is perfect." She leaned back against the arm of the couch with a smile that lit up her whole face. Once again, he was impressed with how beautiful she truly was. He was thankful that the anxiety that had been eating at him for days as he dreaded this moment had already begun to ease.

"Well, that's one way to look at it. I guess I was just worried that you wanted to know whose she was, to find out where she belonged. I mean, do you want to take on somebody else's child, full-time?"

She shook her head, still smiling broadly. "You said it right, to find out where she belongs. She belongs here. Now there is no doubt! Only God could come up with a solution like this as an answer to prayer. Do you not see?"

Sheriff Harper shoved his hat back a little further on his head, admitting his confusion. "No, I guess I don't."

"The prayer was that Immigration would not take her or that the Federal agent would do nothing that would make that a problem. Instead, God sends a completely unexpected answer. Immigration cannot take her because she is American and she belongs here. But even better, God lets you know that she is from this town, or at least her father is and he is not going to take her away any time soon. Now we know we have time to work with her, to really help her, to teach her what she needs to know. And you tell me she is related to your good friend Eddie. That means we know she comes from, as we say in my country, *buena gente*, good people. Eddie will want to meet her, yes? and get to know her, but she will still get to stay here with us. It is a perfect answer to a prayer!" She jumped off the couch in her excitement.

"You have made it a wonderful day, Sheriff Harper! Did you know? I have to go tell Martha and Anna Mae. I will see you later, yes? Thank you so much!" She leaned over and kissed him on the cheek with all the exuberance of a child and then she was gone to share her good news.

"Well, I can't say I did 'til now," the sheriff muttered as he walked out the front door. He touched his cheek lightly and smiled to himself. And to think that he worried he was bringing her something else to worry about!

CHAPTER 11

"I want her fired!" were the first words that greeted Sheriff Harper when he walked into the office the next morning. Commissioner Richard Ravens was standing in front of the counter glowering at Wanda who was clearly not having a good morning. She was chewing her signature bubble gum, slowly and deliberately, as if she were considering her next words particularly carefully.

"Well, Grandma used to say people in Hades want ice water, too," was the only thing Harper could think to say. He knew it was not the right thing at the moment but sometimes when it came to dealing with Dickie Ravens, he could not imagine what the right thing could possibly be.

"She has compromised my reputation with the news media of this town and I want her fired!" The county commissioner repeated himself, his voice rising in tone and volume.

"To begin with, Dickie," Harper tried not to sound as tired as he already felt so early in the day, "Wanda doesn't work for you. She works for me and that means you don't get to make that decision. Now beyond that, I have no idea what this is all about and until I do, I'm not doing anything."

Commissioner Ravens took a deep breath and blurted out, "I'll tell you what it's all about. She compromised me, and—"

"Dickie!" Sheriff Harper interrupted him with a no-nonsense tone he found he only had to use with the most difficult of incoming prisoners. "First of all, I can't imagine how she could have done that better than you manage to do it yourself every day! Now, I'm going to get myself a cup of coffee and then I'm going to get the story from Wanda and then, and only then, I might be inclined to talk to you. In the meantime, I'll thank you to get out of my office. Go somewhere and calm down." And with that, the sheriff opened the door behind him and made it clear that it would be in the commissioner's best interest to leave.

Dickie Ravens left, grumbling under his breath, but the sheriff was simply glad he was gone as he was seriously considering how to throw him out physically.

"Now what in the name of all that is holy was that about?" Dale Harper asked, as he came around the corner of Wanda's desk with a steaming cup in his hand.

"Oh, Sheriff, it's been one of those mornings where the phone would not stop ringing and people were at the front desk and I'm afraid he's right. I did compromise him, or whatever he said, but I swear it was not on purpose." Her breath caught in her throat, and Sheriff Harper witnessed one of the rare occasions in which Wanda was about to cry.

"Excuse me." She choked out the words as she headed towards the restroom in the back of the office.

The phone rang and he picked it up. "Crossland County Sheriff. Hello, Silas. How're you doing? Your bull is gone, heh? From the upper field? When's the last time you checked on him?" He listened a little more. "Yes, I appreciate he's worth a lot of money and you can turn in a claim with the insurance company, but it's like they told you. You will have to come in here first and fill out a report before they're likely to do anything. Yes, five days, I hear you. Did you check with all the neighbors? Nobody's seen him. Maybe he got over into another field. They're prone to do that sort of thing, especially this time of year. Well, you check with all of them and make sure. I can send somebody out to look for any signs of the gates and fences being tampered with. I'll be honest with you, Silas. We've been lucky around here lately and haven't had any trouble with rustling for quite awhile. That's a good thing, of course, but it doesn't mean that it can't change. I'll have Jimmy out your way this afternoon to take a good look around. In the meantime, if you find out anything more, you let us know. And when you're in town, when did you say, tomorrow? You can come by then and file a report about a missing bull. State the value and then we'll have something for the insurance company, if it goes that way. Take care, Silas. Goodbye."

Wanda returned, her eyes still red and moist, but her voice was clear. The sheriff noted that for the moment, the bubble gum was gone.

"Like I said, I can't say he's wrong this time and if you need to fire me because of it I'll understand." She dropped her thin frame into the chair with a dejected air.

"Why don't you tell me what this is all about and let me decide." Sheriff Harper leaned his back against the counter and waited for her to begin.

"This is the quietest it's been all morning. You know how it gets around here sometimes. Dave Weatherly from the radio station called early on and asked me a question about something on the radio log from last night. I had a bondsman in here, the other two lines ringing and somebody wanting to leave off stuff for one of the inmates, so I just glanced at the log and told him what he wanted to know. We're always being told the radio log is public information and I've even heard you say that is true, although they 'bout beat you to death with it sometimes."

She took another deep breath and continued, her voice a little steadier. "They were asking about the bridge that's out down at Piney Creek on Hwy JJ and wanted to know if someone had an accident out there about three or four this morning. When I looked on the log, there it was. Doug Blankenship ran his truck right into the bulldozer the county road crew had pulled across the road to keep anybody from running off the end of the pavement since the bridge is gone. I read him what the night shift radio officer had written and then hung up and got back to the folks at the front counter."

"Okay, so far it doesn't sound too bad," Harper interjected with a smile, trying to lighten her mood.

"Well, there were a half dozen more phone calls and then Dave called again, this time asking about why a bulldozer was put across there like that. And I told him he'd have to talk to the road and bridge crew if he wanted those kind of answers but that it wasn't unheard of. He asked about another radio log entry, this one from six last night."

Harper nodded his head. "I know about this one. I was still here when the call came in from Buzzy Jackson, the road crew chief. He set it up. He told us they put up orange barrels and a set of flashing lights and signs to let anyone know before they got there so they wouldn't go slamming into the bulldozer. Made sense to me at the time. I guess Doug wasn't watching too close when he came through there at three o'clock in the morning. Makes me wonder what he was doing out at that hour anyway."

She sighed again and studied her shoes as she continued. "Well, it gets better. I read them that one and then I answered the other lines, and about then, Sergeant Baker came in with a wild one. You know, one of the things I like about the day shift over the evening shift is I don't have to deal with too many drunks. They usually wait until later in the day before they get caught up in that sort of nonsense, but not this guy. Roy Baker brought him in here and I don't know what he'd been drinking, but no sooner than he got inside, he threw up all over the floor. I mean, I had people leaping out of the way of it, and then the radio station calls again! It was all I could do not to just jump right through the phone at Dave, but you said we need to be nice to those people, so I bit my tongue. I was real polite and asked him what I could do for him, and he asked me to read him the log entry from midnight."

"Now," she let out a long sigh, "how Dave Weatherly already knew so much about our log, I didn't even think about until later. I had a crisis going here, so I just snatched it up and read it to him, real quick. It wasn't until the words were out of my mouth that I realized what I'd just told him. And I guess it was after that the radio station called Commissioner Ravens and, of course, the first thing he did was come flying in here to rail at me and…." She stopped and let out a big sigh.

Sheriff Harper reached for the radio log clipboard and flipped the page back to the night before:

2345 hrs Officer 354 Johnny Morton called in to say

that there were no lights or warning signs out at the Hwy JJ bridge across Piney Creek, only a bulldozer pulled across the road which was pretty hard to see in the dark, until it was too late. Officer 354 informed the caller that an earlier log entry stated that there were lights, signs and barrels. Caller stated that someone must have removed them, kids maybe, because now there were none. Officer 354 called County Commissioner Richard Ravens, who stated that there were barrels and signs. When asked if he wanted to go out there to check or have Buzzy Jackson take care of it, he stated he was quite sure that they were still there and that Morton had simply missed them. He said he wasn't going to go running around out there at midnight and he would take care of it in the morning.

"Now, you see?" Wanda's voice took on a high pitch. "I had no idea what I was reading aloud until it was too late. Of course, Dave, the radio guy, went nuts and asked me to read it again. I told him, no, I was too busy and had to go. He was laughing and said the county would be owing Doug Blankenship a new truck. Sheriff, all I can tell you is I was just sick. I mean, I wouldn't have told him that deliberately, even if it is true!"

Sheriff Harper gave up the battle of trying to suppress the smile that had been teasing the corners of his mouth for the last few seconds and let out a low chuckle. "Well, Wanda, looks to me like Dickie Ravens has done himself in. All we did was write it down and give it to the news media like he's always hollering about anyway. It's not our fault if it didn't all come out the way he wanted it."

He clapped a hand on her shoulder as he headed back to his office. "Try not to upset yourself over it too much, and for goodness sake, if you see Dickie Ravens coming your way, hide! But it sure ain't a firing offense in my book!"

The sheriff continued back towards his office, chuckling as he went. It was one of those situations that really wasn't funny, and yet it was, mostly because if the commissioner would have simply taken care of business when he was called, there would not have been an issue at all. He was glad that apparently Doug was not hurt, as there was no mention of such on the log. He reflected that it was quite possible that the county would see a lawsuit out of the whole business. Still, it was worth a laugh at this point, just because it was so typical of how so many things went in this business.

Sergeant Baker passed by the open door of the sheriff's office and he called out to him, "Roy, are you busy?"

"No more than usual," came the reply as the sergeant stepped back into the doorway.

"What do you know about this accident out on Hwy JJ at three o'clock in the morning? I found Dickie Ravens in here in an uproar first thing. As far as I can tell, he should just be glad Doug Blankenship wasn't hurt or killed."

"Well, I tell you from what I'm hearing, he may have more to worry about than just that. Did you know what Doug was hauling and for who?"

"No. What are you talking about?"

"I just got a report in from the Highway Patrol, as they're the ones who covered the accident at that hour. It seems Doug Blankenship was hauling a small tank of anhydrous ammonia for none other than Dickie Ravens. He told the trooper that he was traveling that late at night so he could go slow and not cause traffic problems since he was hauling that kind of liquid fertilizer. He also claims he'd picked it up for Dickie to save him some money and haul it back himself from up north. Says Dickie's decided to plant corn in those upper fields that his dad hasn't used all these years.

"I dunno, Sheriff," the chief deputy shook his head. "As much trouble as they're having up north with people using the anhydrous ammonia to make meth, and with Dickie always squeezing every penny until Lincoln screams, it's just got me wondering…." He stopped speaking and raised his eyebrows as the sheriff gave him a hard look.

"You really think Dickie Ravens might be involved in a meth-making operation? I mean, I've always thought he was a card or two short of a full deck but I never suspected him of anything that dumb!" The sheriff sat back in his chair without saying anything more.

"They say it's the folks you least suspect sometimes," the sergeant added. "We've certainly had our fair share of cases like that."

"I suppose." The sheriff shook his head at the strange turn of events. "Let's think about it some more and you keep investigating. I just can't imagine Doug Blankenship getting mixed up in that kind of a deal either, but who knows? Maybe I'm the one who just can't see it."

"I'll keep on it," Baker added lamely as he turned towards his own office.

Sheriff Harper sat at his desk, absent-mindedly thumbing through the accumulated papers there when his phone rang. Wanda informed him that a relative of one of the prisoners was requesting to see him. He sighed and told her to bring him back.

Prisoner relatives were often a bigger headache than the

prisoners themselves. At times, they were angry and just needed some place to unload. Sometimes, they were quite certain that the whole problem belonged to law enforcement and not their beloved son, father, brother, or these days, even sister or mother. And at other times, they just needed to talk.

Wanda appeared at the door a moment later, escorting Howard Hulls. He was one of four brothers, and their mother had named them all with an H. Howard was the oldest. Then came Harold, Harland, and the youngest, Harvey. The oldest three were model citizens, and had never been in any trouble with the law but the youngest, Harvey, despite the fact that he was no baby, couldn't stay out of trouble with his drinking. Harold had taken in Harvey's son, Herbert, to raise after Harvey's troubles began, and now it seemed the son had chosen a road similar to his father's.

"Good morning, Sheriff." Howard Hulls, a tall and heavily built man, stepped forward and shook the sheriff's hand before sitting down in front of the large oak desk.

"'Morning, Howard," the sheriff replied. "Can we get you some coffee or something?"

"Oh, no, don't trouble yourself. I won't take much of your time. I just need to talk to you for a minute, if you got the time."

"Sure, sure." The sheriff eased back in his barrel chair. "What can I do for you?"

"Well, Sheriff, I come about my boy, Herbie. Well, I guess I should say Harvey's boy really, but me and the Missus, we've had him now for so long, well, he might just as well be ours. That's how we've always felt about him, especially since we didn't have none of our own. I mean, Harvey has spent enough of his time here in your jail as a drunk and now his son, too. And the Missus, she's real tore up about the fact that here of late, Herbie's been as bad as his daddy drinking, getting into fights at the local watering holes. Well, I ain't telling you nothing you don't already know. He's been here this last time, sentenced to six months in the county jail by the judge for drunk driving. He's fixing to get out in another week or so, and the Missus, she just can't wait. She's all excited about fixing up his room and having him back home and such, and well…"

He stopped speaking and slid his thumbs in behind the straps of his denim overalls and leaned back. "And well, I ain't. There I said it. I just don't want him back. Leastways, not at the house, and I just don't know what to do, because it's gonna cause an awful fuss with her, and well, Sheriff, what do you think?"

Sheriff Harper contemplated the hard-working farmer in front of him. He had known Howard Hulls ever since his own childhood. He was a farmer who lived down the road from his parents' farm. He knew there was not a dishonest bone in his body. He thought about how hard it must have been over the years to have not only a brother like Harvey, but now a nephew who had grown into a son, and neither seemed to be able to leave alcohol alone.

When Dale Harper spoke, his voice was soft and low, with compassion. "I guess my first thought might be, how old is Herbie now?"

"Why, he's 25, nearly 26, Sheriff. He's no little boy anymore. That's what the Missus don't seem to understand. This ain't missing school or skipping a day's work. This is serious! If I understand the law right, about one more trip and that boy'll be on his way to prison for drinking and driving. You tell me if I'm wrong now, but that's about the way I got it figured."

"I don't remember Herbie's case specifics," the sheriff answered. "I'd have to go look and see how many times he's been before the judge, but I'd say you're right or close to it. If not the next time, then the time after that."

"Here's my thinking. His birthday is coming up right after he gets out and I told my Missus I was ready to find him a place here in town. I'd pay to get him started in some little apartment and fix it up nice. I figure to pay for the deposit and first month's rent and get him what he needs to start out, but then he needs to get him a job—something he can walk to, 'cause he ain't got no driver's license with all of this trouble. Now Delores, she thinks that's a terrible idea as she wants him home. But I don't need no grown man out on my farm that's wanting to run to town and drink with his friends. If that's what he's determined to do, having him out on the farm at this age ain't going to change it. He'll just have his worthless friends come and get him, like as not."

"I'd say you're right about that."

"Well, you know I am." Howard let go of his overall straps and leaned forward in his excitement as he continued to explain. It was clear to the sheriff that the man before him had given the entire situation a great deal of thought.

"You see, I got a friend over here that's got the upstairs of one of his rental houses made up into a nice, big apartment, so he wouldn't even have to be in one of those complexes out on the main highway where there's always a lot of parties and stuff. At least that's what I hear goes on there, according to the talk at the Four Leaf Clover. They're always going on about who got arrested, how many times the city police have to go out there, well, you know. Did you have a lot of that when you were on the city force?"

The sheriff nodded. "Oh, a fair amount, there's no doubt. A lot of younger people out there, some with too much time on their hands. They tend to get involved in drinking, a little drugging, domestic stuff. I think you're on the right road here, that a separate apartment might serve a better purpose in this case."

"That's just what I'm saying." Howard gave a tug on his wide-brimmed ball cap, proudly emblazoned with the name Crossland County Feed & Seed, with a John Deere pin fastened to the side. "I think I've about got her figured out, by golly. I appreciate your time, Sheriff. You've told me what I needed to know. It may cause a storm at the house for awhile, but I'm going home to tell the Missus I'm renting that apartment and she'll just have to get used to the idea. Herbie can have his own place in town. It's high time the boy got out on his own. This way, he'll have to get a job and earn his own keep. Thank you, Sheriff, for all your help." He stood up and reached across the desk to pump the sheriff's hand once more before he turned back towards the office door, nearly colliding with Wanda as she came towards him.

"Good to see you again, Miz Wanda," he said as he hurried on.

"What's got him all wired up? I thought he was going to give you a hard time when he came back here and instead he's going out as a happy man!"

The sheriff shook his head with a grin. "It's a gift, Wanda. A true gift from the Heavenlies, as Milagro might say. I didn't do nothing, but that man is convinced I just helped him out, so who am I to argue with him?"

A smile spread across her face as she remembered how many times she had seen the story repeated. She had even told Lou Ann once, when they were talking about the job, that it was amazing how much of his time Sheriff Harper spent serving as the poor man's counselor. He listened, said very little and yet when the person left his office, they felt satisfied to be walking out with an answer to their problem.

"Well, I came back here to tell you there was a nurse from the hospital on the phone. She said you asked her to call about Freddy Ganst, when he's awake."

"Awake?" He was on his feet. "Wanda, get back on that phone and tell her I'm on my way over!"

* * * * *

If the sheriff's boots echoed down the hospital hall today, he didn't notice as he hurried toward the room he had visited a half dozen times in the past several weeks. Upon entering, he found the window blinds were open wider and the morning sunlight was pouring in. Most significantly, however, the young man in the bed was halfway sitting up, with his eyes open, taking in his surroundings. He looked away from the two nurses who were carefully observing the machines that continued to blip and beep as they monitored his changing condition.

"Hey, Sheriff." Freddy Ganst croaked out a greeting from a parched throat, unaccustomed to conversation. "Whatcha doing here?"

"Just stopped by to see how you was doing, Freddy." The

sheriff tried to sound more casual than he felt. "They called and told me you was awake so I thought I'd come by and see for myself."

Freddy grinned self-consciously. "Well, of course I'm awake. Look at that sunshine out there. It's the right time of the day for a man to wake up. Probably past time, knowing me." He tried to giggle at his own joke, but his throat did not cooperate fully and it came out more like a muffled cough.

Freddy tried again. "I mean, what's that to you?" His eyes widened as the realization struck home. "Oh, for all the world, I've gone and done it again! I'm in trouble, ain't I? What is it this time?" One of the machines began to react at a higher rate of speed as he spoke. The blips continued to increase and the older nurse frowned as she wrote down the figures.

"Sheriff, if you've come to question this patient or upset him, I'm afraid you'll have to postpone it. We've just got him back to consciousness and we can't have him--"

"It's all right, nurse. I'm not here to upset him in any way." The sheriff was conciliatory. "Let me continue to talk, if you don't mind. I promise I'll try real hard not to shake him up."

Sheriff Harper turned his attention back to the patient. "Freddy, you got to calm down or they're not going to let me stay. I'm not here to haul you off to jail or anything. I just honestly came by to see how you're doing. You give us quite a scare."

"Sheriff," Freddy's eyes shifted quickly back and forth between the women at the machines and the man before him, "I don't really understand none of this. They ain't told me yet why I'm here or what happened or nothin'. I mean, I can see I'm powerful tore up but just exactly how and why, I got no idea!" Freddy stopped speaking and while the numbers had stopped their upward spiral, they showed no signs of descending any time soon.

"Freddy, look." The sheriff took a step closer to the bed. "Maybe this is not the best time to start asking too many questions. Take a little time. The nurses and the doctors here, they'll tell you what you need to know as far as how you are and all that. Just try to take it easy and not upset yourself."

"Sheriff, I can do that. I can, sure as the world." Freddy took a deep breath, with some difficulty, and slowly let it out again. "See? I'm all calm-like now. I just want to know. Why am I here? I mean, I been terrible drunk before and passed out, sometimes for a day or even two, but this ain't like that, is it? This is lots worse, I can tell. Just let me ask a couple of questions, and you tell me the truth, 'cause I know I can always count on you for that. I'll try not to ask too much, I promise."

Harper glanced at the older nurse, who gave him a small but definitive nod.

"This is the hospital, right? I mean, I can look around and tell that, right?"

The sheriff nodded.

"And this is the Crossland County Hospital, right? I mean, I ain't in any far off city or anything like that?"

The sheriff nodded again. "You're right here at home, Freddy. You was off to the city hospital for a little while, at first, 'cause they were real worried about you but now you're back and looks like you're doing lots better. I mean, you're awake, and you're sitting here talking to me, and---"

"And, and," Freddy interrupted him. "And another thing—what happened to me, really?"

"Well, Freddy, you were in an explosion, a meth lab explosion. You and another feller, you blew up a house." The sheriff tried to say it as gently as possible but it still sounded pretty rough to his ears.

"We what?" Freddy covered his mouth with his hand as he started to laugh, but it quickly turned into a cry of pain. "How could that happen? Meth. Meth. Meth. It's the devil's own drug. There is no doubt that I'm paying him my dues now." He jerked involuntarily and a grimace seized his face as the nerves on the side of his neck with the worst burns contracted.

"And one more thing…" He hissed through his clenched teeth.

"This is the last question for today," the nurse cut in. "After this, Sheriff, he really needs to rest."

"That's fine, that's fine," the lawman reassured her. "I'll go then and come back another time."

"Just one more thing first," Freddy pressed.

"Fine, Freddy, what is it?"

"I gots to know, how long have I been here, Sheriff? Please, tell me that."

Sheriff Harper held his breath for a moment as his eyes fell to the floor. "Well, I'll tell you, Freddy, it's been awhile.

But let's not worry about it now. We can talk about that later."

"No!" The patient's voice was low as it cracked with emotion. "Please, Sheriff, how long?"

Harper sighed. "It's been about five weeks, Freddy."

Stunned silence was the only response.

The visitor reached over to pat Freddy on the shoulder but when he saw him wince from the pain, Dale Harper instantly drew back his hand in regret.

"Sorry, Freddy, I didn't think."

"It's okay," came the soft whisper. "Five weeks, oh my heavenly days! Five weeks in the hospital. How could that possibly be?"

"We'll talk about it another day, Freddy. I promise. Get some rest, some more rest," he finished with a lopsided grin. "I better go."

"Thanks for coming, Sheriff. Thanks for telling me. I'll see you another day." He closed his eyes and all but collapsed back against the pillows piled behind him. Sheriff Harper noticed as he walked out the door, the bleeps on the machine had already begun to decrease.

* * * * *

The visit with Freddy Ganst had not gone like Sheriff Harper had hoped. It might be a long time before Freddy could remember anything, if he ever did. Harper contemplated the white coffee mug on the table before him with the little green clover on its side. He sat in his favorite corner booth at the back of the familiar café. Doreen, crisp and neat in her white starched apron over her pale green uniform blouse, coffee pot in hand, still looked fresh for early afternoon.

"You're studying mighty hard on something," she observed with a smile.

"Been kind of a long day already, you might say," Harper replied, looking up as she poured a topper on his cup.

"Yeah, I heard it didn't start out so good at your place this morning," Clyde Logan, an insurance man with an office up the block, commented from his stool at the counter. He was sitting directly behind Doreen who had to move out of the way for the sheriff to see who was speaking.

Harper simply raised an eyebrow in the man's direction as he peered over his coffee cup.

"Commissioner Ravens was in my office earlier today, going on about how he was going to have Red's job before the day was over. What's her name, the gal that runs your front office? All we ever called her in school was Red."

"Wanda," the sheriff answered quietly, still not certain which direction Logan was likely to take the conversation.

"Wanda. That's it! Yeah, ol' Dickie Ravens was sure fired up on this one. Something about the radio station and how she didn't tell them the truth about him. I'm not right certain what it was all about, but Dickie seemed sure enough she'd be standing in the unemployment line in short order."

"He tends to be that way from time to time."

Clyde Logan frowned as he turned halfway around on his counter stool to look at the sheriff. "What way?"

"Sure of things that he hasn't got any say over." The sheriff continued to keep his voice low.

"Come again?"

"Dickie is all in a big hurry to fire Wanda because he didn't like what she told the radio station. Truth is, she read Dave Weatherly, from the radio station, just what was on the log, nothing more. It's the commissioner's problem if he doesn't like the order of last night's events. That's trouble of his own making. It's got nothing to do with my office staff which, by the way, are my business to hire and fire, not his."

"Well," Clyde chuckled as the sheriff noticed a few other heads turning in their direction to listen, "I figured, like as not, there was another side to this story. So Dickie wasn't telling all of it. Now there's a surprise." Clyde Logan turned back for his lunch special as Doreen set a plate of chicken-fried steak with all the trimmings in front of him.

"That ain't the first time your secretary and Ravens has gone around," quipped one of the retirees who seemed to make the Four Leaf Clover their second home most afternoons. "That seems to me it's becoming a regular event." He smiled, but not in a way that held any amusement for the sheriff who was already getting to his feet.

"All I can tell you, boys, is that it ain't Wanda going over to Dickie's office to pester him. Now you're a bunch of smart ones, sitting here solving the world's problems. Our department has got all we need to keep us busy. We ain't meddling in other officeholders' concerns. Think about that one for awhile." He threw a dollar on the table beside his cup and gave a wave to Doreen as he walked out the door.

"See ya, Sheriff," she called after him. "Hope your day goes better," was all she could think to add. She gave Clyde Logan a stern look for stirring up the whole conversation, but his head was down as he concentrated on the mashed potatoes, gravy, and corn on his plate.

Back in his pickup truck, Sheriff Harper drifted towards the west road out of town. Just driving had long been one of his favorite pursuits to calm a troubled mind and an anxious spirit, a way to forget the Clyde Logans of the world.

This afternoon, however, his truck stopped instead in front of the Foot of the Cross Mission. He got out to circle the building to the west, looking over the path he had taken the night of the fire weeks ago now. He noticed the bright new patch of roofing above and thought that Milagro had not dawdled in getting the needed repairs made once the fire marshal had given his permission. He had to give that woman credit, she knew how to get things done.

He swung a leg over the split-rail fence that formed more of a decorative barrier than a real one between the building, the narrow strip of shoulder, and the paved road. A few yards down, the fence was replaced with barbed-wire fencing that ran all the way to the corner of the lot, where they had cut the wire the night of the fire.

As he slowly walked toward the back porch of Milagro's cabin, he was surprised to see her there, standing alone, with her back to him. He watched her for a moment without making a sound. When he saw the puff of smoke and her hand drop away from her face, he realized why she was out back all by herself.

"I hear those aren't good for you." He broke the silence and she whirled in surprise.

"*Por el amor de los santos!*" she exclaimed. "I did not know anyone was here!"

"Hiding, are you?" He grinned as she dropped the cigarette and quickly tried to step on it. Instead, it rolled off the bottom step of the porch, forcing her to step down to finish the job.

"Oh! I do not want them to see." She tilted her head back towards the main building. "I do not do it very often now. It used to be all the time," she smiled, "but now, well, some days, it is just something you need, no?" She hopped back up on the porch after scooping up the cigarette butt. She dropped it in a small trash container in the corner.

"What are you doing in the back today?" she countered. "The fire marshal said he had all that he needed for his investigation, so we are making the repairs now. Did you see the roof? It looks good, yes?"

"Yeah, it does. Who did that for you?"

She looked surprised. "You do not know? Your Aunt Martha's son, Dennis. He is your cousin, yes? He came here with a friend, another worker, and did it last Saturday. She told me he works for a roofing company in Montgomery City. She asked him to take care of it. They made it look so nice and they did not even charge any money. They came early in the morning and were all done before noon."

"My cousin, Dennis. I hadn't even thought of him. You're right. Those roofers work fast. Gets too hot up there this time of year, otherwise."

She took a few steps out into the yard to stand beside him and gaze up at the new roof. "He was very nice. We fed them lunch and then they went on their way. Martha was funny. She said she does not ask much of her grown sons, but when she does, they are good to come."

"I'd say that would be true," Dale Harper nodded.

"So if your roof is fixed, what's going bad enough in your day that it's got you sneaking onto the back porch for a smoke?"

She shot him a sharp, sidewise look and stepped away to drop down and sit on the porch steps.

"How did you know?" She looked up at him, shading her eyes from the sun with her hand.

"I guess 'cause I'm having the same kind of day myself." He grinned and sat down beside her. "But I don't have no cigarettes."

"Do you want one?"

"No," he laughed aloud. "I've been quit a long time. Don't intend to take that up again."

"Really? I wish I could say that. I do good for a little while, but sometimes…Tell me, how did you quit?"

"Oh, I did it because someone asked me to and at the time, quitting was more important to her than keeping on with it was to me." He leaned back, his elbow resting on the top step.

"Oh, you quit because your wife asked you, yes?"

"Yes."

"That is good but it does not tell me how to do it." She sighed softly as she looked out over the field of flowers that rolled away before them. Wide bands of white and yellow ox eye daisies waved gently in the summer breeze, while clumps of raggedy purple horsemint on slender square stems were sprinkled along the fence line.

"I guess it is like a lot of other things," he mused as he followed her gaze. "You just got to make up your mind to do it and then never turn back."

"I suppose. That is how we do the hard things, no?"

"Yeah, that's the way of it." He picked up a piece of gravel off one of the steps and flipped it out into the field.

"So your day has been *bien feo* as well?"

"Bee-yen, what? Since I'm not sure what that means, I guess I can't say, but it's been an aggravating one so far."

She laughed. "I do not always know the right words. *Bien feo,* pretty ugly, but a friend tells me you do not use the word 'ugly' in that way, so maybe aggravating works better."

She continued. "The roof looks so nice from outside but inside it is not so easy. A man came who said he could fix things but then he tells me that my walls are not plum. That is a fruit, no, so I did not understand. By the time he is finished, he is telling me they are not straight and that I need to tear out this part and that part and rebuild much more than we were planning. He says he works inside the city all the time and if we do not do it this way, we will not pass inspection. So now I do not know. I think maybe he just wants more money, but I am not sure. There are others who have worked on other parts, like the childcare center, and they never tell me these things. He says it is because they are not working on the old motel, and that is true. I just wanted to get the rooms done sooner, you know? And not wait so long, but now I think it will just have to wait."

"So what's this feller's name? If I know him, I might be able to tell you if he's honest or not." He turned to look at her.

"Oh, he is one who stayed here before when he needed a place to stay. He has brothers. You probably know him. Junior, they call him. Junior Ganst."

A wide grin spread across Dale Harper's face. "Yeah, you might want to wait a bit. Junior is not a bad guy, not even a bad carpenter, when he's sober. Probably what he told you about the walls not being true is right, as old as that motel is, what with the way things settle and all. But whether it has to all be torn out or not to meet city codes, that's another story. You ever hear the phrase, a day late and a dollar short? Well, they might have invented that just for Junior, so I know it probably has you in a bad spot but you might be better off to wait for your other workers. Like as not, Junior might get the job half-done and not get around to finishing it."

She nodded. "I see. That may be true."

They sat in silence for a few minutes. The sheriff continued to flick pieces of gravel off the steps onto the dirt in front of them.

"Would you like something to drink? Water, iced tea?" she asked after a few more minutes.

“Oh no,” he sat up straight, “I really should be going. Just stopped to look over the area one more time, last part of the investigation and all.” He hoped the lie sounded convincing.

“I do not mind if you stopped just to talk.” She looked at him directly. “Everyone needs that sometimes.”

“Yeah, they do, don’t they?” He made no move to get up. “So tell me, you said you lived where, San Antonio?”

“Yes.” She dropped her head and studied the black straps of her sandals.

“I always kinda liked that city.”

“You have been there?”

“Years ago, as a soldier. Me and Eddie, we got a weekend pass and went down to the Riverwalk and the Alamo. We did the whole tourist thing. We saw the inside of a couple of cantinas, too, but we were good. Didn’t even get in any fights, just got good and drunk,” he added with a chuckle.

A melancholy little smile crossed her face. “That is quite a distance from the side of San Antonio that I knew. I lived with my father and his wife and their two children in the suburbs.”

“Doesn’t sound like you liked it much?”

“No, it was a difficult time. Now I can see it was that way for everyone, not just me. I was fifteen, a teenager, and not very happy. My mother was dead so I had to come and live with my father, but he did not know what to do with me. We had never met.”

"You'd never met your dad before you came to live with him? Ouch. That had to be tough. How'd that happen?" He focused his full attention on her.

"He had come to El Salvador years before as a church volunteer. He came to work with the poor one summer when he was in college. My mother was the cook's daughter. She and her mother worked for the priests there at the university. They cooked and cleaned. My mother was young, eighteen or so, and very beautiful. I guess you might say the young American did not always keep his mind on his work. After he left, I was born. The priests arranged for my mother to always stay there and work for them, and my father, he sent a little money every month. My mother had a picture of the two of them together, but that is all I really knew of him until she died."

"Whoa. That would be something." Dale Harper shook his head slowly, side to side. "So, here he is the father of a teenage girl from another country who is pretty upset about losing her mother and..."

"And he has an American wife and two little blond children who do not understand much about the girl who has come to live at their house." She stole a sideways glance and grinned at him. "It was pretty ugly. I stayed for almost a year before I found a way out."

"A way out?"

"Well, that is not quite true. A better way to say is that God gave me a way out and I have always been thankful."

He raised an inquiring eyebrow.

"Someone shared with me an opportunity to go to school through the church, where I could live at the school. My father was happy to pay it to get me out of his house, so it was a good thing for everyone. I went to school and then later, I went to work for the church, and now I am here in Serenity. *Serinidad.* It is a good name."

"So, do you still see your dad and his family?" Dale Harper wasn't ready to turn loose of the subject yet.

"Oh, yes, we write or call sometimes. We get along much better, with time and distance. My half-brother and half-sister are in college now. They are good people, even my father's wife, Tracy. She is not a bad person. They just go to work and go to church and do not understand much about the world outside of the one where they live. I have learned to be careful and not talk about things that they do not understand. Then we get along better."

Harper grinned as he watched her hands flutter while she explained. "I guess I understand that better than most folks," he nodded. "There's a lot I see in this job every day that a great many genteel people do not understand and really don't want to know."

"There, then you see exactly what I mean. There are many people like that in the world. It just made me so angry when I was younger. Mostly, I think, because I knew Max could not say he did not know or he did not understand. He lived in El Salvador. He knew. He just liked to pretend he did not." A sigh escaped her. "So now he lives in his world and I live in mine, and that works better. It is more peaceful for both of us."

"So that's what you call him? Max?"

"That is his name. Maxwell Young."

"I heard that but most people call their fathers, Dad

or Pop or Father."

"Most people do not meet their father for the first time at age fifteen," she answered evenly with no smile.

"I suppose that's true." He leaned back on his elbow again, his earlier resolve to leave forgotten for the moment.

"Can I ask you something? Something difficult?" She kept her eyes trained on him as he looked out over the waving flowers in the fields.

"Sure."

"Your Aunt Martha says you were shot when your wife was and that you nearly died. Now you have to go to court for that one day soon?"

"Yeah," he nodded without looking at her.

"That will not be easy."

"No, it won't." He was suddenly on his feet, dusting off his jeans as he stood up.

She remained seated and squinted up at him.

"What?" he asked, as he looked down and his eyes met hers.

"Oh, I just never met anyone before…" Her voice trailed off and she didn't finish the thought.

"Never met anyone like what? Like me?" he asked, somewhat amused.

"I never met anyone before," she held his eyes and chose her words deliberately, "who lived through his own murder."

*****

Dale Harper was back in his truck driving as he mulled over her last words. As fast as she'd said it, one of the older children had appeared at her door, saying the cooks had sent him to look for her. She had invited the sheriff to stay for lunch, and the aroma of steamed rice and hot beans coming from the kitchen was enticing, but her last comment had thrown him more than he cared to admit. All he could think was that it was time to walk away for a little while.

CHAPTER 12

It had been another sleepless night. As Dale Harper lay in his bed well before dawn, he decided he might as well get up despite the hour. He had just put on his undershirt and blue jeans and was pulling on his boots when the phone rang.

"Sheriff, I'm sure sorry. I don't know what else to say to call you so early and with bad news and all, but I didn't want you hearing it somewhere else, and--"

"What is it, Ernie?" The sheriff tried not to sound as irritated with the late night deputy as he felt.

"Sheriff, we got an escaped prisoner. He was one we had upstairs, but I had him moved downstairs last night. It looked like him and one of the Martin boys were going to come to blows up there in the cell, so before that happened, I thought I'd just move--"

"Who is it?" the sheriff interrupted again. "Who escaped?"

"It's that Kroll guy, Bo Kroll. He just pried up the corner of the ceiling in that back cell. I mean, he was back there by himself, and I figured he couldn't hurt nobody but…"

The sheriff hung up the phone and grabbed his shirt and hat as he headed for the pickup truck parked outside his front door.

This was the problem, he thought again, of converted jail cells. Most of the county jails in this part of the country had originally been built with the sheriff's living quarters incorporated into the jail building. In the last half of the twentieth century, most sheriffs started moving into their own homes with the hope of raising their families anywhere but in the middle of a bunch of prisoners. Many counties, like Crossland, simply did their best to convert an old living room and a couple of bedrooms into more cells. For a prisoner who was not intent on escape, that usually was not a concern, but for others, it just led to more problems. He had already pointed out to Commissioner Ravens that the back corner was a weak point that wouldn't need more than a hearty shove to separate the roof from the walls. A clever prisoner could quickly figure how to wriggle his way out. Promises had been made and he thought he had made it clear to the jailers to be careful who they put in that back cell, but then there was Ernie Wilson.

He turned up the radio and listened to the chatter as Sergeant Baker talked back to the dispatcher. Try not to say too much, he thought to himself. Why is it grown men liked to get on the radio and say stuff they wouldn't say if they were standing right in front of you? The next voice he heard was Jimmy's. He and the sergeant were headed in separate cars towards the railroad tracks at the east end of town where the tracks ran through the woods. If he were an escaped prisoner, Sheriff Harper mused, that is certainly the direction he might run.

He caught up to his men where the tracks crossed one of the side streets at the edge of town. Ernie was in the car with Jimmy as the sheriff walked up to the passenger side of the vehicle.

“Wanda came in when we called her so I could ride with Jimmy and help look for the prisoner, too.” Ernie began to explain himself as fast as the window was rolled down.

“I heard her on the radio.” Sheriff Harper looked down at Ernie who squirmed in the seat.

“Oh, yeah.”

“So what do you think?” The sheriff spoke across the top of their car to Sergeant Baker in the next car over as he pulled up facing the opposite direction.

“I thought we’d cruise through these streets down here, along the tracks,” the sergeant answered. “We found his orange shirt a block or so from the jail, wadded up and thrown down by the curb. Guess he was in too much of a hurry to put it somewhere out of sight.”

“He ain’t the brightest boy.” The sheriff grinned. “Just keep your eyes open, and be careful. I don’t want anyone hurt in this. That means lawmen or prisoner.”

“Omigosh!” The word seemed to leap out of Ernie Wilson’s mouth as he grabbed his belt under an ample waistline.

“What’s the problem?” The sheriff looked down at him again.

“Oh, uh, nothing, I mean. Nothing too serious. I just, uh…”

“Ernie, what is it?” Jimmy’s tone was patient.

"I forgot my handcuffs. I took them off my belt when I was sitting at the desk, and I guess they are still laying there. If we catch up to him, I better have them, but…"

"Here." Harper reached over and unclipped his own from his belt. "Take these. I'm going to circle back to the office anyway to start from there and make sure there's no sign he went in a different direction. I'll pick up another pair."

Ernie Wilson simply was not cut out for the road, Harper thought to himself again.

Sheriff Harper climbed back into his truck after the other two cars had pulled out and began to turn his vehicle around. Still, he could not resist one little pass along the tracks.

The spotlight circles of white from the streetlights spilled across the night, illuminating the twin rails that ran behind the tiny homes. The houses remained dark in these early hours, setting Harper's heart to rest that Kroll had not done something even more foolish than break out of jail. There was nothing to see other than a stray cat as it pitter-pattered swiftly across the street when the sheriff turned the corner.

He was two blocks away when he heard Baker's call over the radio. "Subject spotted near tree line just below Taylor's Crossing. He ran back into the woods when he saw us. Must have been waiting there for the next freight train, since it has to slow down to make the curve before the trestle. We'll be leaving the car to continue pursuit."

"Copy, 356." Wanda's voice was clear and calm.

Sheriff Harper whirled his truck in the opposite direction, spitting gravel as he tromped on the accelerator. He saw the sergeant's cruiser in the distance and turned off his lights as he skirted the woods on the far side from where Kroll had last been seen.

The shirtless man flew out of the woods in such a panic that he almost collided with Harper's front fender. The sheriff spun the wheel and slid to a sideways stop.

"Kroll!" He shouted as he barreled out of the pickup. "Stop! It's my only warning!"

Sheriff Dale Harper drew his .38 and fired it into a nearby tree. Bo Kroll skidded to a halt with his hands above his head.

"Down on your knees! Hands behind your head!" Harper scooted up quickly behind him and reached for the familiar spot on his belt only to come up empty. He bit back the curse that leapt to his lips about the worthlessness of Ernie Wilson.

"All right, you." He reached over and pushed the prisoner's bare, scratched shoulder. Running half-naked through the woods had taken its toll on Bo Kroll. "Face down, in the dirt! Spread eagle. Don't move!"

The prisoner complied without making a sound.

Sheriff Harper kept a close eye on the man as he edged back towards the pickup truck's open door. He ducked inside and pulled the radio mike out as far as the cord would allow.

"Sergeant, I've got your man over here. Would appreciate your assistance, 10-33." He spoke the rarely used radio code sign for rush assistance and was thankful he didn't have to use it often.

"10-4," came the immediate reply. He recognized the extra scratchy sound of the handheld radios they used in emergencies and realized that Baker was still outside of his car.

Harper dropped the microphone and switched on the overhead flashing lights. He noticed his prisoner starting to edge back towards the woods.

"I said, don't move!" The sheriff ordered again but Kroll was already scrambling to his knees.

The sheriff took careful aim and shot into the dirt a foot away from the prisoner, spraying him with dust and gravel. Kroll immediately flattened himself back onto the ground.

"Don't kill me! Don't kill me!" The shaggy-haired man began to wail.

"Don't move again!" Harper walked up behind him and nudged his ankles apart with a boot. "Or the next one'll go in you."

"I won't move," Kroll continued to whine. "Don't shoot me, Sheriff. I won't run no more, I swear."

Cars #356 and #357 careened to a stop on both sides of Sheriff Harper's gold pickup, and the three officers scrambled towards the sheriff and the downed prisoner.

"Get some cuffs on him!" Harper barked at Jimmy. Ernie, trailing along behind, hung his head as he reached back and returned the sheriff's handcuffs to him. Jimmy had the prisoner cuffed and on his feet in seconds, and he and Ernie escorted him back to their waiting car.

"Put him in the drunk tank," Harper called out to his deputy as Jimmy climbed into the driver's seat of his cruiser once again. "I think he better be getting used to that cell. He seems to be spending a lot of time there."

Sheriff Harper leaned against the front fender of his truck as he watched them drive away. Sergeant Baker joined him there as they both stood, arms folded across their chests.

"Well, now what?" Baker broke the silence.

The sheriff shook his head. "We keep Kroll in the drunk tank for awhile and then get him back upstairs in a day or two, or whenever we have a more pressing need for the drunk tank. In the meantime, I want a sign on that back downstairs cell that says *Not To Be Used Except In Extreme Emergency*. Hopefully that will keep fools like Ernie Wilson from putting the more dangerous prisoners in there. I tell you, Roy, some days this job will just wear a man out."

Roy nodded. "I hear ya, especially when the day starts at 5 o'clock in the morning! Why, the milkers aren't even out yet!"

* * * * *

Later that same morning, Sheriff Harper sat in his office and laid out the pieces of a puzzle on his desk. He had lab receipts, notes, bits and pieces, but he could not quite make them all fit. He pushed himself away from the desk and leaned back as far as the old barrel chair would allow. He wondered if he was working the whole matter over too much, trying to make the suspects he had fit the crime, rather than letting the evidence tell him what really happened.

The phone rang and he was surprised to be talking to the

hospital once again.

"Freddy Ganst asked me to call you." The sheriff recognized the voice of the young nurse who had spoken to him a couple weeks ago when he had stopped by to visit a still-comatose Freddy. "He says he would like to talk to you, if you have time."

Harper sat up straight as he spoke into the phone. "You tell him, I'll make time!"

* * * * *

Sitting in the back of the courtroom, Dale Harper had watched the whole day as prospective jurors had come and gone. He had listened to the prosecutor's questions and the defense lawyer's objections. It all had such a surreal feeling to it. He had lived through this once. He wasn't sure he could do it again. Cooper James, the young prosecutor, knew he was here, but he had allowed him to sit quietly in the back. That's all he wanted to do. His mother had even called last night from Florida, asking once again if he was sure she shouldn't come. And do what? he had asked her. It was enough he had to live through it all again. He wouldn't ask anyone else to do that. Once the jury had been seated and the judge had given them the preliminary instructions, the judge released them all for the day to begin again in the morning.

It was good to be outside in the brightness of the day. As the sunshine washed over him, he drove back to Serenity in a more leisurely fashion than normal. He had an appointment, but Eddie would be late. He always was.

Dale Harper parked in front of the Foot of the Cross Mission and waited a few minutes before getting out of the truck. Still no sign of Eddie's beat up pickup truck.

"Good afternoon, Sheriff," Milagro greeted him as he came in the front door.

"Good afternoon, yourself," he smiled upon seeing her. "Eddie said he would meet us here, but you know, he is always late."

She shrugged and smiled back. "It is not a problem. There is no hurry, yes? The children are playing out on the patio in the water. We have some chairs on the side where we can stay dry, I hope. I thought we would just watch for awhile, if you think that will be all right with Eddie. Maria plays well with the other children, and that way he can see her, but since she does not really visit, not the way other people do." She wrinkled up her nose as she looked at him.

He laughed in spite of the day he had endured so far. "I'm sure that will be fine with him."

Eddie came in the door behind the sheriff. "Sorry, sorry," he began to apologize.

"There is no need," Milagro came across the room and put out her hand. "You must be Eddie. It is a pleasure to meet you. Please come in."

Eddie relaxed and slapped Dale on the shoulder. "So this is Miss Milagro? Nice to meet you, too. I've heard lots of good things."

"Surely not from this grumpy character," she teased as she cast a sideways glance at Dale Harper.

"Hey, I've been nice, or at least, nicer than the stuff I've told you about him." The sheriff made a lame attempt to defend himself. "He's the one you have to watch out for!"

"If he is a friend of yours that is probably true," she shot back.

"Oh, she is a sassy one." Eddie grinned at his friend.

Milagro ignored both their comments, except for a very small smile. "Come this way, gentlemen. We shall have something cool to drink while we sit and watch the children play."

The men followed along behind her gentle samba as she led them through the building to the back courtyard. Harper was pleasantly surprised to see all signs of the fire had been erased. New walls had been erected at the far corner of the courtyard. Several small children were running through a lawn sprinkler that was providing a cooling afternoon activity while wetting down the concrete.

"Omigosh, is that her? Look at her. She's beautiful." Eddie's hushed voice was reverent as he stopped and stared at the dark-eyed beauty who leapt over the sprinkler with all the grace of a young gazelle.

"I think she is, but then I may be a little prejudiced." Milagro took his arm to gently guide him over to the chairs and small table she had arranged on the far side.

"Oh, no," Eddie continued without taking his eyes off of the squealing, dancing children. "You are right. She really is special, isn't she? You can just see it."

Dale Harper sat to one side and watched his friends marvel at the small child before them. "You're both right," he cut in with a chuckle.

"Oh, Dale," Eddie turned to him, with unexpected tears in his eyes. "I never imagined…" He stopped speaking and took a gulp of his iced tea while he regained his composure. "I'm just glad I came," he finished.

"Me, too. How she's doing?" Dale Harper turned to Milagro who had sat down beside him with a glass of lemonade in her hand.

"As you can see, she gets along well with the other children. She does not speak yet, not really. We know that she is able, but I think more will come with time. She listens well and does many things I ask her to do like come, sit here, take this to our house, and things like that. In this way, I know she understands me. I still speak to her most of the time in Spanish because in the beginning, that was the only thing she responded to, but now she also listens and does pretty well with Martha and Anna Mae in English. I have to say, she still is not very fond of men. They seem to make her nervous, but that is from her circumstances, no?"

Sheriff Harper nodded. "I'd say you're right there. She's had a lot to deal with in such a young life."

Milagro continued. "She loves to listen to Anna Mae read books and she loves to run with the other children. We have not begun any real schooling with her yet, and that will be a new challenge we shall have to begin soon, but I think it will not be as difficult as we first thought. She loves the whole idea of books and I have seen her looking and going over them again after the readings are finished. She turns each page carefully and looks it all over in a very serious manner, as if she is reading it to herself, over and over again. Like I know I have told you before," she stopped to look at the sheriff on her right, "I think she is very smart. It may not take as long as we first thought for her to catch up in everything."

"I hope you're right." The sheriff nodded as he watched her

play in the water with the others. “It will certainly make life easier for her and for everyone else if that’s the way it works out.”

“Oh, I forgot to tell you. I took her to the doctor last week. I explained the circumstances, and she said she is fine, healthy in every way. She says there is no physical reason for her to be silent. She was surprised she was doing so well and that she thought she might be about eight years old.”

Eddie sat and watched like a man mesmerized. “I just never would have thought…” He shook his head slightly as he spoke. Finally, he looked at Milagro. “Thank you so much. Do you mind,” he stopped and cleared his throat and continued in a low voice. “Would you mind if one day I brought my father to see her? I know it would mean a lot to him.”

“Of course.” Milagro smiled at the simple request. “That would be wonderful. He should see his granddaughter, yes?” She turned back towards the children and called Maria by name. The wet, glistening child trotted over towards Milagro, followed by two of the others. She stopped partway, however, when she recognized the sheriff and saw the other man with him.

“Está bien, está bien,” Milagro encouraged her. *“Ven aca.”*

Maria continued to move forward, but hesitantly. When she got close enough, Milagro reached out and pulled her close and whispered in her ear.

Maria instantly put out her hand to Eddie and he took the tiny cool, wet hand and solemnly gave her a proper handshake. He told her how pleased he was to meet her.

She murmured a barely audible, "'ello" but stepped away, closer to Milagro, as soon as he released her hand. A breeze swept across the patio and she shivered as did her two damp companions who stood back a few paces watching the proceedings with great curiosity.

"It is almost time to turn off the water. You can play a few minutes more, but then it will be time to find your towels before you are too cold." Milagro spoke to all of the children in English and then repeated the same phrases in Spanish for Maria. The children whirled and ran back to their make-believe waterfall and began leaping once more through the falling water drops.

"I love watching them like this," Milagro mused, her attention focused on the sprinkling droplets and those who danced beneath them. "They are not bothered by the problems of the world when they are like this."

"No, they certainly aren't," Dale Harper agreed. "Maybe we all need to be running through the sprinkler once in awhile."

"It might be nice," she nodded with a smile.

Eddie finished his glass of tea. "Thank you so much." He took one of Milagro's hands in both of his. "Thank you for taking such good care of her and for sharing her today. My father has told me more than once that he still prays that he might have grandchildren in his old age. Now I can tell him that his prayers have been answered."

"That is part of the business that we do here." Milagro patted Eddie's hands with her free hand. "Sometimes, I think it is the best part of what we do."

Eddie looked back at his newfound niece. "She even

moves a lot like my brother, Albert, when we were kids. He always looked like a deer running through the woods. Do you remember that, Dale?"

"You know, I had forgotten until you mentioned it, but it's true. He could always run well. Of course, as I remember, we were always after him for something, so maybe he learned to run so fast because we were always chasing him."

Eddie grinned and stood up. "Maybe so. I've got to go. Hey, I'll catch up to you later this week, Bro'." He headed towards the doorway leading to the front door. "It's all right. I'll show myself out," he told Milagro as she started to follow him.

"Are you sure?"

"Yeah, yeah. It's fine. Thank you again." And he was gone.

She turned back to Dale who was still seated watching the yellow and green lawn sprinkler as it spun around. "Do you think he is all right? I mean, he left so suddenly. I just hope he was not upset or…"

"No, at least, not in the way that you think. If he could get his hands on his brother right now, that might upset everybody but since that's not going to happen, I think he'll be okay. It's just going to take some time for it to all sink in. It'll probably be the same for his dad, but overall it'll be a good thing. After they've had a little time, I'll sit down with some of the jail records and we might be able to narrow that time line down for you. We should be able to get pretty close to when she was born."

He shifted his attention from the children to the woman at his side. "So you're an answer to prayers now? That's pretty good."

"Oh, I imagine you have been many times, too, when people are in one kind of trouble or another." She deflected the compliment with ease. "But that is not what you were thinking about just now, no?"

"What?" Her question brought him up short.

"Just as Eddie left, you were watching the children and the sprinkler, but I see you are thinking of something different. Something more serious."

"You are so right." He snapped to his feet. "It took me a minute, but I just realized that something has been bothering me and I couldn't put a finger on it before. Sorry, no time to explain. I've got to check something out. Thanks for being so good to Eddie…and Maria. I appreciate it." He leaned in close as if to embrace her but then checked the impulse and drew back abruptly. He turned towards the door and was gone before anything more could be said.

Sgt. Roy Baker found his boss making his way through the items they had confiscated when they searched Carley Dunstan's place of business. With Dunstan's employee, George, as one of the suspects in the meth operation at his own house on Polk Street, they had secured a search warrant and gone looking, but they found nothing that matched up with the methamphetamine operation. The sheriff had considered getting one of the narcotics officers from the state patrol to come in with a drug dog, but he didn't have anything to support it and he didn't really want to do battle with Carley's lawyer if he didn't have anything more substantial. Still, sitting at the mission this afternoon watching the yellow and green plastic parts of the sprinkler going around reminded him of the yellow and green sprayer they had taken into possession at the same location.

It occurred to him that there might be something more to that part of the investigation.

"What are you doing back here?" Baker asked as he stepped into the storage locker attached to the back of the sheriff's department where they stored items held in evidence.

"Looking for that weed sprayer we picked up at Carley Dunstan's place. Which one of these cubicles is it in? Do you remember?"

"Well, sure. Just check the log right there in the computer. I tell you, Sheriff, I have this organized. I really do," Baker began to explain himself.

"I'd rather you check the stuff in your own computer," came the flat response. He could do what he had to with computers when the need arose, but he didn't like to admit he wasn't as comfortable with them as most of his staff.

Roy Baker walked over to the laptop sitting on the evidence room desk and pulled up the page he was after. "You knew the city cops picked up George this afternoon, didn't you?"

"What?" came the surprised reply.

"George O'Brien. The city found him trying to sneak into the back part of his house this afternoon. I'd heard you on your radio earlier, telling Dispatch that you were back in town from the court proceedings in Miller County so I thought you knew about it already."

"No, I didn't know. I was out of the truck for awhile, down at the mission with Eddie and Milagro. A bit of personal business really. So where is George now?"

"I'd say he should be in a holding cell about now, all booked in. The city was bringing him over to lock him up on our warrant for questioning."

"Good. We need to have a chat with young Mr. O'Brien as soon as I get another look at that sprayer."

"Sure. Here it is, right over here in bin #16." He walked over, tilted out the basket, and pulled the sprayer out.

Sheriff Harper walked over, unscrewed the top and took a tentative sniff. A flat smile of confirmation spread across his face. "Have a whiff yourself," he said as he extended the plastic container towards Baker. "Tell me if that smells like any insecticide you ever heard of."

* * * * *

George O'Brien looked like the proverbial scared little boy in his oversized jail oranges as he was led into the interrogation room. The sheriff stood at the one-way window and watched him for a few moments before turning towards Baker.

"Give me a few minutes and then bring that sprayer in from my office, if I need it," were his only instructions.

"George." The sheriff nodded to the prisoner as he walked in and sat down across the table from him. He laid a piece of white typing paper and a small tape recorder on the table between them. He clicked on the tape recorder and then flipped over the paper and carefully read the prisoner's rights to him.

"You got all that?"

George nodded and exhaled a barely audible, "Yes, sir."

"Whatcha been up to lately, George?"

The young man's eyes frantically circled the room looking for a way out. A sheepish grin crossed his face as he looked down and then back up at the sheriff. His eyes continued to flit from side to side, as if he was having trouble controlling them.

"Oh, Sheriff, you know me," his voice came out, half an octave higher than usual. He cleared his throat and tried again. "I'm not doing nothing. I let some guys stay with me 'cause they said they didn't have nowhere to go, and they went and blew up my place. Suzie's gonna be so mad when she finds out."

"Where is Suzie?"

"Huh?"

"You heard me, where is Suzie?"

"I dunno, Sheriff. I sure don't. I mean, I ain't seen her now in a couple of days and…"

"George, it's been weeks since your house blew up, and you and her have both been missing all that time. Now why don't you tell me where you been and what you've been doing? You know we're going to find it out one way or another, before it's all said and done."

"Now, Sheriff, it ain't like you think. We ain't been up to nothing all that bad. We were just having a little fun and it got kinda crazy is all. We didn't mean nothing by it. We never meant for nothing bad to happen to nobody."

"Like, nobody who? Like Freddy Ganst?"

"I don't know what you mean, Sheriff." George swallowed hard and his eyes began to roam the four walls around him again.

"What I mean, George, is I found Freddy on your front lawn, closer to dead than alive, after your house blew up. I got a word or two out of the other feller involved saying he was supposed to shut somebody up. Now was that you or was that Freddy? Maybe he was supposed to blow up both of you. What do you think?"

"Oh, I don't think it was me, Sheriff. I didn't do nothing. I wasn't even there when it happened. He sent me over to the shop to get some…" George stopped speaking and hung his head.

"He who? Who sent you where?"

"Booger," came the barely discernible whisper.

"Booger. Who's that?"

"Booger. The big guy with lots of hair. You got him in the cells upstairs. You ain't gonna put me in with him, are you? You can't do that, Sheriff. He'll kill me if he gets the chance. I know he will."

"I thought you weren't worried it was you he was trying to hush up. Changed your mind, have you?" The sheriff leaned back in his chair as if he had all the time in the world.

George remained quiet for a few minutes more, but he began to twitch as he sat on his chair.

"Well, I just don't know, George. Cell space is pretty limited these days, and I don't know where everybody is liable to end up, you know."

"Oh Sheriff, you gotta protect me. That Booger, he's a bad one, I tell you. You can't put me up there where he can get at me. You've known me all my life. You know I ain't a bad one like that."

Dale Harper brought his hand down flat and hard on the table, making the prisoner leap at the slamming sound. The tape recorder nearly jumped off the table. "Dang straight I've known you all your life, George, and I gotta say I've never seen you mixed up in anything like this before. But there's always a first time. Now give me some straight answers quick, before I escort you upstairs myself!"

"All right, all right." George took a deep breath and made an attempt to calm himself. "What is it you want to know?"

"I want to know what your part is in this meth-making operation, for starters."

The sheriff leaned back and listened as George spoke and the tape rolled on. When the prisoner was finally silent, the sheriff nodded. "That's good, George. We need to know it all."

"I just thought…" George started again. "I mean, you've always known me, Sheriff. I ain't never really had nothing. They told us we could make some money with this, me and Suzie. I just thought if we could get ahead a little bit, you know, but when they started cooking that stuff in our house. Oh man, nothing was ever right after that."

"I don't doubt that, George. I don't doubt that at all. Now I got just one or two more questions for you." He waved his hand, and Sergeant Baker appeared at the door with the sprayer canister.

Although it did not seem possible, George sank even lower in his chair at the sight of the garden sprayer.

"What can you tell me about this thing?" the sheriff asked.

"Where did you find that?" George's voice was barely a whisper.

"Where do you think we found it?"

"Well, it was at the house at first. I mean, it was part of the makings, you know, but after that…" His words trailed off.

"After that, it was at your place of employment. That's where we got it. I want it all, George. Where's the truck and who was with you?"

"I knew it. I knew it. He said he was taking the truck back to Montgomery City, and I started to throw that thing back in there, and then he pulled it out and--"

The sheriff waved him off. "He, who, George? I need names here."

"Well, Mr. Dunstan had the truck. He told us where to go and how to do it, but it was Booger who pulled the sprayer off at the last minute. He said we might still need it at the house. I told him it was all ruint, what with having the diesel mix in it, but he said he'd clean it. Stupid, that's what he is. Stupid. For a lousy twenty dollar sprayer, he's pulled it all down on us." He sat there with his hands tucked under his thighs and leaned forward to rest his forehead on the table. The sheriff wondered briefly if he was going to cry. He hated it when they cried.

"George, back up a little more."

The sheriff continued until he got the details he needed on tape and then he called for Sgt. Roy Baker to escort George back to the jail cells.

"There was a phone call for you while you were in there, but I went ahead and took it," Baker explained briefly while he cuffed George's hands behind his back.

"Who was it?"

"Suzie."

"Suzie called me?" The sheriff frowned in his confusion.

"Well," Baker chuckled a bit, "she was really calling for George."

The prisoner picked up his head as an expectant look came over his facc. "Is shc okay?" he asked.

"Seems she's in jail in Montgomery City, but they allowed her to call because the judge is letting her out."

"He is?" George looked surprised.

"He's letting her out of jail because she signed herself into thirty days worth of drug treatment. She called because she just wanted to find out where you were and let you know what she was doing."

The sheriff cleared his throat. "Sounds like Suzie is doing the smart thing, George. If and when you get out of this mess, you'd be wise to do the same."

George hung his head but not before Harper caught a

glimpse of the tears in his eyes. "Suzie, oh Suzie," came out in a whisper.

Sheriff Harper finally had the pieces of the puzzle he needed. Now to make them fit.

* * * * *

Twenty-four hours later, Sheriff Harper was sitting back in his own office. Another day spent in Miller County court, watching and listening to the proceedings, was behind him and this afternoon Carlton Dunstan was coming to his office. It had not taken a lot to convince Judge Billy Joe to sign a warrant charging Dunstan with conspiracy to manufacture methamphetamine and another for conspiracy to commit arson. He had taped information from two men, George O'Brien and Freddy Ganst, as well as bits and pieces of information from Bo "Booger" Kroll. To get more, however, the sheriff knew he would have to move carefully. He could have gone out to Carlton Dunstan Enterprises but Carley would simply have shut his mouth and called his lawyer. Sheriff Harper wanted more, a lot more, and he was hoping that the casual approach, might be the key.

His phone rang. "He's here," is all Wanda said.

"Bring him on back," he said and hung up the phone.

"Carlton." The sheriff stood up, welcomed him to his office, and showed him a caned chair in front of his desk. "Have a seat. I appreciate you coming by. I just had a few questions to clear up in regards to this case we've been working on."

Carley Dunstan tried to look less nervous than he felt, but the attempt was not particularly successful. His hand shook slightly as he reached into his jacket pocket for a cigarette pack and lighter. “Do you mind?” he asked as he lit up.

“No, not at all,” the sheriff lied as he pulled an ashtray out of a bottom drawer and passed it across the desk. “Hey, you don’t mind if I record this, do you?”

The sheriff whipped the same small tape recorder out of his desk drawer that he had used earlier when talking to George. He set it in the middle of an otherwise empty desk and clicked it on. “I mean, it’s just a few little things, but I want to be sure I get them right.”

“Well, I suppose that will be all right.” Carley Dunstan seemed more than a little confused.

“This is a conversation between myself and Carlton Dunstan on June 30…” The sheriff droned on with a few more details.

“I’m sure you know we’ve got a couple of your employees here in jail,” Sheriff Harper began.

“A couple? You have George O’Brien here, I believe, and he is a former employee. I hardly know a thing about the boy, really. I mean, I hired him at a time when we were short of help. Who knew he was involved in such illegal activities? It’s like I told you the day you came over to serve that search warrant I was completely in shock. You know, one expects that this sort of low level employee may be involved in some illicit activity from time to time but certainly nothing like this. I mean, it is just such a shock--”

The sheriff leaned back in his barrel chair until it creaked loudly. “Carlton,” he said softly, “I got statements from George and Freddy Ganst and even from Kroll. Now you want to go on with this?”

"You got nothing from Kroll! He wouldn't dare tell you a thing!"

"He wouldn't, heh? Now what makes you so sure?"

"Kroll wouldn't tell you anything," Carlton took a long draw on his cigarette and then leaned forward with a conspiratorial whisper, "because I know where he's got a body buried."

The sheriff smiled, but there was no warmth behind it. "We've got the body, too," the sheriff continued. "I've got statements from George and Freddy linking you to their meth operation and I'm sure to the one Kroll had going up there on the Federal land. You're no insurance salesman, Carley. I had a little chat with Clyde Logan the other day and even your own cousin, Commissioner Ravens, doesn't buy insurance from you. And you ain't repairing mobile homes over there either."

"Now, you can't prove that." Carlton Dunstan waved an unsteady finger at the sheriff.

"I don't have to. When we came with the search warrant we thought maybe you were making the stuff there, but you were too smart for that. No, you're using the mobile homes to ship it in from California and the Mexican border, in addition to the stuff you make here. Now that means you're shipping it across state lines, and that has the Feds interested. As a matter of fact, they should be arriving at your place in short order with their warrants. They will, of course, have dogs and some pretty sophisticated equipment."

Carley gave up the battle of trying to conceal his true feelings. "What kind of a scam are you running here, Sheriff?" He jumped to his feet. "I don't have to sit here and listen to this! You say there are Federal officers at my place? Then I'm out of here. I have a business to protect." He threw his cigarette on the carpet and stomped on it as he turned to charge out the door.

The sheriff was also on his feet, coming swiftly around the desk. "Sorry, Carley, but I'm afraid you do have to stay just awhile longer." He brought his hand down roughly on Dunstan's shoulder and pulled him momentarily off his feet. He caught him against the wooden door with a loud crash, which brought a deputy headed his way from near the front desk.

"No problem, no problem." The sheriff waved him off. "We're just having a little discussion back here. We're doing fine." He turned his attention back to the thin man in front of him, who seemed to be shrinking with every passing moment.

"Come on back in here and sit down," Sheriff Harper continued in an even tone. "I've got a couple warrants to read to you." He returned Carley Dunstan to his chair, sat back down at his desk, and proceeded to read the warrants aloud to him, as well as his prisoner's rights statement.

Once finished, he laid the papers aside and looked across his desk at Carley Dunstan, who was hunched forward, slowly shaking his head from side to side.

"What I really want to know here, Carley, is why? Why burn the mission? I can understand the drug dealing and the cooking as a money-making operation but the mission? What was that about?" The sheriff leaned across his desk, imploring the man before him to give him some answers.

"Because she just wouldn't shut up." Carley Dunstan had started to rock gently back and forth in his chair, his feet planted firmly on the ground. “She shoulda never come back here, that old lady, getting people all stirred up over that old case. I mean, they were talking about it everywhere. When I went into the Four Leaf Clover one day they was talking about it, and at the post office, and the bank. Everywhere I went. When I’d walk in they’d stop talking and they’d look at me, like they thought I didn’t know. But I knew. I always knew. She just needed to go back where she came from, that’s all. Then people wouldn’t have to think about it no more.”

Harper kept a close eye on his prisoner in case he decided to bolt for the door again. “What old case is that?” he asked in a hushed tone.

“Oh, Sheriff, you know.” Carley turned his face up to meet the sheriff’s and the look in his eyes reminded Dale of his conversation months earlier with Milagro about the meaning of *malicia* and the presence of evil.

“You’ve been asking about it, too,” Dunstan continued. “I know you have. Too many questions, too much talk.”

“Tell me which case, Carley,” the sheriff repeated.

“The one with that dumb kid, out there at my mother’s place, all them years ago.”

The sheriff noticed the longer Carley talked the more he sounded just like what he was, what he had always been, one of the local boys. “Where she went and got herself killed and the kid, too. If that old lady had just not come around, nobody would be asking, nobody would be talking, I tell you. People had done forgot all about it until she showed up.”

“You think your sister forgot?”

"Carol? Miss Perfect? Well, of course not," he snorted, "but even she don't talk about it. She never says nothing. She just don't talk to me at all. She's too good for that."

"Is that what she says?" The sheriff raised an eyebrow as he played into Carley's psychosis.

"Oh no, she would never say anything like that," Carley went on as if they were discussing something as inconsequential as the weather. "She just looks at me and she knows. And I know she knows that's what makes it so hard." He dropped his head and looked at the floor again as if he had found something quite fascinating there.

"Well, Carley, I got to say you're right. I have been asking a few questions and I found a few things." The sheriff opened his top desk drawer and pulled out the lab reports he had collected and the papers his father had left behind in the old case file.

"You see, here's a note left in the file from all those years ago. It shows that the gun found at the scene was in Rupe's right hand. Rupe was the boy who got shot that day. But the thing is, when I started talking to his people, I found out Rupe was really left-handed. And then here's a report I just got back from the state lab that shows your DNA is a match for the skin that was found under your mother's fingernails the day she died. Did you know about that, Carley? See, the sheriff back then, he left me some notes and--"

Carley Dunstan looked up slowly. "That sheriff, he was your dad, wasn't he?" He didn't wait for an answer. "I remember him. He was a big man, not like you. He was lots bigger."

"I don't know, Carley. Your dad is always bigger, if you know what I mean, just because he's your dad."

"He asked me a lot of questions, back then. Kinda of a scary guy 'cause he just kept asking." Carley Dunstan squinted at the sheriff. "Maybe you are like him, after all. You just keep asking questions, too."

"Well, maybe so." Harper's head was reeling at the surreal conversation, and yet he felt compelled to continue.

"So here's these other reports I got. One from the state highway patrol showing most of the serial number of that gun, that Walther PPK. Did you know it was one of the first ones imported and sold out in California all those years ago? Did you know the state of California has gun permits going back for years? That's where this report is from." He laid out another page from the desk drawer. "It tells who the original owner of that gun was. A guy named--"

"Do you know how dumb that kid was?" Carley's eyes were roaming wild, and this time, Harper suspected their conversation would soon be coming to an abrupt end.

"What?"

"Do you know how dumb that kid was?" He repeated. "I mean, he was watching me for I don't know how long. That's why I had to do it. Me and my mother got into it. Really, we were into it ever since I first got back from California. Nothing I did was right, but that wasn't no surprise. She was always on me, like a duck on a June bug, but when I found out she was going to sell the property to the highway department and put all the money in Carol's name, now that was too much! Didn't I have as much right to any of it as she did?" His voice rose to a high pitched whine as he continued.

" She was my sister, but I was born first. Don't the first born have some rights? The Bible even says so. She was such an all-fired mighty fine Christian but then she was going to cut her first born son out of everything. How do you like that?" He slapped his thigh as if he had just told a good joke.

"We got into it and she jumped on me, screaming that she was sorry I ever came back! She put a big ol' set of scratches down my neck, and they hurt like the devil, so I went and got that gun. Yeah, I brought it back from California with me. You never know when you might need something like that. I wasn't going to do anything with it, except let her know that I could take care of business if I had to. And you know what she did?"

Harper held his breath as he shook his head slightly.

"She laughed at me. She called me a little boy and told me I was a fool. She said she'd tried her best, but I would never amount to nothing, and she wasn't going to leave her money to nothing. Now I can't say I meant to shoot her but when she said that, well, it's like I just couldn't take no more and I pulled that trigger. Just once but it was enough." He closed his eyes, leaned his head back against the wall behind the chair, and put his hand to his forehead like he suddenly had a headache.

"I didn't see them scratches until afterwards, and then I knew I had to do something to cover 'em up. The boys she'd hired had been out in the field all day haying. She'd sent me out there to help, and I did for awhile. We were picking up them little square bales like we all used back then, and when I fell off the hay wagon, them boys all laughed at me. That's when I knew I'd had enough and I went up to the house to tell her so. And that's how we got into it all again." He stopped speaking and dropped his hand to his side, but his eyes remained closed.

"What about Rupe?" the sheriff dared to ask. "What did he have to do with it?"

The crooked grin that spread across Carley's face was made all the more ominous by the fact that his eyes remained closed as his face was tilted towards the ceiling. "That dumb kid. He stood there and watched me in the barn as I threw myself out of the hayloft to hit that last load of hay still sitting on the wagon down below. I figured if I had enough scratches from the hay 'cause those boys all seen me fall off that wagon, it would account for those long scratches on my neck. Had to throw myself out of that loft a couple of times to get scratched up enough. Then I turned and there was that kid, standing at the barn door, watching me. Never said a word, just watched, he did. When I finally saw him, that's when he asked me, what was I doing that for?" A distant smile crossed his face as a derisive laugh rose up from deep in his throat. An icy chill swept over the sheriff at the sound of it.

"After that, I just walked him into the house. He was so busy worrying about her being on the floor, he got right down beside her. He never knew I was coming up behind him." He stopped speaking and the sheriff was thankful for the silence. He had heard and seen a lot of dreadful things in this job. He would forever consider this to be one of them.

Sheriff Dale Harper reached over and clicked off the tape recorder. He picked up the phone and quietly told Wanda at the front desk to send a deputy back to his office to take Carley Dunstan into custody. He finally had some answers for the Jensen family after all these years.

Chapter 13

Dale Harper sat ramrod straight, in the first row of the Miller County courtroom. True to his word, Eddie was ready bright and early to make the long ride with him. Side by side, they were immediately behind the prosecutor's table. The courtroom had been nearly empty when they entered. As they waited, Dale Harper listened to the stirrings and noise behind him that let him know that more people were coming in.

The young prosecutor assigned to the case by the state, Cooper James, offered Harper a seat at the front table, but he had declined. There was no need. He could see more than he cared to from where he was and he had no desire to be any more in the spotlight than necessary. The young prosecutor had treated him with respect and decency from his first day on the case and Harper had spent enough time with the attorney in the last many months to come to respect his talent and education. The elected Crossland County prosecutor, Fred Sutherland, who was just a year from retirement and a long time associate in law enforcement, had recused himself from the case from the beginning. Harper didn't blame him. It was a case that offered nothing but misery to all of them.

Harper's attention was directed to the left side of the room as the silver-haired Walter Barrington made his way into the courtroom. He looked as calmly impeccable as he always did on television, the sheriff thought. Not so for his younger associate, Charles Graham, who seemed to be everywhere at once.

Eddie leaned over and gave voice to his own thoughts. "That kid looks like a flea on a hot griddle. I hope he don't keep jumping around like that once this thing gets going. Although I guess if he does, it'll make things pretty interesting."

Harper shot his friend a sideways glance, but the look on Eddie's face said he was anticipating a long, uneventful day.

One of the two bailiffs escorted the defendant, Rodney Sherwood, into the courtroom from a side door. It had been almost a year since Harper had last seen him, and he was impressed, as he was certain the jury would be, that he looked quite presentable in his trim brown suit. His hair has been cut and he, or rather his lawyer, had apparently secured permission from the judge for Rodney to wear street clothes to his trial instead of his prisoner oranges. The defendant wore no handcuffs or shackles of any kind, which Harper did find surprising until he noticed that his former brother-in-law walked with a newly acquired limp. It was then that the sheriff realized he was wearing a stiff-leg, a special leg brace that fit under a man's clothing, out of sight of the jury, but that would not allow him to run if Rodney decided once again to flee. The bailiff seated him at the defense table and Walter Barrington immediately leaned over to confer with his client.

Harper's former in-laws, Rodney's parents, Preston and Brenda Sherwood, sat directly behind him. They had done their best to avoid making eye contact with Harper since they had arrived. Harper wasn't sure he didn't feel the same way about them, but he didn't have time to think about it.

The judge entered the court and everyone rose at the bailiff's instruction.

The judge promptly reminded all present that the day's proceedings were the continuation of an ongoing trial. "Mr. James, call your first witness."

"The prosecution calls Dale Harper to the stand," came the young prosecutor's booming voice.

As he stood to walk forward, Dale Harper noticed his knees felt funny, the way they did sometimes after a big rush of excitement, like the night Bo Kroll came running out of the woods in front of his truck. He forced himself to walk calmly, hold up his right hand and repeat the oath. He sat down in the witness chair as he reminded himself he had testified in court before. It always made him nervous, and while today would be different, he knew he just had to get through it once.

For the first time he looked up at the standing-room-only crowd. How it was that he could pick her out of the crowd so quickly he had no idea, but just the same, there she was, sitting next to his Aunt Martha. Milagro! She was the last person he expected to see in the crowd, and now Cooper James was speaking to him. He had to concentrate on what was being said.

"Please state your full name for the record."

"Dale Thomas Harper." His voice sounded extraordinarily flat, he thought.

"And what do you do for a living, Mr. Harper?"

"I'm a county sheriff," he tried again, but it still sounded strange.

"For which county?"

"Crossland County."

"So," the prosecutor swung around on his heel as he asked Harper the questions, but directed much of what he was saying to the judge, the jury and the roomful of spectators, "I should be calling you Sheriff Harper."

"Objection." Charles Graham, the younger defense lawyer, stood up.

"On what grounds?" The prosecutor sounded almost offended.

"Prejudicial."

"Judge, I assure you," Cooper James began to debate, "this is the man's occupation and proper title, and I see no reason--"

"Overruled!" The judge answered the defense counsel, cutting off the other's argument mid-stride.

"Very well. Sheriff Harper, I know this will be difficult, but would you lead us through, step by step, the events that took place at your home on June twenty-third of last year?"

Dale Harper took a slow, deep breath. He looked up once more to see his Aunt Martha and Milagro, seated side by side. The back door of the courtroom opened quietly, and he saw the unmistakable tall, lean figure of Judge Billy Joe

Randolph quietly enter the courtroom and stand in front of the doors. The judge looked up the long aisle and his gaze rested kindly on the man before him on the witness stand.

After a second or two, the sheriff brought his eyes back down to his hat which he held lightly in his lap with both hands. “Yes sir, I’ll do my best. My wife and I were up and starting on the day, getting dressed, making coffee, that sort of thing. She said she thought the outside door, the front door, was banging in the wind, and she went to close it. I remember she opened the door, and the next thing I knew Rodney had taken a step or two into the living room. He had a shotgun. I don’t really know what he wanted or intended ‘cause he never said a word. He just leveled the gun on the two of us and pulled the trigger.”

“Thank you, Sheriff. Now just a few additional questions. And we should point out for the record, Rodney is Rodney Sherwood, the defendant, who is, or was, also your brother-in-law, your wife’s brother, is that correct?”

“Yes, sir.”

“Do you know how many times he fired the gun that day?”

“No, sir, I can’t say that I do. The only one I heard was that first one. I saw my wife go down, and part of it caught me in the ribs. That’s the last thing I knew or heard until I came to in the ambulance on the way to the hospital.”

“I see.” The prosecutor stepped back towards his table and studied his notes for a moment.

“Sheriff Harper, can you tell us, did you or your wife have some sort of problem with Mr. Sherwood that this court is not aware of?”

“Well, I had problems with Rodney, everybody did, one way or another. He was in trouble all the time, drinking, using drugs, wrecking cars. It had got to the point that his sister had told him the last time he called from jail that she didn’t want him calling the house no more--”

“Objection! Objection!” The young defense lawyer was on his feet again, sounding nearly hysterical. “Judge, this is all hearsay. He is trying to testify to my client’s criminal history.”

“Not too many people know it better than he does!” Eddie suddenly called out from his seat.

“This sort of disruption will not be tolerated in this courtroom!” The judge’s gavel came down as his voice thundered throughout the chamber. “The jury will ignore that outburst. I am quite certain there will not be another!” The judge slammed his gavel once more as he glared directly at Eddie, who squirmed in his seat. “Another like it, and I’ll clear this room.”

The judge returned to the business at hand. “Overruled,” he stated as calm returned to the courtroom.

Dale Harper resumed his testimony. “It was a personal problem as well as a professional one. I mean, he’s my wife’s brother, so when he got in trouble I couldn’t very well lock up my own brother-in-law in the county jail. I sent him to another jail. That’s the usual procedure that most law enforcement officers follow when we have a relative who gets into trouble. It makes for both a personal problem as well as a law enforcement one.”

“And so that was what you did with the defendant, your brother-in-law, Rodney Sherwood? You sent him to another jail?” The prosecutor’s gentle questions continued.

"Yes, sir. I sent him to the Chisolm County Jail, the next county over. That way he's still handy for any court proceedings and it doesn't make it any harder than necessary on the family for visiting and that sort of thing." Dale Harper continued, listening as much to his own disconnected voice as to the prosecutor's questions.

Why did he sound so strange, even to himself? But more importantly, what was she doing here? He glanced back at Martha and Milagro. His mother had called and asked about coming all the way from Florida, but Aunt Martha, she hadn't said a word. He was beginning to wonder but Cooper James' questions kept coming. What was he saying now? Why could he not concentrate? Would he have to ask him to repeat the question? How embarrassing! He would have to concentrate harder. He couldn't be asking the man in front of him to repeat every question.

His gaze drifted to Preston and Brenda Sherwood. Preston looked as if he was made of stone-cold, hard, and unmoving but Brenda's face was contorted, like she was ready to cry, but he could see no tears. He thought she looked like he felt on the inside.

Another question was coming his way. His head was swimming, as if he was trying to come up for air but there was none. Is this what it felt like to faint, he wondered vaguely? Was he losing consciousness? He'd heard people say that the world turned dark just before that happened. Nothing looked dark. If anything, the light was brighter than it should be.

Suddenly, he heard the shriek of a metal chair against the tile floor as Rodney Sherwood jumped to his feet, upsetting his chair, and screaming.

"Make him stop! No more questions! I can't stand it. I shot

her, but I didn't mean it. It was the drugs, they made me crazy all the time! I just wanted her to know she couldn't talk to me like that! She couldn't tell me not to come around no more!" He was crying and yelling and moving around the table towards Cooper James, who stood staring, transfixed in front of the sheriff who was still seated in the witness chair.

The closest bailiff grappled with Rodney and the other lurched towards the defense table as Charles Graham reached out in an attempt to control his client. Walter Barrington smoothly moved out of the way as Rodney tumbled sideways. As Rodney fell, he pushed roughly against the younger attorney, who fell backwards over his own chair and hit the floor.

"Get that man under control!" the judge bellowed.

"I wanted her to know she couldn't tell me what to do! I wasn't going to hurt her. I just wanted to scare her! She shouldn't have come at me like she did. She had to know. She had no right to tell me that. I'm her brother. She was supposed to love me no matter what!" Rodney's tirade continued even as he lay in a heap on the floor.

The bailiffs had a grip on the babbling man and placed him in handcuffs. Clumsily, they tried to pull Rodney Sherwood from the courtroom, but they could not control him and quiet him at the same time.

"Rodney, oh Rodney, we never knew!" Brenda Sherwood's shrill sobs could be heard above her son's blubbering.

Dale Harper watched the family tragedy unfold in the crowded courtroom. As Brenda Sherwood cried, her husband, also on his feet, collapsed back into his seat. The stone facade had crumbled.

The fog that had temporarily enveloped Dale Harper seemed to dissipate.

The judge's gavel had finally stopped its incessant pounding.

"The defense requests a short recess, Your Honor," were the first words heard as Walter Barrington finally spoke out over the din of the still disrupted courtroom.

"Granted! Thirty minutes." With that, the judge was on his feet and headed towards his chambers.

Dale Harper looked at Cooper James who had not moved. The prosecutor motioned that the sheriff could return to his seat behind the prosecution's table. Harper did so quietly, but the prosecuting attorney turned and quickly left the courtroom by one of the side doors.

Eddie immediately leaned over to ask, "Now what, Bro'?"

"I don't know, Eddie. I've never seen the like, to be honest." Harper shook his head as he slumped forward in his chair, studying the floor.

Several people began to move about in the courtroom, and within just a very few moments, Harper saw a pair of shiny black cowboy boots standing directly in front of his. He looked up to see Judge Billy Joe Randolph.

"Well, son, you've got yourself quite a circus going here, don't ya?" Judge Billy Joe commented dryly as he leaned down to speak close to the sheriff's ear.

"Yeah, you could call it that." A crooked little grimace crossed Harper's face.

The judge continued, "I'd say you'll have some lawyers doing some serious conferring behind closed doors for the next little while. Your part in all of this may well be over."

"I certainly hope so." Dale Harper shook his head from side to side, still staring at the floor.

Judge Billy Joe had figured it right. At the end of the thirty minute recess, the lawyers returned to the courtroom and it was announced that the defendant would accept a plea bargain, which included a guilty plea to first degree manslaughter. He and his defense team also accepted a sentence of not less than twenty years in prison. The jury was excused by the judge after he thanked them for their willingness to serve.

The room began to spin just a bit once again for Sheriff Harper by the time the whole proceeding had come to an end. He and Eddie found their way out into the hall. A few people Dale Harper recognized from Crossland County grabbed his arm and shook his hand. He heard, "Congratulations, Sheriff," more than once. It all seemed like something happening to someone else, like he was watching from a distance but then he caught sight of Martha and Milagro again at the end of the hall.

He cut his way through the crowd to catch up to the two of them.

"Dale," Martha greeted him almost curtly, "Glad it's all over finally."

"What in the name of glory are you doing here, Martha? Why did you come?" He glared accusingly at Milagro.

"Well, what do you think we're doing here, Dale?" Martha frowned at him. "Your mother called me last night. She was most upset about not being able to come. She asked me if I would do so in her place, and of course, I asked Milagro if she would drive me. You know I don't drive any distance any more, and--"

"Martha!" He tried without success to keep the anger from his voice. "I told her I didn't want her here. What part of that do the two of you not understand? I told her that last night on the phone! I didn't need anyone here to watch this. Wasn't it bad enough that I had to come and take care of it without the rest of the family being drug through it again?" His voice rose and several people nearby stopped speaking to look in their direction.

"Dale, for heaven's sakes!" Martha crooked her arm through his and started towards the door. "Come along outside and stop this nonsense!" He walked with her but with a hostile air that said the issue was far from settled.

Eddie and Milagro trailed along behind, trying to keep up and not get too far separated by the crowd.

Once out the door, the sharp exchange between the woman and her nephew continued. Milagro and Eddie stood a short distance away, trying not to hear the family squabble and yet finding it unavoidable.

"Why, then, did you have to bring *her* along?" His angry words could be clearly overheard despite Eddie's feeble attempts to make jokes.

"I told you before," Martha snapped back, "I needed a driver. She volunteered, if you really want to know. Much as it seems to bother you, there are still a few people in town who care about you, although heaven only knows why on days like today!" With that, the older woman spun away quickly on her heel and stormed towards Milagro and

Eddie.

"Milagro," she commanded, not unkindly, "let's go. There's nothing more for us to do here." She never broke stride as she called back over her shoulder, "Eddie, good to see you again."

"Miz Martha," Eddie touched the brim of his baseball cap as she breezed by.

Eddie strolled on down to the sidewalk in front of the courthouse and took up a comfortable position leaning against a city lamp post. He waited there, watching the human and vehicle traffic moving by until his friend joined him for the drive home several minutes later.

They drove back towards Serenity without speaking for the first several miles. After a time, the silence began to wear on Eddie. "So, hey, you want to go fishing one day next week or even next month?"

When Harper didn't answer, Eddie took a good look at his friend's face. Dale Harper's eyes were barely open and for a moment, Eddie was afraid he was falling asleep despite the fact that he was driving.

"So it was all between Bonnie and Rodney. I'd just kept thinking he came after us, after me, and killed her instead, but it was never about the law enforcement or even being in jail…"

"Dale," Eddie interrupted. "Let it go, Bro'. It was between them all along. You just have to let it go now."

"I guess you're right." A heavy sigh escaped him and he kept his eyes fastened on a distant point somewhere down the road.

Eddie didn't bring up fishing again. He just told Dale to call him if he needed anything at all when his friend dropped him off at the River Emporium.

* * * * *

He didn't like being out of sorts with anyone but especially not with his Aunt Martha. He wasn't sure why. Maybe it was because she reminded him so much of his mother. He didn't like being in a long-running disagreement with her either, although it seemed to be an ongoing thing with her pretty much ever since she married her second husband. Harper decided he might as well go find his aunt and get it over with.

She was just leaving the Foot of the Cross Mission when he brought the pickup to an abrupt halt in the parking lot.

"Got a minute to talk with me?" he asked through the truck window as he pulled up beside her car.

"Maybe," she answered without smiling, "but you may not like what I have to say."

The couple of hours since they left the courtroom had done nothing to quell her anger or improve her mood, Harper thought to himself.

She stood beside his pickup truck with her arms folded.

"Look, I'm sorry, okay?" he began lamely, looking at the steering wheel. "I just did not expect to see you there and especially not her. I still don't know why…"

"You don't know what? Why she came? I told you. I wasn't going to drive that far, but there's something more you should know. She *wanted* to come."

He pulled his eyes away from the steering wheel and turned in his seat to look directly at her as she continued to stand beside his truck. "What does that mean? She wanted to come. Like it was some kind of spectator sport or something?"

"Oh Dale, for pity's sake! You can be such a fool sometimes!"

"What did I do now? I swear, Aunt Martha, this is making less sense to me by the minute!"

"Because you don't think, or you think like a man or at least a lawman! You have no idea why she wanted to come? What do you really know about her, anyway?"

Now Dale Harper was really confused. "What do you mean? What does that have to do with anything? Why would she want to come and watch a man squirm in a courtroom proceeding that was going to rip his guts out?"

His aunt crossed her arms across her chest even tighter, if that were possible. "Dale, I can't believe you. The two of you had a conversation on the back porch a few days ago. Do you remember?"

"Well, yeah, I do, but what does that have to do with--"

"It has everything to do with everything," she continued to explain as if to a small child. "I asked you what you really know about her, about how she came to the United States, because after your conversation the other day all she could talk about was how hard today would be for you." She shook her head slowly while never taking her eyes off of him.

Harper let out a sigh of frustration. "She told me she came

to the U.S. to live with her father after her mother died. Her mother was Salvadoran. Her father is American and he still lives in San Antonio. She said she'd never met her father until she came to live with him. That's it, I guess."

"That's it? Hardly. Did you ask how her mother died and why she had to come to America?"

"Well, no, I can't say I did. She didn't seem real anxious to talk about it. I can't blame her. She was just a kid, and…"

"That's right!" she snapped. "She was just a kid, a fifteen year old girl who helped her mother, cooking for a rectory of priests. A bunch of murdered priests! She and her mother were amongst those shot by the soldiers who went to the rectory early one morning to kill the priests. They considered the priests to be anti-government because they were helping the people fight for their rights. Her mother was the cook, and Milagro was right there with her when they shot them all. The only thing that kept Milagro alive was that her mother threw herself across her daughter when the bullets started flying. Milagro was injured badly but she wasn't killed. The soldiers didn't know that, and some of the nuns in the church made certain they got Milagro out of the country before anybody knew she was still alive. A few years later, when the government finally changed and they put the soldiers on trial, they brought Milagro back to testify against them."

Martha's speech slowed as she emphasized each word. "That made her a twenty year old kid, and they brought her in as a witness where her very life was in danger every minute she was in the country. When she realized that you had also lived through your own murder, as she calls it, and would have to testify about it, she insisted she had to be there to support you! And instead, all you did today was yell once you found us there!"

Dale Harper turned to lean his forehead against the steering wheel. "Oh my aching head," was all he could manage to say.

"Your aching head! I'd like to kick your backside and make it ache, if you really want to know." Martha leaned forward and took hold of his shoulder with both hands and shook him as a sad little chuckle escaped her.

"Oh, Aunt Martha, why didn't you say something… *anything*!"

"Well, excuse me, it's not the sort of thing that generally comes up in polite conversation!"

He sat up and then fell back, straining the truck seat with his complete collapse. "No, I suppose that's true." He let out a long, ragged breath. "I'd better go, I guess. I'm sorry. I just had no idea."

"I know, I know, but you wouldn't let me explain, either. Well, I suppose what's done is done." She leaned with both arms straightened against the pickup door for a moment.

"I gotta go." He sat up and started the truck.

"Where are you going?" She seemed surprised.

"I don't know exactly, somewhere, anywhere. Maybe back out to talk to Eddie. I'll catch up to you later, tomorrow maybe."

"Dale, are you sure you're all right?"

"Yeah, well, as good as can be expected, I guess, at the moment. I don't know. I'll talk to you later." He waved slightly as he backed out of the parking lot.

CHAPTER 14

"What do you want, Dale?" Milagro stood on the top step of the porch at her back door, her back straight against a support column. "Please do not be so loud. There is no reason to wake the children."

"I want some answers, by God." He staggered, his arm making a wide arc with the neck of the fifth still tightly clenched in his fist.

"I am sure God would be happy to give you some. Have you asked Him?" Her voice was tinged with more than a touch of angry sarcasm.

"Yeah, sure. Isn't that what you do? Give answers for God."

"I have answers for my own life only, at times," she responded, more evenly this time. "I cannot speak for anyone else."

"Well, I don't talk to the Heavenlies on a regular basis, like you. I mean, why should I?" He stumbled to the bottom step.

She watched him without answering this time.

"You've been drinking, Dale. Surely you are not driving? How did you get here?"

He snorted in amusement. "Can't have that, can we? No, I ain't driving. Eddie is out front. He's driving. He don't drink no more, he says. He wouldn't drink with me tonight, that's for sure. But so be it. If he don't want to drink, that's his loss. Me, I need some answers. I need to know about a lot of things. Things like why. Why this all happened, with Bonnie and Rodney and now you!"

"Me? I do not have anything to do with what you are struggling with," she answered even more quietly.

"Oh no? That's not what I hear now." He negotiated another step towards her and stopped. "I hear you know all about it, one way or another. Living through your own murder. Isn't that what you called it? Why didn't you tell me before?"

Her tone was low with a deadly calm that carried its own menace. "The day you told me, we were right here. Do you remember? I was going to tell you, but you did not give me a chance. I told you the truth that day. You are the first person I ever met to live through your own murder, but before I could tell you why that was important to me, you were on your feet and gone. So," she shrugged her shoulders, "I let you go."

"And that's it then?"

"What more do you want from me?" The strain could be heard in her voice with her rising level of exasperation.

He continued in a loud voice. "I want to know about you and me and what it all means. I want to know why. I want to know…"

"You want a lot for someone who tries to find those answers in a bottle," she hissed at him as she lost her patience. "You are a good man, Dale Harper. You are good and kind and funny and everything a woman might want when you are not like this! But I do not want what belongs to someone else!"

"Someone else? I ain't married. I don't belong to nobody!" he bellowed in defiance.

"You cannot give what still belongs to someone else, and whether you know it or not, your soul still belongs to a dead woman." Angry tears stung her eyes despite her best efforts to fight them.

As fast as the words passed her lips she regretted them, but the damage was done and she could think of no way to undo it.

He fell backwards off the porch steps as if he had been hit. "That's a cold thing to say, woman. How could you be so…so hard."

"It may be hard, but it is the truth and that is the only thing that matters now," she managed to choke out the words.

"And what if it is? What can I do about it?" The emotion in his voice did nothing to bring down its volume. "I didn't choose this, but it's killing me just the same!"

"Then who did choose it?" Her voice resumed its earlier deathly calm.

"How do I know? Isn't that a question for your God?"

"Oh, you blame Him, but you have that part wrong. God does not murder our loved ones. People do that and sometimes…" She stopped speaking.

"What do you mean? Sometimes what? What do you know about it anyway?" He heaved the bottle into the field of flowers behind him where it shattered and, once again, he started up the porch steps.

Milagro stood her ground and when he was beside her, he brought his face close to hers but she turned away.

"You need to go home, Dale. You have surely awakened everyone by now. Go home. I will talk to you another day when you feel better." She turned abruptly and stepped inside her cabin, leaving him alone on the porch with his hands balled up into fists in his blue jeans pockets.

* * * * *

She stood in the clear moonlight on the back porch of her cabin two nights later, looking out across the fields of flowers and down the long ribbon of highway. She lit a cigarette and drew deeply on it.

"Those aren't good for you, you know." Dale Harper's soft voice startled her as he stepped out of the nearby field.

"What are you doing here?" In spite of her promise to herself that she would hold him at some distance from now on, she found she was smiling as she asked, "Are you all right?"

"Yeah, I'm okay. Just got back from a meeting up the road a couple of hours."

"A meeting? A sheriffs' meeting?" she asked with a slight frown on her face as she put out her cigarette.

"Well, not exactly, although there was another sheriff there." He stepped closer to the porch and she could see a paper sack in his hand.

"I do not understand." She shook her head.

"It's the kind of meeting where you tell everybody your first name and you also tell them, like I did tonight, that it's been two days since my last drink."

"Oh, that kind of meeting," she nodded. "A quarter of the men in my country go to those meetings. Many who do not, should. They have some of them here in Serenity, no? Or do you need to go far away?"

He grinned self-consciously. "Oh, there are some people here who know that I go. That's not news, but it is better to go somewhere else. Kinda hard to be sitting next to a feller today that you might have to arrest tomorrow."

She laughed softly. "So what are you doing out in the field in the middle of the night?"

"Gotta clean up the mess I left the other night. Or at least, the part that I can." He shook the paper sack and she could hear the shards of broken glass inside. "What are you doing out here? It's late."

"I was just feeling a little…" She stopped and glanced over at him.

"A little lonely?" He finished the sentence for her. Her hair formed a soft halo around her face in the moonlight and her long, golden earrings sparkled in a way that made his heart leap, and reminded him of the night the mission caught fire.

"Yes, that was it."

"Didn't you tell me once that God is always with you?"

"Certainly He is," she grinned in spite of him, "but all people feel alone sometimes. Even Jesus in the garden was lonely and terribly sad because his friends would not stay awake and keep him company. People are just that way. Sooner or later, we need to be with another person."

"Well, I wouldn't blame you if you didn't want my company anymore after the way I acted the other night."

"Do not be ridiculous," she chided. "Come and sit. What do you remember of the other night?"

He sat down next to her on the top porch step and let his arms stretch out straight over his knees. "I remember I was shocked to find out why you came to the trial, why you wanted to come. Did you really go back to El Salvador and testify against the soldiers that killed your mother and shot you?"

"Oh, yes, that." She let out a long, slow breath. "Yes, I did that. It has been a long time now, more than ten years."

"Still, that's a real brave thing to do. Mine was bad enough but it wasn't like I had anybody waiting to kill me on my way to the courthouse."

"Yes, it was not any easy thing, but I knew I had to do it for my mother and for the priests Padre Dionisio and Padre Guillermo. They were always so good to me. They helped to raise me. It was like a debt that I could not ignore. Besides," she shrugged as if it was of no consequence, "I thought if God wanted me to live no longer than that, then at least I would live long enough to put them in prison first! I even thought maybe that was why God had let me live that day when everyone else died, so that I could tell the truth in court. I told myself that if they killed me, it would be that much sooner I would be with my mother and our friends, the priests. Losing them had hurt so badly, I decided that nothing else could hurt any worse than that. The nuns, they told me I was simply living out my name--*Milagro*, miracle."

Dale Harper watched her tell her story, sitting by her side in the pale moonlight. "I can't imagine it," he spoke softly. "I am glad you made it through and came to Serenity instead."

She gave him a full genuine smile. "Me, too. So, what else?"

"What do you mean, what else?"

"What else do you remember from the other night?"

"Well, I remember I asked you something but you said you were not interested."

"That is not what I said. I told you," she slowed her words and continued in a deliberate manner, "I do not want something that belongs to someone else."

"That was it," he replied. "And what does that mean? I think I asked about that, too, only in a not-so-polite way. I'm sorry about that."

"You do not have to be sorry. I feel sad that you are still hurting so, but it means what it means. You are not free yet. Your wife is not here with you anymore, but my friend," she turned towards him and put her hand lightly on his forearm, "your life has to go on."

"And how do I do that? I can't just forget her. I wouldn't even if I could."

"And no one wants you to." She patted his arm once again and dropped her hand. "But you do have to understand exactly what happened."

"Oh, I know what happened. I was there and---" He stopped.

"You were there, but that is not the same thing. I did not understand completely until the other night, but now I think I do."

He was quiet for another moment. "Tell me what you think."

"What did Bonnie tell you when she helped you in the campaign to become sheriff? Wanda said she heard her tell you that you were the best thing to ever happen to this town. She said the best use she ever made of any of her money was to help get you elected, to give you to the people of her town. That is an incredible thing to say, yes?"

"Yeah, well, I guess so." He frowned at the difficult memory. "I remember when she said that in the office that day, it was kinda embarrassing, so I told her to hush and to get going." He sat, staring at the shadowy field of flowers cast in the ghostly light of the moon. "It made it sound like she bought me into the office or something. I know that's not how she meant it but it sounded funny, just the same."

Milagro continued, "As I understand it, Bonnie worked very hard on your campaign and that was even before you were married. Wanda said she supported you even when her family would not."

"That was pretty much the way of it. They weren't hard against me or anything, they just didn't know much about me. I mean, I'd been a city cop for years, not a bad one, not a great one, no hero or anything. I can see why her folks weren't crazy about the whole thing. I just wasn't anything to them, one way or the other."

"But you were something very special to her." She took a deep breath. "Now this is the hard part."

"What?" He turned to face her.

"Tell me."

"Tell you what?"

"Tell me about the day Bonnie died."

He stared at her. "Why would you ask me that?"

"To help you understand what really happened. Go slow, but say it out loud. Tell yourself the story about what really happened that day."

He turned away towards the moonlight and the darkness. He remained still for so long that she feared he might not say another word, but instead, after several long moments, he dropped his feet down another step and leaned forward. He seemed to be talking less to the woman at his side and more to the ghostly flowers before him.

"We made love, morning love, the kind when you first wake up." A crooked, melancholy smile tugged at the side of his face in gentle embarrassment at the sweet memory.

"There was a noise at the front door. The outside storm door didn't always catch, and Bonnie went after it. She had on one of my old shirts. It had buttons up the front, and she was doing the buttons as she went down the hall. I had on a towel because I was headed for the shower and then on to work. I was just a few steps behind her. Her hair, that long, blond hair, I remember it moved so pretty with the sunshine coming in the front window." He stopped for a moment and then took another deep breath before he continued.

"She reached for the outside door knob and I was standing in the doorway of the bathroom. I started to call her back, to tell her to check and be sure no one was there before she opened the door, but she was saying it was just the wind and--"

His voice got lower and more ragged but he continued. "It all moved fast after that, yet it seemed so slow at the same time. I saw the shotgun first, I think, the barrel. Then I saw that Rodney was the one holding it and I knew. I knew we were dead. He was supposed to be in jail, the next county over. He raised that 12 gauge and..." He put his hand up to his eyes as if to shade them from some invisible sun.

"Do not stop, Dale." Her soothing voice was softly insistent at his side, "Keep going."

"I know I called her name. I don't know if I even said anything else. There wasn't time. By then, she knew too. She must have. She heard me because she turned and looked at me. Oh glory, I didn't remember that before! She turned and then..."

"What, Dale? What did she do? Do not stop now!"

"She looked at me," he gasped, " and gave me that little smile, the one she always saved for good-bye like when she was driving off and I'd catch up to her later. She gave me that smile and then she stepped away. I jumped towards her but she stepped between me and Rodney."

He leaned heavily against the porch post, his face hidden in his hands. A silent sob shook his body.

Gently, Milagro slid her arm through his. They sat in silence for a time. She listened to the night sounds of peeper frogs, insects and a lone owl calling at the far side of the field. She cast her eyes towards the silver moon, now high in the sky, and said a silent prayer of thanks. The soft summer night's wind wrapped around them and caressed her cheek.

Finally, a whisper escaped him. "How did you know?"

Milagro answered in a voice barely louder than his. "Wanda told me what Bonnie said that day in the office. She came from one of the richest families here and yet she considered you the best thing that ever happened to her town. She was a woman who made her own choices. Who would know that better than you? She chose you, yes? She chose to share you with her town and she chose to give her life for yours. Jesus said there is no greater love than to lay down your life for the ones you love. You are the gift that she gave back to her people. She knew what she was doing and it was her choice."

She hesitated for a moment. "Remember what I told you that first day we had lunch here? Between the star and the cross we each have to choose, and we hope that what we choose will make a difference."

The flowers before them waved in the soft breeze. Dale Harper shifted his position and a small sigh escaped him. "Her choice," he whispered. "It was always about the choice."

"Look, there is still a candle burning in the chapel." Milagro pointed to the small stained-glass window at the far side of the building where a candle's flame danced against the darkness. “It is time.”

They stood up together to make their way inside. Milagro knew that for the first time in a very long while, Sheriff Dale Harper would sleep that night in peace.

OTHER BOOKS BY LAURA L. VALENTI

Novels

Between the Star and the Cross: The Promise
Between the Star and the Cross: The Election

~~~

The Heart of the Spring
The Heart of the Spring Lives On
The Heart of the Spring Comes Home
The Heart of the Spring Everlasting

~~~

Las Palomitas: The Little Doves
A Story of El Salvador

Non-fiction

Ozark Meth: A Journey of Destruction and Deliverance
By Dick Dixon and Laura L. Valenti

Made in the USA
Columbia, SC
07 February 2025

52716992R00163